Ignoring Alva

Ignoring Alva

Emilie Khair

CURRENT WORDS | LOS ANGELES

Ignoring Alva

Published by Current Words Publishing, LLC.
Dianne Pearce, editor and publisher.
David Yurkovich, design.

This is a work of fiction. Any similarities between actual places, events, or people, either living or deceased, are entirely coincidental.

ISBN: 978-1-957224-45-9 (paperback)
ISBN: 978-1-957224-46-6 (epub)

Printed in the United States of America.

FIND US AT
currentwords.com

Dedication

To my loving mom and fellow writer, Carolyn Eklin, who asked daily for an update on my novel, even as those days spread to years. And to my sweet dad, who will never see the finished book, but continues to inspire me from his new place in the stars.

Ignoring Alva

She touches it with the toe of her orthopedic sneaker. Finger bones protrude from the sleeve of a larvae-chewed wool sweater. "I used to have a sweater like that," Alva says. "I bought it at JCPenney during that cold snap we had right before Irvin died."

"Is that all you have to say right now?" The other woman stares down into one of the eye sockets. The other eyehole is filled with dirt. There are little lines on the dull yellow skull like a spider's web.

"Mine had a blue stripe, but this one's more of a coral color."

"Alva, holy shit! I don't like to be out here." She jerks around, looking for ghosts or maybe her ex-mother-in-law.

"I've seen my share of dead people," Alva says, nonplussed. "You get to where most of your friends and family are dead. You know what I'm talking about."

"I don't know."

Alva sighs. "Dead is dead. Those morticians have some talent putting eye caps on eyeballs and the makeup, of course, but we all know it's just dress-up, and the bones are waiting underneath." She taps her toe. "Look, her little arm is reaching out for something. I hope when they bury me next to Irvin, I'll reach out and try to hold his hand, maybe do a little dance in the dirt. I've thought about it a lot."

"What are you talking about? Who is she? Who put her here?"

"I don't know," Alva says, "but I know who she's not."

Alva

They said it was just a small stroke. A month or so went by, and after that, I was pretty much back to normal on the outside. But inside my head, there are changes. I have these visions, not dreams; I'm not even asleep, although my body gets still. Truthfully, the images come like a slideshow. You know those clicker things that the kids used to have, where you peek inside and the small square frames in the circles become panoramas of the Grand Canyon or Florida? It's like that. *Flash!* I see myself manning a boat beneath the spray of a waterfall. My face up, I feel the torrents of water pounding over my yellow plastic coat. *Flash!* I am atop a steeple, brandishing a sword and slicing at the sky. *Flash!* Not just pictures; my senses are all involved. It's like I am right there, the captain of my destiny. I told my sister Millie about my visions—or whatever they are—and she seems intent on researching symptoms of dementia. Yet, these are not delusions, more like glimpses of a more exciting me. Maybe they are better versions of my past, or maybe I'm conjuring up my future. There's a bigger story there.

Millie is 81, older than I am by a year and a half, but she's agreed to take a little trip with me, go out and see more of the world. Before we leave, I look fondly out my back window and see a pear clinging to a sagging branch. It is August, and that's a little early for a pear to turn from green to yellow, but this one has turned gold. It is Minnesota, after all, and most people don't think of fruit trees when they think of snow. Even though my husband Irvin's been dead now for nine years, that tree of his is high on living.

Flash! *I am in a lovely orchard with branches heavy with pears ready for harvest. I have my apron on and am going to collect those pears and make a pie.*

Crows are circling the skies above. I flail my arms, a distraction, and try to shield the fruit from an onslaught. The birds are menacing, after more than just the fruit. I need to protect the crop and myself, stand tall. I beg Prometheus for fire or a little smoke. Then one of the birds cocks her head and says very clearly, "Alva, there's more to you than that apron."

I'm standing in Millie's kitchen. A weird feeling envelops me, like a promise.

"Alva," she says and pats my shoulder, "get that bruised pear off my counter."

We should go, I say to myself. Then to Millie, quietly, "We should go." There are pictures swirling around my head. I am a walking View-Master.

Alva

I sit down on the front steps, waiting for Millie to finish her packing. There my house is, just next door, centered on a little lawn that is kept dutifully mowed by a child down the street. Irvin was fastidious about *his* lawn. I am feeling nostalgic. My husband died almost ten years ago from emphysema. His cigars were probably the final blow, but he used to drink plenty, and the chemicals in the ink shop had to have contributed. Bad air, he called it. I remember his long fingers, stained deep blue, caressing his Dutch Master. And I recollect the smoke curling around the recliner like some Van Gogh sky. But memories aren't always the same as being there. I've got fine pictures in my head about those cigars, but they killed him all the same.

Millie is finally out of her bedroom, yelling for my help, dragging an immense suitcase to rest next to two others. She is a sight, with her newly-permed hair looking like a cross between a halo and a helmet, and she is looking like an old Clara Bow. She is taller than me and I guess more stylish. Today she is in a navy tunic and soft jeans, an inharmonious fur draped over her shoulders.

"Gosh, Millie, what has taken you this long?" She spent most of the day packing, and our quest for something *more* is late getting started. "How far do you think we'll be able to drive before it gets dark? I mean, look at those bags. How'd you get all that in them in the first place? And what's that around your shoulders? That old fur coat is mine. And you won't need it because it will be warm."

Millie huffs, "You didn't appreciate this coat; you put it in the garage sale after Irvin died. Remember? I took it. The fact is that even in the warmer months, I get a little chilly with the air conditioning. I want to be prepared for anything. And now," she looks at the suitcases dramatically, "I am ready for any adventure—or, for that matter, any disaster. Ooh, I hope we have plenty of escapades, maybe even some sexy ones! I have a first aid kit in here because you know how clumsy you are."

"You shouldn't try to get up my goat, Millie. You might need that first aid kit!"

Look at us, two old ladies starting up a quibble. So, I concentrate on piling things in the oversized trunk. We need both of us to hoist up Millie's bags. Millie puts the golden vintage fur coat over her head, so she has two free hands and looks every bit like that Cousin Itt. In a way, though, I am glad to see it after all this time. I had been wavering back and forth about whether I wanted to give up that fur, so I was okay when Millie took it off my hands. We have a complicated history, that coat and me.

I say, "I heard that they make some of the not-so-pricey furs out of cat and dog hair. They skin them alive. In Asian countries, I think. I read it. There is some talk about importing the hair of small things too, like hamsters. My great-grandson told me he was worried about his hamster getting killed for just that reason. I can't see, as there is a real comparison to be made between dog hair and rodent hair. If a coat was made from hamster hair, I doubt people would buy it." *Truthfully, though, I wouldn't miss that hamster.*

"Oh my gosh, Alva! It *is* a mink, and you know it."

"I don't know. I heard that Dayton's Department Store imports fur from China or someplace where they don't care about pets like my Sweetie Pie." I remember the neck of my old, fat dachshund, her belly barely hovering over the shag carpet. Now I've gone and started reminiscing in full, and I really don't remember that article on vintage fur. A tear is threatening to drown our happy day.

"Hold on for a minute; I just need one more look around," I say. "Need to check that I turned off all the lights." I leave the car in her driveway and walk back over to my house. Unlocking it one more time, I pass through the porch and head downstairs first. In the basement is

Irvin's workroom, just like he left it, as neat as an operating room, his tools hanging on a brown pegboard in precise rows and a giant saw stationary in the center. Never a bit of sawdust, but it always looked ready for any violent creativity. Around the corner, I take in the immaculate rec room with its mismatched fittings: a wrought iron daybed, an old wicker rocker, a child-sized pool table, and a wet bar done in pseudo-stained glass. Irvin dusted those bottles regularly, even though he didn't touch alcohol in his later years. I poured out the contents once he passed, but I couldn't get rid of the bottles. I still come down here with my dust rag every Saturday. My built-in Baldwin looks forlorn against the back wall. Maybe when I get home, I'll try to play a little.

I come back upstairs, sit on the couch, and take stock. The house is still decorated in burnt orange and avocado green. It was all the rage a long time ago, and I haven't really kept up with the latest trends. Shag carpeting and a recliner, a tiny organ in the front room, plastic flowers on the doilies that centered each table—each embellishment, I suppose, contributing to a future decorator's nightmare. Millie takes credit for the doily idea, and I let her. It is the best I could do and, at least at one time, pretty stylish for Crystal, Minnesota. A couple of Irvin's paint-by-number masterpieces are hanging on the walls. The bathroom door is ajar, and I can see the maroon tiles and pink towels.

It feels like I'm peeking back into a life that isn't all that familiar anymore, like even the ashtray sits in the middle of the coffee table, but I don't even know why. Nobody's smoked in the house for years. Melancholy rears up and then falls to ashes. A train blows its horn. It rumbles past the green patch of grass and the trees. The tracks mark my property line in the back, and even though there is no whistle stop, they have a habit of jarring me at the most inopportune times or in the middle of the night. *Move on.*

Millie pops her head in the screen door and says, "You promised this was going to be an adventure, not a permanent change of address. We are just heading east and exploring for a few weeks."

"I hope I don't have to stop in the bathroom every five seconds," I manage. For some reason I wanted to say something profound about family or planting roots or train lullabies, but I suddenly didn't have the words. *Never mind.* This is a step toward the future, instead of just talking about it. Walking out to the car, I pick up the fur coat fondly and pull it around my shoulders, sinking into the smells and the history. It is a layer of protection I have missed. "How do I look?"

"Like a woman wearing a hamster costume." Millie smiles. "It's my posture. It only looks like a *real* mink on me."

"Oh well . . . you know," I say, out of habit. And it hits me— how I always let my thoughts trail off.

"Get in the car Millie," I command. I don't need a fur coat to be fierce.

Millie

"Oh well . . . you know." My sister Alva has always ended conversations with that phrase. I'll give you an example. This is a true story, I swear. When I moved next door to Alva, she had a parakeet named Pudge. I'm not a big bird person, but Alva loved that thing. She let it fly around the living room, and admittedly, he was careful (perhaps) not to make a mess. He was a smart bird. Alva taught him to talk, and begrudgingly, Irwin did the obligatory recitation: "Pudge is a pretty bird. Pudge is a pretty bird." And Pudge would rotate his head on his little neck and repeat, "Pudge is a pretty bird." Pudge knew a few other colorful words as well, but they tried not to let him repeat those in front of company. Pudge could say other sentences, too. "Goodnight, everybody. Pudge is tired." And my favorite, "I can talk, can you fly?"

They were an odd family unit: Irwin, not quite six feet tall (missed it by a half inch) with a mustache and strong shoulders, and my sister Alva, a short, plump woman with soft folds in her neck and rosy cheeks shadowed by large, black, wire-rimmed glasses. Behind those glasses were intense, concerned eyes, hazel, with gold flicks sparkling like sunshine when she smiled. Her skin was flawless, a soft cream color in good contrast with her dark hair. Pudge, the bird (and not pudgy at all), was bright green and flamboyant, and later they added a honey-colored dachshund named Sweetie Pie, who was lazy even as a puppy. Of them all, Pudge *was* the prettiest—a pretty bird.

And Pudge knew it. Pudge would hover and stare at himself in the large, over-the-sofa mirror. He would glimpse his beaked profile in the windowpanes and in the gold-tinted frame of the little fireplace. He whistled at himself and got all puffed up. He was in love with his own reflection. For years he sat admiring his exceptional silhouette. And then, I remember, the day it happened, Alva had been making a little supper for us all after church. While Alva cooked in the narrow walk-through kitchen, Pudge always kept her company. She knew I didn't like him coming too close to my food, but Pudge didn't seem to mind that, sat happily on the far counter in front of the copper-plated old breadbox admiring himself. "Pretty bird!" he had exclaimed for the final time because, just then, the magnet that held the breadbox door faltered. Pudge's reflection came falling down onto his fabulously feathered head. And he died right then and there, under the weight of his own admiration.

Alva was devastated. I tried to make her feel better. I held one hand while Irvin held the other. We told stories about Pudge and what a good life he had. I talked about Pudge's hunt for attention and mentioned something about irony. Then she nodded and murmured something about hubris and a winged Narcissus (because she is smart like that), and then, maybe recognizing how different she was from her bird, said, *"Oh well . . . you know."*

That time, I came out and asked her, "Alva, what am I supposed to know?"

She shrugged and said, "The things that I don't."

"You know so much, Alva. Don't be silly," I said, trying to placate her.

"Well, even if I do, my opinions are not that important. I'm not feeling sorry for myself, though. Just Pudge. *It's tragic.*" That was just like her, always thinking about others.

Bookish is what our mother called her. I am not sure I've ever known things that Alva doesn't. I can't complete the Sunday crossword, memorize an entire cookbook, or play the piano by ear. Alva can, but she doesn't ever flaunt that knowledge. She is a quiet sort with a large brain but no confidence to go out and conquer the world. Maybe that's why no one really listens to her. She doesn't ever say things forcefully. Never the loudest in the room. In the 1960s she had two tiny sons and a husband. Women were burning their bras right when Alva was realizing she needed one to hold up her milk-laden breasts. She lived in a house of men, and when her boys left, she busied herself making Irvin's life comfortable. He'd come home; she'd listen intently about his day. She'd watch him puffing his cigar and watching *Wheel of Fortune*. He never tried to solve the puzzles, and his eyes would get sleepy. Alva knew all the answers, but she would look at Irvin then at Vanna. He wasn't listening to her, and Vanna never was. *"Oh well, you know . . . ."*

While she is steadfast, I am the carefree one, the true "fly-by-the-seat-of-my-pants" one. Prettier, too, if I do say. I am taller, with admittedly big bones, but my cheekbones are sculpted, I have good teeth, and my eyes are bright blue like our mother's. Alva and I were the last two girls in a line of siblings, and we were very close but different. She was always studying, always trying to do the right thing. I was trying on dresses. I had so much fun in the little pond we call Crookston! In high school I had solos in the Advanced Choir all three years, and I was in the Girl's Glee Club, presiding over the senior mixer: the Girl's Frolic. Alva was on the Debate Club but more the researcher than the debater. Alva, like I said, was always a little short and a fair bit overweight. She lost most of the weight eventually, but she stayed short. She also had a great smile but didn't use it often. She covered her face with her wire-rimmed glasses and her brunette, unkempt bob. Alva never seemed that interested in boys. I had several boyfriends, some at the same time, and after high school I went to the University of Crookston for one year before I fell in love with Steve Kochman. He had been the quarterback for the Crookston Aggies and then went to work for his father, breeding livestock. Oh, did he woo me! Pretty racy back in the day. Steve had a great sense of humor, and we had lots of friends. Summer barbeques and winter snow fests; every day was joyful. At least that's how an old woman like me remembers it now. Alva headed to Minneapolis with her friend Shirley (which, in truth, was a pretty big adventure on her part, but I think Shirley talked her into it, and she just went along) while I was on my honeymoon. I wish, now, that she had headed to other places, too, before she met Irvin. Steve judged lots of livestock contests, and I traveled with him. One time all the way to Texas! "What the heck," I'd say. "Let's go!" Then our twins were born, and every day got even better. So much love.

I won't go on about those years, but they are my heart and soul. When the kids turned seventeen, Steve fell off a horse, and my dreams fell with him. Eight years later, Alva asked me to move to the suburbs of Minneapolis, the house next door. "What the heck," I said, but with a lot less enthusiasm.

Then our kids were grown, our spouses gone. Even our brothers and sisters. We were the youngest. Not that you can't die out of order, but we didn't. We just had each other then. And now? I'm still the fun one, but Alva has changed. She is still quiet, more content with reading and doing puzzles than joining a cause or hosting Bingo. She overthinks things. But she has a slow burning fire underneath her. Something is definitely different. I'm not planning on following her down any old rabbit hole, but I will sit back some and enjoy the ride.

Alva

My granddaughter, Margaret, travels quite a bit. She sends me lengthy letters about all her journeys. I answer each one with my postcards, the ones with little birds on the front, or the state flowers. *You sound so busy,* I write.

Gram, she replies, *You need to get out and see the world. Visit new places. You need to send me some postcards from wherever life takes you.*

Okay. Okay.

I've got the creepy crawlies, like when we watch one of those CSI's and I know who did it, but don't want to ruin it for Millie. But next time I'm just going to tell her. The stroke did a number on me. I think I'm like a drug addict in recovery, but my nemesis is not drugs; it's my own low expectations. Isn't that what the bird was getting at about me and my apron? I am keeping a journal with me at all times to write down all the places we see and things we do. I am also writing down those odd moments where my brain takes a vacation on its own. Might make a great book one day. It's odd. I'm a Swede, and I heard somewhere that we are supposed to be sensible. Ha! Like I always say to Millie, "If you can't be content with what you have received, be thankful for what you have escaped." It's some adage I found in a book. But now, I think I want to see what I've missed. My head is tingling!

Behind me, my little house in Crystal is invisible. Millie decided to drive the first leg of the trip. The old Buick is jammed with luggage, plus a lot of junk: old ink pens with no tops, lots of Kleenex, two bottles of Geritol, an empty bottle of Plavix, lots of 325 mg aspirin, and boiled peanuts from the little stand on the corner. I've got the most important thing in the world to me tucked under my left hip—my journal and my copy of Christie's short story collection, *The Labors of Hercules*, under my right. I was a reader mostly of what some would call romance novels, but since Irvin died, I haven't been much for the romance part. I read the books we always kept on the shelf downstairs for guests. Old books like *Huck Finn* and *Mystery on the Orient Express*. Anything Agatha, really. I've always been partial to Miss Marple, but I think it's funny that Hercule Poirot imagines himself a hero ala the mythological Hercules. I wonder if there is a famous Alva that *I* can become. *I doubt it.*

Oh well. Alva and Millie flying by the seats of our pants. We've got a couple of weeks before people will get worried about our whereabouts. And by that time, we will be back home. We said we were staying with Jane and Harriet, old friends living in Morehead.

The dashboard is awash in maps, so I choose one, pick up a red pen, and scratch its point back and forth to get it to write. We agreed not to make any destination plans until we were underway, so it would really feel like we were flying without a net, except we did pick a direction to head. So exciting! I wait until we are on Interstate 94, heading east toward Stillwater, and draw circles around things I always wanted to see. Well, I don't know if I always wanted to see them, but I think it is time now and even though the places aren't some of the biggest wonders of the world, my hands are shaking. God gives every bird a worm, but he does not throw it into the nest . . .

"Whoa, Millie, look at this here." The pen stops circling and presses into Southern Wisconsin. "I know you were always jealous that I got to see Niagara Falls and you didn't. I was going to surprise you and say we should go there, but let's start off with a stop at these Wisconsin Dells and head to one of those Indian casinos. The Cherokee run it."

"Not the Cherokee," Millie corrects. "I think the Dakota?"

"Well, some kind of tribe. But I think that I should try to meet some of those Indians. You know my son, Robert, married Agnes. She is part Cherokee you know. I remember it made me nervous when I first heard. But she's turned out fine."

"Alva, she's just a little bit Indian, and that might just be a rumor, but mostly I think she is German."

"The point being, I was always a little worried about the Indian part." I continue to trace an invisible line east over the Mississippi into Wisconsin, through Michigan towards Upstate New York. "And then we can head to the Falls. When I was there with Irvin, it was really wonderful: impressive. Only place I have ever visited outside of Minnesota. But I was such a ninny back then and kind of let Irvin tell me things. I just agreed, 'Oh really? Take a holiday scenic bus tour? You mean we should just stay on the bus, so we don't get wet?' This time, Millie, I want the spray on my face."

I sit back against the vinyl seat and indulge in some reminiscing. Irvin was the cut-and-dried kinda guy once he had his life together, after he stopped drinking and mellowed. He liked to be organized, and it was more important for him to be in control than to fully experience things as they happen. Nothing wrong with that; he didn't mean to be condescending. He always tried to be good to me.

Now it's going to be *me* looking out for me. And I'm coloring outside of the lines.

Flash! *I've got my golden fur coat wrapped tight around me. Someone is trying to yank it from my shoulders, but it has become part of my skin, part of my purpose. The impenetrable lion hides, bravely shields me from an invisible aggressor and the cold day. It has weathered all kinds of storms. I nuzzle it and breathe in the memories. And then it disappears. No ransom note.*

Millie is poking me in the ribs. "Alva, you are doing it again. You were muttering about Irvin and then you just went quiet. Where'd your mind go?"

Maybe I am a little crazy with all of this; maybe I sense danger. I jot the lion pelt incident down into my journal and chuckle. *Probably a little crazy.* I go back to the map. The route will take us 963 miles, which is approximately seventeen hours of driving, which is more like a week for us. At seventy-nine, the bladder goes. Several years ago, my granddaughter took me to the Guthrie Theatre. It was wonderful! But the drive home ended up with me panicked that I mightn't make it to the bathroom. I was worried, but I saw that nice Dr. Worrell down by the hospital, and he has me on some medicine that seems to help. I will *not* wear the diapers. Millie says that she won't mind stopping quite a bit. That way her legs won't get all crampy and full of clots. She is always complaining about her legs.

"So, are you excited to see it? We don't have to go all the way to the Canadian side. But I think there are Indians there, too. I think Niagara is named for an Indian tribe." I reach for the Sunday paper. "It is, and as a matter of fact, it is in today's paper—39 across. I knew it."

"Drop the puzzle and pay attention to the map." She mulls it over. "Since you were the one to decide to become an explorer, I guess you can have first choice as to what we discover. But I'm picking next. You sure you don't want to tell someone where we're headed?"

"Wouldn't it defeat the purpose? They are done letting us be in charge."

"You're right. Okay, I'm for seeing where our journey takes us."

"Great, so long as it's in the general same direction we decide on, you know?"

"I *do* know."

I busy myself looking at the other state routes of Wisconsin, Illinois, and Ohio. Out of habit I start poring over the points of interest. Maps are vital to knowing. The coffee is starting to work on my bladder. So, I bounce my legs and envision the tremendous possibilities splayed before us. There are mysteries, not just in books but in life, to be solved.

The car purrs along, and we fall into a companionable silence. I skim travel books while Millie hums a little tune. I think it's "I am Woman Hear Me Roar," but maybe that's a refrain stuck in my mind. I don't know. It's another lion thing.

"Here's an interesting fact," I say. "Do you know that Theodore Roosevelt was once shot in the chest before he was going to give a speech in Milwaukee? It says here that he walked outside after dinner and was shot by the bartender! The bartender was crazy and said a ghost made him do it!!"

Millie gives a little shake of her head. "You can't trust those guys who pour drinks for a living. I just know." She giggles. She did like to go to the VFW with a "friend" and have a sidecar on occasion, so she *does* know.

"I guess it didn't do too much damage. Says here that President Roosevelt went on and did his whole speech."

"I always liked Teddy." Millie smiles. "Now there was a M-A-N." And she sort of wiggles in her seat.

She said it like she knew him. *A little presumptuous,* I think, but don't say it. And that wiggle? *What in the world is she doing?* "Maybe we could stop by the Hyatt in Milwaukee. They have a little plaque and things about it."

Millie continues, "I liked everything about him because he seemed like such a free spirit in his younger days and then such a courageous spirit in his older days."

"Did you know that Eleanor was Theodore's niece?" I start.

"Well, that doesn't sound right. Doesn't that make it true that he married his cousin, or second cousin?"

"No, you are all mixed up. Franklin was Teddy's cousin. Fifth, once removed. Eleanor was Teddy's niece, like I said. Teddy walked Eleanor down the aisle when she married Franklin."

"It makes me feel happy to know more about Teddy than Millie. "Perfectly acceptable. But I'm not sure that they were meant to be married. Says here Franklin was a cad back then, had some women on the side. Oh, and he got us through the Depression and the war by saying he'd balance the budget with beer."

"Beer? I think that he did plenty more wonderful things for our country, and you focus on *beer*."

I reach for my trusty journal, but it's no longer on the seat beside me. It is my lifeline. "Oh, dear! I don't see it. Pull over, Millie, so that I can reach my book." I write all my trivia down just for these occasions. I don't care if I lose a lot of things, but I absolutely can't lose that!

"I'm not stopping, Alva; if I stop, I won't want to keep driving. Besides, I do not want you to test me on the presidencies of our time."

"Why? You always tell me you're a history buff, even though I've seen no evidence. Millie, goodness' sake, pull over for a minute; I think it slid under the seat."

"I'll do it only because I don't want you leaning over with your skirt out the window. You're blocking my mirror! If you cause an accident, Franklin's ghost won't be the only one rolling about in a wheelchair."

I pictured us airborne, a flying Buick, maps fluttering out the window, landing in a waterless spring. No recuperative powers there.

The car slows, and I thrust my hand underneath the seat, touching a few soggy boiled peanuts that escaped the bag and pulling out the book. Millie rolls her eyes.

"I loved Eleanor, too, but wait . . . oh, here it is." I am so relieved. "Did you know that people believed that Eleanor loved another woman?"

"Like you always say to me, Alva, sometimes the truth you hear is not complete. But I don't think you can just imagine the rest."

I do not let her get under my skin. "They really kept their personal lives separate from each other, but they were a team in politics. I'm sure that she helped him make all the important decisions and handled all the press and critics. I bet that she was the one who made sure no pictures of him got out after he had polio. You could keep things quiet back then. It's not like today, thank goodness, where people have to be in everyone else's business."

"People do, yes." Millie glances at me and raises her eyebrows.

"Repeating important information is not the same as gossiping," I say.

Millie

We'd journeyed forty-two miles and stopped at a roadside recreation area to have a little stretch. Not too far from Hudson.

"I'm not sure we'll make it all the way to the Dells today; looks here like we have hours of driving left, and it's almost three. If you are right with all that map plotting, we might make it to Eau Claire. I just saw the sign for the exit in sixty-two miles."

"Which would still be wonderful," Alva says with a grin. "Do you know what Eau Claire means, Millie? I mean, have you heard the story?"

"No, Alva, I don't remember any story about Eau Claire." I know I sound a bit testy, but my share of the adventure so far has been a bigger share of the driving.

Alva doesn't recognize my frustration. She continues, "Well, it came about because of some pioneer traveler sorts. They were paddling up some muddy river when they came across a littler river, and it was very clear. They were French. They said something like 'Voile, it's Eau Clair,' which meant Clear Water. I think I have that right."

"You don't speak French," I say.

"I *know* I don't speak French. I said it was something *like* that," Alva snaps.

We head back to the car, and Alva gets back in on the passenger side and pulls on her seatbelt. "Alva, if you have to stop every fifteen minutes, we're not going to make it anywhere. I was going to tell you it was your turn to drive, but now I'm so hungry, and I drive faster, so we will get somewhere to eat sooner." And then I smile slyly. "All that talk about 'Eau Claires.'" I draw out the 'e.'

"*Ha!* Okay, Millie now *that* is quite funny," she giggles.

"I meant to be funny," I chuckle. "See, you are not the only one who can play with words."

"*Eclairs?*" Alva is cackling. "*Yowzer!* Oh, now I'm going to wet my pants!"

"*Terrific,*" I snort, "*another* rest stop. Maybe a gas station where they have some of those little doughnuts."

Alva goes back to the map, but I keep one eye on the road and the other on the lookout for a station with a little grocery attached. It's midday already, and we've eaten the sandwiches we packed.

Alva finally looks up and seems resolute. "Well, we could pick up some pretzels or doughnuts, but they will ruin our appetite for later. Millie, why don't we just go all the way into Eau Claire? Have an early dinner and a good night's rest. I tossed and turned last night, had a few nightmares about getting older, becoming extraneous. Must have been a little anxious about this adventure. I didn't want to worry you, but things are starting out swimmingly. Let's celebrate our first day of freedom."

"Swimmingly, huh? Well," I note, "so far, we haven't drowned. But Alva, we haven't really accomplished anything as of yet. No adventure as far as I can see."

"Millie." Alva gets serious. "The mere fact that we left is a kind of dangerous undertaking for women our age. Good for us—to stave off security! It means we are part of the living; we can be measured as people who still take charge of our imagination. See, Millie?"

"Um, I guess. You seem different, Alva."

"We are in for a pound, pushing away our fear of dying, making our mark, and all of that," Alva says, waving her arms in big circles.

"Taking charge of our *imagination?*" I repeat her words with all the sarcasm I can muster.

"Most certainly. Imagination can run wild. We can follow it and then rein it in when necessary. Oh, and we need to be curious about *everything.* We will discover plenty on this trip." She says it with such surety.

Alva

It is almost 3:30 when Millie exits the highway and heads towards Eau Claire. I switch to the state guidebook, but I really can't find tourist attractions that might whet our appetites. And now *I'm* hungry.

"Millie let's stop at that Cracker Barrel. They have the best biscuits and are always very clean. We can look for souvenirs in the gift shop because I will have to bring things back for Robert, Carolyn, and Margaret. Maybe salt-and-pepper shakers painted with different states' names? I want them to know—I mean when we get back—that we were thinking of them on our adventure."

"I don't think they will care," Millie says while swinging into the parking lot. "Besides, they have a Cracker Barrel right down the street in Minneapolis. Same merchandise."

"It is the thought—"

"Okay, Alva, whatever you want. I am too hungry to think about shopping."

"That counts." I continue, "Maybe the waitress will have some good ideas about motels and museums."

"The waitress will most likely be a teenager working for tips to buy shoes instead of saving for a college education," Millie says more irritably than ever.

I knit my eyebrows together. "You are very grumpy right now."

"I could eat a dwarf," she retorts.

"That is a terrible thing to say," I admonish, and then, "Darn it, Millie!" as she hits the speed bump hard on the way into the parking lot. When she wrangles the car into a spot, I get out and slam my door. Millie locks the doors, practically runs through the parking lot, and pushes in front of me towards the hostess stand.

"Hello, we need a table for two," Millie demands.

"Maybe by the window?" I ask, trying to act more dignified.

"All the windows look out over the parking lot," Millie almost yells. "Any table will do."

The poor hostess looks a little alarmed at the redness creeping all over Millie's face, so she grabs two menus and bids us to follow her. She hurries to a table (next to the window, I might add) and hurries away just as quickly. Appeased for the moment, Millie stares at the menu. It takes her less than a minute to decide, and she puts her hand up to call back the waitress. She starts to order before the poor girl gets back to the table. I am appalled.

"I'll have the Southern Fried Chicken with the green beans and mashed potatoes, and those biscuits, really as fast as you can," she says loudly to the young waitress, with seemingly new shoes, heading to our table. There is *such* desperation in Millie's eyes.

I wait for the girl to get all the way to our table. "I will have… hmmm, let's see…" I glance up at Millie. She knows I'm just being a bratty baby sister, and I know, if we were a lot younger, that she would have already punched me in the nose. "Okay, I will have the same. But I want a baked potato instead of mashed."

We wait in silence after that. It's best that way.

Alva

Our food comes out shortly after the order is placed. I'm never sure that's a good thing. The chicken and potatoes were probably sitting under those warming lights for an hour, waiting for just the right unknowing customer. But it tasted okay. In a much better mood, Millie decides that we should split a piece of German chocolate cake with our decaf coffee.

"Now this," Millie is almost swooning, "is delicious."

I spy a new tourist map in the gift shop and ask the waitress if it is free. She says yes, and I am up and back in my seat in a flash. I open it up all the way and spread it over the table. After staring for only a minute, I cry, "*This!*"

"Don't scream in a restaurant, Alva. People will think you see a mouse or a cockroach. It is bad for business."

"Waldemar Ager's house is here, right here!" I jab my finger at a spot on the map very close to this very Cracker Barrel.

"Who *in the world* is Waldemar Ager?" Millie exclaims.

"Only the most interesting Norwegian to ever come to America. I cannot believe you don't know that!"

Coffee spurts out of Millie's mouth. "The most interesting Norwegian? Like the beer commercial? 'The most interesting man in the world,'" she says in a low, deliberate voice. "Isn't that a misnomer?" She is laughing so hard that the cake falls off her fork. "I'm sorry, Alva, I am proud of my heritage. I am. But let's be frank, it conjures up a picture that just doesn't fit, you know? Interesting and Norwegian . . .." She trails off when she sees my face.

"He *was* interesting. Very. He was a newspaper publisher and a writer of both fiction and nonfiction. He tried to preserve our Norwegian language and culture, so we didn't forget all of it."

"Nobody I know can speak Norwegian, so he couldn't have been very convincing."

"Well, that's because we all let Waldemar Ager down! And he spoke often in support of Prohibition. We let him down there, too."

"Doesn't sound very exciting to me. A teetotaler? I am not for drinking in excess, but a drink every once in a while? Can't hurt you."

"Millie, you are missing the point. He was a wonderful storyteller. He tried to keep our stories alive for future generations. He was even a poet. And he supported equal rights for women!"

"Well, that's something. So, what are you saying? You want to go visit the dead Norwegian's house? Is it haunted?"

"Millie! It is a museum! But now that you say it, I guess all museums are a bit haunted. They'd have to be. *We are going.*"

Millie pops the last piece of cake in her mouth and mumbles, "*Greit,*" which is "okay" in Norwegian. Good old Ager.

Alva

Our stomachs are full. Taking the advice of the young waitress with new shoes, who we tipped well but who probably didn't have any background in motel recommendations, we head down a couple of blocks to the Traveler's Lodge. The waitress was a little bit snippy when we didn't let her use our phones to use Google Maps. But Millie and I decided a long time ago that we would just use those new phones our kids got us to make calls. I think you get lazy when you stop trying to read a map or go to the library. That, and we didn't understand how to use them.

Anyway, we park in the weed-grown lot in the back of the "lodge" and head down the sidewalk toward the front office sign. The motel is painted a strange, streaky, aqua blue, like maybe they painted over some other color and didn't do a good job. And it has twelve small rooms that surround a pool with no water, and a tiny playground. The play area has all the prerequisites: a slide, two teeter-totters, three swings, and a merry-go-round. I remember taking Robert to just such a place when he was a boy. His bright blond curls, the same ones that turned to a deep gold as he grew, would ripple in the wind as I pushed him faster and faster. I can still hear those giggles, those sounds of total glee, and I wondered how long it had been since I had let loose and yelped with excitement. And then I wonder how long it's been for any old woman.

I sit down on the antiquated metal circle and begin to walk my feet around. It spins slowly. The circular motion lulls me into a serene acceptance. The visions I have tend to make me uneasy or spur me to action. But this rhythm calms my anxiety about this excursion of ours: the cyclical nature of life is beautiful.

After a bit, I stand unsteadily and grasp one of the metal bars. "Millie! Give me a push!"

"Alva, I don't think your sense of balance is all that great." She says it, but then the corners of her mouth raise up a bit. "Do you think that if I gave it a spin, I'd be able to jump on?"

"Won't know until you try it," I say with delight.

"Thank goodness I am wearing trousers," Millie replies and grasps the bar in front of mine. "Okay, hold on!"

The first push was hardly a push at all.

"C'mon Millie," I cry, "put your back into it!"

With a great big heave, Millie gets the old dinosaur of a ride going. I make a full rotation, and she grunts and pushes again, this time pulling herself up as it spins.

"I did it!" she cries with pure joy, and I yelp my approval. Our gray hairs blow a little bit in the wind. We are not spinning very fast, but we are revolving and evolving. Time stands still, or maybe it goes counterclockwise for a minute.

It finally stops. Millie is snapping her fingers in my face.

"Alva." It's one of those daydreaming things again. They are really making me nervous. You just stop talking. You are getting rust on your skirt. Can you get up?"

"I'm fine. It wasn't one of those things. Just mulling over life, the beginnings, and *endings.*" Shaking my mind free, I take her arm and continue to the front office to inquire about a room. Millie keeps looking at me with concern and nearly trips. We are both dizzy but don't want to admit it. The bright red neon sign, also framed in aqua blue, is blinking *VACANCY*, but the door is locked tight.

"Look Millie, we should have noticed. Not a car in the lot. And that slide looks dangerous. Someone is mowing the grass around the front, but I don't think this place is open for business."

"Sign should have just said *VACANT,*" says Millie absently.

I spot a man leaning against a landscape truck. "Wait, okay, I am going to ask that man over there."

"What are you going to ask him? 'Why is this motel closed?' How does that help us?"

"I don't know. But it can't *not* help us." My mind now clear, I stride with purpose over to the man. He looks about our age, with graying hair cut short like in a military style, and he is dressed all in khaki. "Excuse me, sir, we were referred to this property by a nice young woman down there." I point toward the Cracker Barrel even though he doesn't know we ate there." I smile pleasantly. "It looks permanently closed. Do you have any other suggestions for where we could spend just one night?"

Millie walks to my side as the man takes off his hat and scratches his head. "Doesn't that sound like you just propositioned him?" she whispers.

I think about it and then almost faint with embarrassment. "Oh, my goodness, that didn't come out right at all," I stammer. "We are just in the area for one night and do not want to get too far away from the Ager House where we are going tomorrow, and we just need to find a motel close by." I am as red as neon and babbling.

"What?" the man says in a gruff but sincere voice and then removes his earplugs. "Sorry, I use these when I use the edger. Makes a lot of noise. What can I do for you?"

I let out a long breath and steady myself. *Saved by earplugs.* "We are disappointed that this place is closed," I say more assuredly. "Do you know of another motel in the area?"

"Oh, this place is owned by my daughter. She got it in a divorce settlement, of all things. A big bunch of nothing if you ask me. It's a crazy story if you want to hear it. She and her new husband decided they wanted a smaller investment with better bones. This here motel has an ugly history, so they opened a bed and breakfast instead, right down there on Wicker Lane." He gestures down the street lined with big elms to our left. "I'm trying to keep this property up. We need a buyer. Are you interested in motels; you say?" He talks quickly and loudly. His ears are probably still ringing. I hope.

Millie steps up to the plate and pushes me aside. "We do not want to buy a motel, but we do want to find lodging for tonight. Does your sister's bed and breakfast have vacancies? You say it's just down the street?"

His eyes brighten. They are nice eyes, blue with little specks of gray that match his hair. "Oh right, I get it! You need a place to stay! Come with me, you lovely ladies. My daughter will be very excited that I have drummed up some business for her." He takes Millie's elbow and starts in the direction of the big trees.

"Sir, we have a car," Millie says. Maybe she wants to sound businesslike, but she's tickled that the man took her arm. I can tell.

"It is just right there," he says again and points enthusiastically to the third house on the right. "We can walk over, and you can meet her, and she'll give you a little tour. In the morning, she makes a dynamite breakfast: eggs any way you like *and* waffles."

"Alva, why don't you follow us over with the car. I left the keys right in the ignition." And Millie turns and walks away with the stranger without a second glance. I am steaming. She accused me of doing the propositioning, but here she is, doing the follow-up. And she is swaying her hips!! I note that there is nothing quite as distasteful as a flirtatious octogenarian. I watch as Millie, her tunic wrinkled from hours in a car and with a little stain of gravy on the sleeve, throws back her head and laughs. Ick. Like a *really* old schoolgirl. I turn the key and rev the engine a few times to get the frustration out and, admittedly, drive a little too fast down the half a block. The car slides on the gravel driveway and I almost kill one of those trees, but luckily no one notices. Millie disappears through the front door, and I take stock of my surroundings.

Okay, it's pleasant enough. Reminds me a little bit of our house in Crookston. It is white with two wide front porches, one up and one down. There are three dormers with three little stained-glass windows on the top. The yellow and red panes glow as the sun nears the horizon. There is a circular drive, gravel as I said, that embraces a careless garden of wildflowers. Big broad steps lead to a heavy brown wood door, lacquered with obvious care. The elms on either side frame the residence with protective branches. It feels good.

I walk up those steps and see the hand-painted sign decorated with drawings of flowers inside hearts. *Come into our Garden,* it reads. *Not very original,* I think meanly, but then I notice the sign art is rosemaling, a special kind of Norwegian folk art. *One needs to be kind to kin,* I think, and then the smell of those chocolate chip cookies hits me, and I'm in a better mood just like that.

My nose leads me right through the front door and into a large parlor/dining room. There is a Victorian table and chairs on my right, seating for at least ten, set with blue and white plates on crisp white linen. There is another table that holds a coffee urn, water cooler, and what looks to be lemonade. *And those cookies!* I know we just had that German chocolate cake, but there is always room for more chocolate. There is a grand staircase dividing the space that I assume leads to the guest rooms. On the other side of the room there is a grouping, of all things, of furniture upholstered in blue velvet. The rug is a mix of creams and blues and is on top of a polished wood floor. The room is both old-fashioned looking and contemporary, all at once. The mower man is standing in the middle, making introductions.

"Sweetie, this is the lovely—oh my goodness, we haven't exchanged names yet! I am Sam, and," he smiles, "this is my daughter, Laura." Then he reaches out for Millie's hand. She takes it and, I think, squeezes it instead of shaking.

"Hello, my name is Millie," she says, taking the lead role, "and this is my sister, Alva. It is so nice to meet you both. What a wonderful place you have! And you have a room for us tonight?"

I shake their hands in a dignified manner, but I suppose I look hopeful because I really want to stay in this place with the cookies.

"The pleasure is mine," says Laura, beaming. She is tall, taller than her father, probably about five foot nine, with an easy, quick smile. She wears a navy checked apron over jeans and a white dress shirt, her long blond hair in a ponytail. Yep, a Scandinavian. "And yes, we have room at the inn!" She winks. She moves gracefully to a desk that is hidden underneath the staircase, lit by a glass lamp that has multi-colored panes, much like the windows above, the same warm color illuminating this space. An old computer monitor blinks as she sits and types in our pertinent information.

"Your full names, please?"

"I'm Millie Johnson, and this is my sister, Alva Eklund," Millie announces.

I feel like we are both still Wilsons—pre-married, pre-kids, pre-old. Quietly, I say into Millie's ear, "Maybe we should be using our maiden name, Wilson, like an alias."

Millie chuckles but ignores me. "Just for one night, please."

"Certainly. And a credit card?" We both exchange looks, secretive sister looks, and shake our heads.

"You see," begins Millie, "we are on an adventure."

"We will pay cash," I say.

"An adventure? How mysterious! Will you share it with us?" Laura eyes us a bit suspiciously but with a twinkle. *She'd be one to enjoy a good story,* I think. So, I say "Yes." And then I say, "You see, we are both widows, and, well, I had a stroke, and I now see that my life has been a bit more—well, I mean, *less*—significant than I thought before. More just small. And I talked my sister Millie into taking a road trip. We didn't really tell anyone where we were going because we didn't want them to worry, and we didn't know where we were going."

"It's not devious or anything," chimes in Millie. "We are not going too far, and we just don't want to use our credit cards in case our children notice we are not with our friends in Morehead. Her older son Robert is awfully protective."

"He worries," I say.

"He does all her bill paying. And he's a bit nosy."

"Is *not.*"

Laura and Sam seem amused. "How long do you expect to be gone?" asks Sam.

"I came up with the plan."

"Not the *whole* plan," Millie complains.

I think she does that because she notices that Sam is looking at me with curiosity.

Millie continues, "I told the kids that we would be gone three weeks. That way, I will be back for my doctor's appointment in plenty of time. I have a bit of arthritis. *Just* a bit. Our friends in Morehead are in on it. We told them we would call with updates, and we will."

"We just want to visit a few places," I say. "And it's more than a bit of arthritis. Her legs get crampy. And her fingers."

Millie turns a shade of pink; she never likes it when people look at her as "really old." But let's face it.

"Do you want to share that *you* have a doctor's appointment too? Next month for that bladder—"

"Millie!"

"A true adventure then." Laura interrupts what was bound to be an uncomfortable couple of minutes. "Okay, cash it is. I'll give you a discount, too, provided you give us a few updates on all your escapades. Do you have things you want to see?"

"We are heading in the general direction of Niagara Falls. Alva has seen it, but I haven't."

"Oh!" I say, because I had nearly forgotten. "And we want to see the Ager House! It is near here, and I love all things Norwegian!"

"Not my first choice," Millie grimaces. "But when in Rome…"

"Or when in Eau Claire," I start to giggle. Millie joins in, and we are back in sync.

Millie

Our night at the bed and breakfast was one of the best ones I can remember. Laura, her husband Don, and Sam, that beautiful man, sat with us till the wee hours—almost 10 p.m.! They told us all about the history of this old house. It was built in the 1930s and was sagging in all the wrong places when they first purchased it. Don (Laura's new husband) and Sam are do-it-yourselfers. Sam is ex-military and an engineer by trade. Retired now, he is thrilled to have a new son-in-law who enjoys working with his hands. When Don quit his job as a carpenter for one of the big construction companies and bought into this idea of his wife's, they all got down and dirty. Laura is, yes, an artist, but she is a welder too! I didn't even know that women did that sort of thing, but I'm a little behind the times. The three of them reconstructed the house from top to bottom, to its old grandeur, and, I expect, even a little more than that.

We were only the eighth and ninth visitors since the opening, and because we were the only ones staying last night, we got the royal treatment. After we got settled and explored a little, Laura insisted on putting on a spread of beef stroganoff and big hunks of homemade sourdough bread. I didn't think I was that hungry since we had that late lunch at Cracker Barrel and a few of those chocolate chip marvels, but I plowed through and even had some room left for the lemon meringue pie. Alva, equally hungry though she acted a bit more ladylike and left some on her plate, relished her pie as well. We retired into the little parlor with the blue velvet furniture and had decaf and more conversation. They wanted to know where we were planning to go.

Alva was uncharacteristically talkative, said that she was escaping from something, but she just wasn't sure what it was. And she was sure she was meant to do something important. I knew that, but I didn't think she would share it. My sister still surprises me sometimes. We retired to one of the suites, with a big queen bed and a smaller bed too, probably meant for a young family. I said I'd sleep in the small bed, but as we discovered the big one had a featherbed mattress, I pushed Alva over, and we doubled up. It felt like, well, I don't know. Childhood, maybe.

Alva

I had been sleeping blissfully, and then, in the early dawn, I got up, uncharacteristically edgy. I put my feet on the floor and walked around the room in small circles, listening to Millie's snores. I returned and sat on the edge of the bed. I was awake and burning up. I tried to remove one of the quilts from the bed and, in doing so, had to move Millie.

"Millie." I shake her a little. "Millie?"

Flash! *It is a murky space. Smoke swirls, and I have to clean my glasses. A crowd is forming. Too many strangers are here, and a lot of lies are being told. Necks crane and are replaced by more. Serpent-tongued men spread deceit. Exaggerated claims muddy the truth. I cut to the chase and challenge their words with sharp ones of my own, metaphorically lopping off the wits of the dishonest. I am not usually distrusting, but this game is not being played fairly.*

Sitting stock-still, I come back to the unfamiliar bedroom. It was an odd portent to experience right here with Millie muttering beside me. I get up and dig in my big purse for my journal and sit at the little desk by the window to write it all down: the shield of fur from before and now the reprobates. With each augury, there is an accompanying shudder in my shoulders. I squirm around in the chair, a narrow Victorian number not all that stable. I fall back but catch myself before hitting the floor. I reach for another piece of furniture to steady myself but end up knocking my glass of water off the nightstand.

"What are you doing?" gripes Millie. "I heard a thud."

I am on all fours, blotting the water on the rose-colored carpet with the hem of my nightgown. Not so much water, and thankfully the glass didn't break.

"Oh, Alva! Did you fall out of bed?" Now there is alarm in Millie's voice.

I'm embarrassed and always feel a little lightheaded after such an episode. I try to sound unfazed. "No. I thought there was a fire, but then I realized the radiator is just turned up high. So, I was going to turn it down and tripped on the leg of this table. Spilled my water."

"You thought there was a fire, but you were just feeling hot? Are you running a fever? I'm a little chilly myself."

"Just forget it." I'm uneasy. "Go back to sleep."

"Weird. And no," says my sleepy sister. "Now I am already up. Let's go down for breakfast. I swear I smell those waffles!"

Out from underneath the blankets, it *is* chilly. We take turns in the bathroom, fix our faces, and dress in good pantsuits. After all, when breakfast is over, we are heading to the Ager House. Down in the dining room the table is set with a different set of bone China. This one has birds and botanicals. A goldfinch peers up at me through the syrup as I cover my gorgeous waffle. *Well, hello, Pudge,* I think. I swear the little bird is trying to tell me something, but I can't decipher it.

I push my lingering thoughts of liars, and now this little bird's apparent secret, out of my head. I need to concentrate on the objective of the day. It's too bad that we must leave this place. But of course, an adventure would have to include all kinds of new people. And these people were the best kind to meet. There might be more new friends in our future. Sighing with contentment for both food and company, I bring up the morning's plans.

"What I was going to ask you," Sam interrupts the conversation, "is if you would allow me to accompany you? Laura and Don have their hands full with this place today, but I've never seen the Ager House. And I looked it up. They are sponsoring the Pie and Ice Cream Social today!"

Millie jumps up from the table and claps her hands. She takes Sam's hands and pulls him up with her. Now the two of them are just standing there face-to-face and obviously a little uncomfortable. Think before you act is what I always tell her. Don and Laura look bemused because no one is saying anything.

"I'm sorry," Millie stammers. "It is just that I love ice cream—and pie." She is blushing but recovers when she drops his hands and smooths her hair. "Well, the cat must have got my tongue for a sec. I got overwhelmed. It's just that I really do love ice cream. I think both Alva and I would be happy to have you join us. What's a social without a lot of people? The more the merrier."

God, I think, *she must stop with the clichés.* I look from one to the other and break out a smile. "Yes, it would be wonderful if you could accompany us, Sam." I am proper *and* patronizing all at once.

Millie

I feel a little off-kilter today. Started with Alva falling out of bed (I'm sure that is what happened, and she is just too stubborn to admit it). And now, that scene with Sam? What is going on? I was almost giddy! Maybe it's like Alva has been saying, that this adventure is to discover new things, but maybe it's to rediscover old things too. For goodness' sake, I haven't made a new friend in decades.

"So, what are we waiting for? Alva let's go up and pack up our overnight bags. Get ready for more fun."

"Millie, we have time. It doesn't open till noon, and it's only 9:30 a.m. Checkout is at 11, right, Laura?"

"Sorry. I can't wait to get started. I'm filled with fun!" It's something my grandson says.

"I'm filled with coffee." Alva drops her napkin on the seat and heads up the stairway.

Laura starts to clear the table while Don sits down at the desk and busies himself with paperwork. Before the platter of cinnamon buns is swept away, Sam grabs one and pulls it into two parts. He hands one half of the sticky thing to me and licks his fingers. I imagine him licking my fingers and visibly shake off the image. *Dear me, I am a little crazy this morning.*

"I am so glad that you stopped by the old place yesterday," Sam begins. "I am always a third wheel around here. Not that Laura and Don don't want me around, but I feel in the way sometimes. My wife died a couple of years ago. Marcy. We lived down the street." He gestures to the left. "Raised Laura there. I stayed in the house up until a couple of months ago. Sold it so I could invest in this charming inn. So now I live in the back"—he gestures to the back— "in what's known as the carriage house. It's comfortable, but the kitchen's not finished. I'm over here a lot. I have another child, a son. But he's married with an adorable set of twins of his own. No room for me at *that* inn."

"You are lucky to be so close to family. But I can see where it might be too close sometimes. It's hard for me to imagine. I've lived by myself for so many years. Alva is next door, but my kids and their families are in different towns." I pause. "I forgot that I was lonely. I swear, Sam, I haven't even paid it any mind until last night. And today." I try to chuckle and wave it off. But I can't.

So, in an adventure that only began yesterday, I have already experienced a roller coaster of emotions. *Where had I put them for all this time?* Never too high, never too low. Now I am as restless as Alva.

Sam seems genuinely touched. After a long pause, he says, "You are lucky to have a sister. A companion. Let's be a travel trio today. Eat ice cream and pie and dive into the history of Mr. Waldemar!"

"Sounds like someone who is not to be named."

Sam throws back his head and belly laughs, a deep chortling sound that is contagious. "Well Millie! I read that book with my granddaughter. You are very funny!!"

"Filled with funny!" I smile a big smile. I like this man.

Alva

Millie drives, and Sam sits on the passenger side. She pushed me into the back seat. Leaning over Millie's left shoulder, I feel like I'm the odd man out, but I try not to complain and focus on the Victorian cottage ahead of me. It is white—lots of white here in the North. I guess people are warding off the winter's darkness. Or want to camouflage their abodes when it snows. *What are they hiding?* The house is narrow but deep, with the most adorable, lathed balusters around the small front porch and above on the tiny second-floor balcony. *A fully frosted gingerbread house!* The sign says they moved the whole house from down the street when the local hospital needed the lot. The Agers raised nine children in this house. Not such a big thing since ours in Crookston was about the same size and we had thirteen. Ah, but the history! I can't wait to get inside.

"I can't get past the whole temperance thing," chatters Millie. "A good Scandinavian would know that a bit of the hooch can keep a person quite warm in the winter."

"Did you really say hooch? What a slangy word for an old bird!"

"*Alva,* I am *not* an old bird."

"There, there," Sam interrupts. "Neither of you is remotely an old anything." He turns and winks at me, and I smile back at him.

"You are a charmer, Sam. Now let's get out of this car and see what's what. Just remember that Waldemar Ager was so much more than just sober. He was a journalist. There is nothing more attractive than a man who can write," I say without really knowing why. I believe it, though. "And he was a witty storyteller."

"Even better," laughs Sam. "I love a good story. Okay, ladies— shall we?" Sam leads the way up the steps, past the sign that says *Center for Nordic Culture,* and opens the door. There is no fee because today is the Ice Cream and Pie Social, and there is faint laughter coming from the backyard. I would have expected a larger crowd, but it is not so lively; there are only about six people milling around.

"Oh, look! They still have the knitting exhibit!" I cry.

"Wow," Millie says with an eye roll. She *obviously* doesn't understand the significance.

"It is the world premiere of these amazing sweaters and such, with embellishments that are significant to the actual Vikings!" I cannot contain my glee.

Millie groans. "Well, you can ogle to your heart's content. Sam and I are going to get some ice cream."

I can tell that neither of them is going to change their minds about this whole experience, so I wander alone through the old house alone with its charming, patterned wallpaper and warm, colorful carpets. I know it says *Do Not Touch* but I can't help but stroke the expertly woven jacket on the mannequin in one of the upstairs bedrooms. It's history, you know? I have that intangible feeling you get when memories connect you with other people, other people's memories . . . the dusty smells.

I am standing in the room, breathing in the past, when Millie takes my elbow and nearly scares me to death.

"The ice cream is delicious. You should go down and get some. I think there are a few people out there that share your passion for the old Norwegian and your passion for knitting, even though you don't knit."

"Please, let's go up to the third-floor library first and see the gallery. I know if you just learned a little more about Mr. Ager, you would come to appreciate all that he did." I beg a little more, so they follow me to the room filled with copies of his books and speeches and even his newspaper. Millie reads a few translated articles on how Ager tried to get Norwegian women to get involved in politics. Sam is curious how they moved the house and spends the next thirty minutes examining the gallery blueprints. I read a poem that is dedicated to the renowned Norwegian:

If you through strife and tears
Keep your childlike gleam to the last
Then you have a rainbow over your tears,
Then have you the halo over your coffin.
　　　　　– Johan Welhaven

All in all, we each get something out of the excursion.

"The renovations were really remarkable," says Sam.

"And okay, Alva, he was ahead of his time with his political viewpoints. Even helped the farmers and labor unions. He really *might* have been an interesting Norwegian," Millie admits.

Good enough, I think. We head back down to the ice cream. I have my pie ala mode, and Sam and Millie get seconds. There is a lot of both pie and ice cream because it isn't very well attended.

"That's the problem," Millie says between spoonfuls. "I think history is mostly appreciated by the generation that was closest to it. I mean, look around. We are the youngest people here, and that's saying something. It's ominous, don't you think? Maybe we are about to be history ourselves."

"That's morbid. On a beautiful day like this."

"I don't like to think about the future," Sam adds. "I'm okay with the history and the present, but look too far ahead and well, at my age. . . and well. . ."

We are all solemn.

"Let's talk about something else," I say. And we all remain silent, looking from one to the other.

I try again. "Sam, didn't you say that there was a story behind the motel? Can you tell us that?"

"I'm not sure it's very uplifting," he says, *rather mysteriously,* I think.

"Can't be worse than talking about our imminent demise," Millie pitches in.

"I don't know," Sam says. "It might be."

Millie and I cajole him into telling it. Maybe we shouldn't have.

"So," Sam begins. And he tells us everything.

"Laura—my daughter, you know—was married before. I know I mentioned that. He was not a very nice person, and my wife and I couldn't really understand her attraction. He was the kind of guy who always had a plan, usually a bad plan, on how to get ahead. What I'm saying is that he was a conniving bastard, excuse the language."

I tut-tut about the language, but Millie sniggers, and so he goes on.

"Fred, he was her husband, worked for some men who owned a chain of nursing homes. When Laura married Fred, he always boasted about his position in the company, always wore fancy suits and went to community chamber meetings. Laura thought he was a stand-up guy, but a father has a feel for those kinds of things. Fred was the manager on duty when one of the residents fell out of bed and died. There was an investigation, and no malice was found, but they did note the uncleanliness of the place and that a few of the people were full of bed sores. You hear about stuff like that, but it's hard to imagine it."

"Hmm?" *I didn't mean to interrupt. But I think that, even if you are old, the risk of dying from falling out of bed would be low. Breaking a hip is a different matter.*

"I have my reservations as well, Alva. Some people thought that Fred should have done a better job managing the place. Some people blamed the corporation that owned it. Anyway, long story short, they took away the license and Fred got let go. He just sat around and drank and blamed everyone else for his problems. A year went by. My wife got sick, and Laura and I took turns caring for her. We needed more help, but there wasn't any. Fred went to the bars in town rather than lifting a finger. My wife passed at home, not very peacefully. Anyway, that is a different story, one I am not ready to discuss."

Sam gets quiet, then shakes his head from the memory and continues. "Then, one day, Fred comes to Laura and says he has a plan. Somehow, he makes a pitch to the CEO of the nursing homes and gets them to sell the one property to him. No one else wanted to buy a place that still smelled faintly like urine, so he got it for cheap. Fred turned it into a motel. New sheetrock, some paint. They got a loan with Laura's good credit and bought furniture and things. The local Women's Club donated the playground equipment. It did a little business for the first two years, enough to pay off some of the mortgage. But, just like how no one wanted to buy it, no one really wanted to stay in it either, no matter what got fixed up.

"Laura should have probably quit her job and helped at the front office, but the money wasn't there. It was rumored that Fred cut corners, if you know what I mean. The housekeeping wouldn't wash the sheets, just made the beds, didn't sanitize the glasses, and filled up water bottles with the tap and pretended they were new. He ended up getting together with the daughter of the old company. A maid found Fred and the girl rooting around like pigs in room eight."

"Ugh," I say. "Adultery is such a common vice when it comes to villains."

"Man, I hate that little weasel. If I could get my hands on him now! My girl finally got wise and divorced his sorry ass. But she got saddled with the motel. Still paying off the last of the mortgage with nothing to show for it. We've been trying to sell that motel ever since!" Sam ends with a smile, but underneath, I can tell he is a very bitter father. We all sit in silence.

"What *a snake* he was!" I say with disgust.

"Whew," Millie says.

"See, not such an inspiring story," agrees Sam.

"He sounds very deceptive, and his corrupt actions poisoned all those people: the old ones, your family, you. And what about the employees? And the unsuspecting guests? Wow, I know things like this happen, but my spirit breaks every time I hear about them just the same. A *snake*," I repeat. I don't know why this story of predatory behavior affects me so strongly. But it does.

"There are a lot of snakes out there," Millie confirms my worst fear.

"Whatever happened to him?" I am curious, but I also want to make sure our paths never cross.

"Slithered out of town. Haven't seen him since." Sam stands then, ready to be done with this chapter.

Our spirits and the last of the ice cream eaten away, we get in the car and drive back to the bed and breakfast. I sit back against the worn leather seat, and my gaze drifts out of the window. The streets are lined with quaint little houses, children playing, a curious cat weaving between flower beds.

I think about my own trials and tribulations with our children. My two sons weren't angels but closer to heavenly than the other. There is no guarantee with kids, or with anyone for that matter. Even though things seem okay one minute, life can throw that proverbial wrench in pretty quickly. Once, I had a dream, when I was much younger, that my kids were actually tigers that lived in our basement. They were the sweetest tigers, but sometimes I forgot to feed them (in my dream, you know), and when I remembered, I'd wait at the top of the stairs and see those great big teeth and think, *They might eat me.* Silly. But you can't be careless with children. And you especially have to keep an eye on their friends. It sounds like Sam's girl had found herself a smarmy reptile.

Millie yells from the front, "Alva, why'd you get so quiet? We're back. Let's go in and pack." The afternoon is upon us. I blink fast and follow her.

We meet Laura in the hall. "You should name this place," I tell her. "Like the Ager House, but maybe not with your last name. It's Ekelson, isn't it? Maybe after a songbird or something."

"A wonderful idea," Laura laughs. "I will let you know what we come up with when you call. The Dells are not too far a drive. Remember, you promised to keep us all apprised of your whereabouts, and we can't wait to hear the stories."

"We did promise," replies Millie and gives Sam a reassuring smile. "The last leg of our journey will have us landing back on your doorstep."

"I will look forward to that," Sam says with emphasis. "Here." He takes a pad of paper from the little desk and jots down his phone number. "Please call me and tell me some good stories. I will live vicariously through you." Sam hands Millie the piece of paper but has the good graces to smile at both of us.

"Maybe you should go with them," Laura says offhandedly. Sam seems to be seriously considering it. Millie hadn't heard her, but I did. I wanted this adventure to be between sisters, so I pretended I didn't hear her either. We walk down the driveway, the gravel getting into my shoes.

Millie gets in the driver's seat, rolls down the window, and continues to wave until our new friends are out of sight.

I wave, too, but not for so long. I could swear that I saw Sam head for the garage. Surely, he wouldn't follow us. He insisted we take his phone number, and I didn't want to use it for anything but emergencies, but now I figure we should call him later and make sure he stayed put. It starts to drizzle, and I hear sirens, so I close my window. I say, "Millie, please put both hands on the wheel; it seems a bit treacherous."

Alva

We take turns driving and napping for the rest of the afternoon. I circled the Wisconsin Dells on the map; we really wanted to know what a "Dell" was. I guess I was a little tired from the morning, and I nodded off.

"I think I passed it," moans Millie.

"What?"

"It's getting dark, and I have trouble making out signs in the dark," complains Millie.

"For Pete's sake, Millie, it's not even dusk, but why didn't you wake me up sooner? There are plenty of bad things that could happen to a couple of old ladies in the Wisconsin woods." And I could see those bad things lapping at my consciousness—a bear tired of just raspberries to eat, an armed group of hapless hunters, a melee of mosquitos looking for unsuspecting hosts. "Whoa!" I say a bit too loudly.

Slowing to a near stop, Millie sighs grumpily. "I saw a sign that said Wisconsin Dells, so I took Highway 12 to the east. I'm sure that's right. But I didn't see any 'Dells.' Must have passed them."

"Okay, but what little town is this? There's a place right over on the corner, um. . . the Spinning Wheel Motel. That's a nice name. Do you remember? Mom used to have a spinning wheel on the second floor of our first house in Northfield. Well, not a floor exactly, more of an attic. But I remember the *whrrrr* it made. Maybe we should pull in and call it a night. Look, it's got a diner next door. 'The Broadway Diner. Good Eats.' Looks perfect."

We pull into the tiny parking lot between two old log cabin-like buildings, get out, and stretch our legs. The way I have it figured, we didn't overshoot the Dells by too much. There are billboards pointing the way just out of town. Checking in is not so scary this time. The Spinning Wheel appreciates cash without question. Millie stays with the car while I pay.

The room is clean and has a television and a mini fridge. We walk over to the Broadway and end up ordering too much food, but luckily, we have a place to save it for lunch tomorrow. I have the blue plate special, the one with mashed potatoes and shredded beef, and Millie orders the meatloaf. Good eats.

When we get in the room, I spend some time writing down more details from the visions, a few notes about the Ager House, and add that story I remember about the tigers.

We share a bed again. A king-sized bed with a button that, if you pushed it, would make the bed vibrate. I'm not sure what that was all about, but I don't have a quarter, so we don't try it out.

"Millie, we forgot to ask the name of the town we're in."

Alva

Elephants. I am not dreaming. I hear elephants trumpeting. "Millie! Come out of the bathroom!"

"What is it? What's all that ruckus?"

I'm staring in disbelief at acrobats and massive gray swaying trunks. I'm frozen in time. Magical transports are rolling past my window and clowns are calling after them. Chinese tumblers are next. Then white horses with gleaming manes and hats with feathers. The carriages are ostentatious, the first with gilded carvings of wild beasts and serpentine women and wheels like pinwheels of pink and purple. The next carriage is an audacious red with bright white block letters: *RINGLING BROS.-- WORLD'S GREATEST SHOWS*. That one has its own barred caboose with a lion roaring its discontent.

"It's a *huge* circus parade." Regaining reality or not, I can't tell. "Right here in front of us." And I knew she wouldn't believe me, like I was lost in my brain somewhere. *I* didn't believe me. Pulling on my pants but forgetting my shoes, I stumble into the street, lined by spectators seemingly more prepared for the sight of something so amazing and so nostalgic than me. It was fairy-tale-like to me because I always wanted to be in a circus. Yes, it is a common aspiration for many, but unusual for me, being *me*. I knew a girl named Carolyn once, and everyone called her Carnie, for short. She was sweet, like cotton candy, and ethereal. And every time I heard her name, an image of a carnival popped into my head: a carnival that moved from place to place, probably to start and stop young love. I guess I didn't want to be a circus performer as much as to be Carolyn. "Millie, come join me. I'm not making it up. The Spinning Wheel is in the path of a parade!"

Millie, who does put on her bedroom slippers, joins me in awe. The question remains: are we two old ladies who have both lost their minds, or is there a reason for a morning circus in the middle of a tiny town in Wisconsin near the Dells?

"Golly, Alva, go ask that person over there why this is all going on."

I look to my left and see a woman with a baby nestled in one arm and a toddler hanging on to her other. The baby stirs with the clanging of cymbals but doesn't cry, and the older boy has his mouth open like he is catching flies. "Excuse me, we are just here for a short time. Got a little turned around last night and didn't pay much attention to where we finally landed. Where are we? For goodness' sake, why is there such a celebration?"

Anyone could have seen the contradiction. This was such a big hullabaloo to be barreling down a narrow main street. You might have expected a lemonade stand and a game of kickball, but caramel corn and the Elegant Equestrians? No.

The woman pulls her eyes away from a tiny green car with six big fellows in it and looks curiously at me. "You are in Barbaroo, ma'am. And the parade is 'cause the Ringling Brothers invented their circus right down by the river and wintered here for some thirty-four years. I mean, some people still call the town Ringlingville. It's an annual thing. You can go over to the museum called Circus World and learn more about it if you want."

I'm just tickled. "Millie, this is an enchanted place. What a find! We can skip those Dells and stay here a couple of nights. I think I belong here."

"Alva? It will delay our date with the Niagara, but okay, we will stay at least one more night and maybe go see that Circus World tomorrow."

And so, we stay on the side of the street, one of us in stocking feet and both of us wearing nighties tucked into our pants. The oddity of the show upstages *our* costumes. We stand for so long my stomach stops growling, and Millie's legs are cramping, but the things we see! A tall wagon housing a giraffe clicks past us, pulled by four Sorrel Belgians. At least, that is what the sign says about those brown, beautiful horses. Three royal Bengal tigers glare at us behind their protective glass; one wobbly carriage contains only an enormous bell. Playing atop one wagon is a twelve-piece band! And following behind the band, two motorhomes: vintage behemoths with large windows. They show signs of wear and tear; the once-bright circus emblem is washed out, and there are dents and scratches all over them. These travel trailers look so out of place that someone has thought to have them escorted by horses on either side. Posters taped on the passenger windows promised in one, *The World's Shortest Man,* and in the other, *The World's Fattest Lady.* Through the window, I see one portly arm waving rather lackadaisically from beneath a flowering sleeve. I wonder if she *is* all that fat or if *he* is all that short. It seems a mystery. Following those disappointments is a children's section full of clowns in naval uniforms and a patriotic section with some (possibly) local teamsters waving tiny flags. And the three elephants are decked out in designer red and gold capes, each with a girl in a matching gown riding atop.

Later, after finding my shoes, eating some of the leftovers, and putting on blouses, we followed the crowd to the small square. A little courthouse and a few great big elms shadowed the patch of lawn, giving us some relief from the hot sun. We purchased caramel corn and lemonade and sat on a bench listening to hometown talent. A barbershop quartet serenaded wannabe jugglers and up-and-coming magicians.

And much later, sinking into the worn armchairs in our little room, we evaluated our day. We reread the brochures and rested. First, we needed to put our feet up, and second, we needed an early supper. Tomorrow, we figured we would go to the museum, and if we had enough energy, we would ask how far we were from the Dells. Then, on to the Falls. It was a plan.

"Alva, what part was your favorite?" Millie liked this game best because all you get is good.

"Hmm. I think the one in the kid's section, the wooden farm wagon carrying Cinderella's stepmother and stepsisters. Too bad

Cinderella was on foot, but she was lovely. I thought it was perfect to have those mean three women pulled by donkeys instead of horses. They looked so . . . ignoble."

"You and your words," Millie groaned and started reading a flyer. "Says here that in the 'nineteenth and twentieth centuries . . . the parade, with its yet unadorned wagons, was a way for wary townsfolk to judge whether the circus would be worth the admission fee to see the show. Realizing the value of this, circuses began to add ornamentation to the wagons.' The only ones that weren't that pretty held the 'Fat Lady' and the 'Short Man.' Sure, they were accompanied by some fantastic horses, but the wagons looked an awful like the RV Uncle Dave had, except for the circus posters. Or was it a Winnebago?"

"I don't know anything about campers, Millie, but did you know horses can be included in the pachyderm genre?" I asked without any humility. And then I picked up where she left off. "Says *here,* what we saw this morning was a 'prestigious procession of ponderous pachyderms!' How wonderful! Who do you suppose thought to use all those marvelous Ps?" It was a real question, but Millie didn't respond.

"Are you curious about the fat lady, Millie? I am."

Millie nodded sleepily.

"She was a star of the show, but I guess she didn't feel that way. Maybe she didn't feel well at all and that is why she hid in her camper. I don't think I would like to have all that attention focused on me, especially on a part of me I'm not too happy about. Like being old, for instance. I wouldn't want to be touted as the oldest lady in the world and then have people pay to count my wrinkles. Millie?" Millie was taking a nap. So, I guessed I would, too.

Later, with full stomachs, good eats again, this time in a little diner recommended by a real carnie delighted that we were "out-of-townies," we curled up, almost touching, sharing dreams of sugarplums dancing. It was not Christmas, but what a merry day we'd had!

Alva

This morning hasn't been quite as festive. Beads of rain hit the window of our room. We just make it back from Circus World before the clouds break open. I am lying on the bed watching the weather station.

Flash! *I am chasing a buck through the woods. There is no bow and arrow at my back; I am trying to catch it, hold it down. It is a big animal and way too fast, yet I am always just at arm's length. It is a ridiculous venture; doubtful I will be successful. But I cannot give up. I am so close.*

"Alva?" Millie comes out of the bathroom and finds me creeping around the dresser. "What are you doing?"

"Looking for my sweater," I say in a thick voice. In and out. I remind myself to take deep, cleansing breaths after these little spells. Such strange little scenarios, I just can't get over my mind's handiwork. Shaking my head to rid myself of the vision but grabbing my pencil to remember it as well, I scribble down an account. I'm sure it doesn't mean anything, probably a response to my current boredom and the rain. Except, come to think of it, a fur coat, serpent-tongued man, and now chasing a deer? There's a thread of something there.

The museum was a letdown after yesterday's extravaganza. Lots of big top memorabilia and some live shows in the hippodrome by tired or sobered performers who miss the smell of canvas. A bit of excitement came about when some trick riding by Annie Oakley almost caused Buffalo Bill to go to the local hospital instead of finding his way to the stagecoach hold-up. I wondered what people were thinking after reading the banner *WILL BUFFALO BILL SAVE THE DAY?* It was meant to be rhetorical. The rain turns to drizzle. I add some notes in my journal, circus lingo for later puzzle-solving, and go throw it into the car with our bags. We skip out on the Broadway and find an old A&W about a mile out of town. After lunch we get back on the interstate.

"I think we are lost again." This time I am driving, and things look so familiar that they are out of place.

"You're not lost, Alva. This is still Baraboo, Wisconsin; says it right on that sign, so you've just made a big circle. And look, there's a camper in the next lane with that circus poster pasted on the window: *B_ the W_rld's Fa_test W_man*. Most of the letters are too faded to read. Is it the same one that was in the parade? Maybe it's her driver. Or the circus administration decided to retire it. I still don't know why she got the big billing; she never came out of the wagon."

"Guess some of the parade people are still in town, still high on all that excitement. Anyway, you probably went the wrong direction after our stop and went back to the west instead of east. The root beer float went to your head. We are on the outskirts of town, back near the hippodrome. It might be an interesting stop. Or, if you glance up, you will see that we are right near a place called Ho-Chunk Gaming. But . . . this can't be owned by an Indian tribe; they've got to be Chinese, right?"

I understand her train of thought, but. . . "Okay, Millie, think about how nonsensical that is. I must have gotten a bigger part of the Norwegian gene pool, and you got the bulk of the Swedish side. Remember what Irvin used to say? 'Being Swedish is like being Norwegian with your brains knocked out.' Why would there be a Chinese casino in the middle of Wisconsin?"

"The same way there were elephants in the middle of Wisconsin," quips Millie. "Okay, smarty-pants, then you explain the name. I have heard many names of Indian tribes up here in the Midwest, and I have *never* run across one with such a foreign name."

"Foreign to who? I mean, *whom*? I suppose to you Swedes, everything around here sounds complicated. But it's your turn to pick the place, so I guess we will have to investigate the roots. I'll park the car, and we can just pop in for a second. Maybe find somebody to explain the origin."

"If everyone inside is Asian, then we are going to look out of place." Now Millie looks nervously at the other cars as I glide into the parking space. Most of them are Hondas.

"Uh-oh," I tease, "you are right; there are Japanese cars everywhere!" Every once in a while, I am too clever. I step out of the car, and Millie follows, both with our sweaters draped, purses clutched in our hands. With cautious steps we move toward the neon lights pulsating in the daytime heat. Such a big entrance for such short people.

The blast of air conditioning sends our sweaters off our shoulders to wrap tightly around our torsos. They are just cotton, not cashmere or anything, but then this is Wisconsin, not Las Vegas. And as it turns out we were not underdressed.

"I'm going back for my coat."

"It is cold, I'll give you that, but it is *not* winter, and you will look very foolish. Besides, Millie, people might take you wearing the fur coat as pretentious." But I follow her out anyways. "Why do we need to call attention to ourselves?" I say to no avail because she is already pulling the thing out of the trunk.

Now she is overdressed. Looking around, I do not see any Asians, which is too bad because I really wanted to ask them whether they use pet hair instead of real fur in their coats, and both Indians and Caucasians are dealing the cards and pulling the slot machines. There are a surprising number of women that look more or less like Millie, sans the mink, and me, but maybe a little more resolute about their whereabouts. A few wear translucent surgical gloves while feeding pennies into the slots. A very large woman, impossible to tell her lineage, with knee-high supportive hose and a very colorful getup resembling a kimono, is donning one rubber kitchen glove: a terrible apparition of that music star kid who only wore one white lacy number, I think. She looks familiar. I turn to look at Millie and see relief washing over her. She is not the only non-Asian in the place. Satisfied, she is not wasting any time heading for the ATM.

"Millie, what are you doing? We are on a budget! Let's just go talk to one of those people at the info booth. We are here to get insight, not lose our life savings."

"I've got more than a few Indian nickels in my fund," she quips. With a fistful of coins, she pushes me toward the *Ding! Ding! Ding!* Each machine plays its own melody, and the combined cacophony is hypnotic.

Later, glancing at the clock on the back wall, I see it's been over an hour that I have been watching Millie. Even with the respite of my day reverie, I've reached my limit. The appeal of dropping what *could* have been groceries into a trash can is plainly silly. I get up and head to the bathroom again and overhear a conversation between a few women on a tour group excursion.

"Excuse me, I am sorry to be a bother, but did it say in any of your tour information, just who owns this casino?" I ask casually.

"It says it right on the sign outside, the Ho-Chunk. Local Indians. Good group when I'm winning!" says a woman hurrying out while stuffing one-dollar bills in her wallet.

I follow them out to the floor, doubting whether any of the patrons really care about the Ho-Chunk story, so I decide to ask an expert. I order a pop from a young lady who looks fairly disinterested in her job.

"Have you been working here for a long time?"

"During the last few summers. I go to college in Milwaukee."

"Oh, good for you. College is so important these days. In my day, it wasn't so important for girls. I got a good job at the Honeywell plant not too long after high school. One of the lucky ones. What are you studying?"

"American Indian Studies. I like the outdoors, plants, and things. I'm studying Ethnobotany," she says.

That tone is arrogant, I think. Well, I might be wrong about her tone. It's just that I feel a little insecure about my science education. I persist, "You may be just the person to answer a question of mine then. It's just that I'm curious how the Ho-Chunk got their name."

"Hm?"

"Well, it may sound naive, but Ho-Chunk . . . well . . . my sister said it sounded Chinese."

She doesn't laugh. I thought she would. And she isn't angry, thank goodness. I don't mean to come off like a nut. Instead, she tilts her head, trying to recall the hidden knowledge left by an overzealous teacher.

"You know, there is a story about that. We are obviously not Chinese, but some explorers, way back when, thought because of our name that they were on the right track to discovering some passage from the rivers here all the way to China. Boy, were they wrong! Most people just call us the Winnebago anyway. Like the RVs, you know?" With that, she wanders away.

"Yes. I know!" I shout after her over the slot machines. "Thanks for helping me understand." I hope that I sound appreciative.

I head back to find Millie, but she has drifted toward the pit and is now firmly rooted at a Blackjack table with a small stack of chips near her left elbow. I didn't even know she knew how to play. Crazy Eights and a little bit of bridge, yes, but betting? "Millie, what are you doing?? I just talked to a nice girl who told me some history about these parts. We can go now."

"*Hinikaragi.*"

"Huh?"

"It's Ho-Chunk for 'hello.' I learned it from Peter Werner here," chirps Millie.

A wiry, dark-haired man—he's probably about 70—raises his hand and nods. "Call me Pete. I've been coming to this spot for years now. Have a few friends in the tribe who told me about the progress they've been making in restoring the old language. They are trying to make a program on a computer that can translate it."

"Huh?"

"Alva, a computer program." She smiles knowingly at Pete. He must have told that to her, too, and I know she has no idea what it means. She wants to feel more hip. "You know, computer programs, Alva."

I don't know. All of a sudden, I feel much older. The smoke inside the casino is getting to me. Reminds me of Irvin.

Alva

It didn't start out like it finished. Millie isn't a card shark, maybe a dangerous bingo player, but nothing with a full deck. The thing is, she is just having an especially lucky day. Have you ever tried to do something new and you find you do it really well, and people say, "Oh, it's just beginner's luck"? That was Millie.

Pete, with his scaly complexion and thinning hair, is smiling at Millie. It is not altogether a sly smile, but it seems disingenuous. The dealer is barking out, "Place your bets!" and, "Winner, winner, chicken dinner!" The phrase seems silly if you ask me, but *Maybe,* I think, *you can actually win a ticket to the buffet. I don't know the rules.* Several people sit at slot machines nearby. They are trancelike, pulling on the handles with gusto. *Didn't they call those things one-armed bandits back in the day? Most of the people look as if they haven't left this place since "back in the day."* The gent closest to the table is actually sleeping on the machine, his head resting heavily on the buttons. *The sad thing,* I think, *is that when he wakes and stumbles out, another will take his place.* There are too many people like Pete, and the handle-pullers, and the dealers. All of them are hoping for something tangible in a world full of false hope.

"We need to get going, Millie," I say to her at last.

"Alva, I don't think that it will hurt one little bit to stay in these parts for a little longer. I am just getting the hang of this. You add up the points on the cards to equal as close as you can get to twenty-one. If you think you have the right cards, you put a bunch of chips down. Pete, here, says I am a natural. You remember when I was in grade school?

Top of the class in the math department, I do believe. I have an uncanny ability to count quickly. Always been that way."

Resigned, I sit down on a little stool just behind Millie and Pete and watch them put cards down and tap the green felt for more cards. Now that I think of it, I am probably the one with the better math skills.

I was in algebra once, the only girl in ninth grade allowed. Alas, I fell in love with a blond Hungarian boy named George. He was the smartest boy in class and always got to bring home extra work. I'd follow him to his house and sit in their front yard on the bench of an antique covered wagon. I didn't mind when he got the answers faster than I did. My crush seemed to consume my affinity for calculations, and I was sent back to regular math not long after.

It's stifling in here.

Curiously, Millie's pile of black and white chips continues to grow and is joined by a few red ones. *Millie is hot, too.* She has tossed her coat cavalierly on an empty stool between herself and Pete. The ostentatious French label on her coat looks out of place. Pete doesn't appear to be doing as well. But Millie and Pete are getting along famously. She is telling him the story of the doilies.

"I had no use for coasters," Millie starts to explain to Pete, "or at least I didn't think so, but our sister Harriet was such a clumsy thing. She always put her tea down on the table with such emphasis when she talked. The cup would take chips of varnish from any table. Her own furniture was full of pockmarks. I never did that. My furniture was in good shape; no chips, scrapes, or rings. Even my kids knew how to set down a cup, with or without a saucer. Well, Harriet was visiting one afternoon and was going on about something when I realized that she was going to make her point by slamming her cup down. She was about to absolutely ruin my new coffee table. In desperation, I ran over to where my daughter was struggling with white felt, cutting out snowflakes for a school project. I just grabbed one of those snowflakes and popped it under Harriet's cup just before it landed."

I feel my head pound.

"And you know what? Once I saw that pretty little snowflake peeking out . . . protecting my best furniture, I thought, *What a marvelous idea to crochet delicate little spirals for all over!* Coasters with their brown cork were not fashionable at the time. They were so manly. But this idea? Everyone loved them! My doilies (that's what people call them now) are still the best gift given for wedding showers and the like."

Does she realize that she wasn't the first to think of doilies?

Pete laughed or sputtered. I couldn't exactly make it out. It was a silly story, but he seemed to enjoy the chatter.

"My wife used to like lacy things, too," he said wistfully, and I was surprised at his sincerity. He raised his hand, and the drink lady handed him a Coke with a cherry in it. He immediately gobbled down the cherry first.

"So, you're a widower?" I ask. Millie is too busy looking at her cards to notice the show of emotions. Pete doesn't reply to me, so I try again. "Are you hungry?" I smile at him. "Millie and I are going to get a bite to eat in a little while."

"Not now, not now." Pete scowls. "I need to do better on the next hand."

"Well, if you are a widower, you probably don't have to worry about making enough money to buy pretty things," says Millie. I guess she was kind of listening. "In my opinion, a widower has it a lot easier than a widow because most of the decorating is all done, and there's more money available for new hobbies and such." Millie is insensitive, in my opinion, but she says that when you get to be our age, you don't have time to mince words.

I am thinking, *Why did Pete say "need" instead of "want"? And why do Pete's hands shake so?* He is uncomfortable with Millie's question and answer. The more agitated he gets, the more his hands shake. He reaches for one of those awful cigarettes he is smoking from a half-crumpled pack and looks for his lighter.

"Where's the darn thing?"

"You shouldn't smoke those," I tell him. "My husband died from just such a habit."

"I may die not having one just as well," says Pete.

And I believe him. He wipes his face with his tobacco-stained hands. Looking more closely, I see that his dark hair is oily, like he needed a good shampoo. He hadn't been home for a while, I'd guess. He is glancing slyly at the very big lady who had just sat down to the left of him. Her immense body is balanced precariously over two stools. Her size is accentuated by the yards of fabric draped around her: *a housecoat suitable for the Met Gala.* I'd seen something like it in a magazine once. Her stubby arms hold her cards high on her belly, and a large tattoo of a deer is evident on her forearm. The antlers of the deer quiver as she wobbles, making it appear that it is getting ready to charge right off the table. *I think Pete is trying to peek at her hand.*

I refocused on him. "Someone trying to kill you over a game of cards?" I asked. I meant it to sound like I was joking, but it came out kind of whispery.

And right then, he starts to choke, a coughing fit so intense it rattles the table along with his chest. Arms outstretched, grasping for support, he knocks piles of chips from the table as he falls to the ground. Panic ensues. The dealer, whose nametag identifies him as McGregor, calls for the floor manager as he steps away from his post. The large lady (there is no more polite way to say it) in her flowery kimono slides off her stools in a feeble attempt to help Pete but lands on top of him instead. His lady luck. As they struggle, the abundant fabric covers his torso entirely. The dealer and several people from nearby tables rush to pull Pete from under the fabric garden of camellias, petunias, and tulips. Not really concerned with his rescue, I watch her thick fingers and think, *Is she pocketing other peoples' winnings in her own oversized pockets?* An ambulance is called, and Pete is whisked away to the local hospital.

Millie and I are unnerved: she, because of the sudden departure of her new friend and her poker chips, me, because *I have witnessed a robbery.* I think. We totter toward the door. No one pays us any attention.

Alva

"Follow that ambulance!" *I feel like a police detective or maybe Perry Mason.* Millie is settling behind the wheel without my same urgency.

"Alva, what are you talking about?" Millie is irritated, not outraged. "I need to park over there nearer to the lodge. They said they would give us a free room because of all the action. I still don't think it makes up for me losing my chips. They'd better be paying for the buffet as well," she sniffs.

"I was waiting to tell you, but it was a secret I had to keep until now. I saw what really happened!"

"Mind you, Alva, if you start dreaming up things right now, I may just let you out here. I need to put my feet up. In the morning, I am going to find out poor Peter's last name, and maybe we can send him a card and maybe a doily."

"I am not making anything up. That casino and you were robbed—on purpose! I saw Pete go under the table and help that woman fill up her pockets with those poker chips. She was in on it. Pete was a desperate man."

"Desperate? He looked a little unkempt, but I doubt he is a thief." Millie is eyeing me warily.

"It won't even show up on the surveillance, I bet." *My mind is reeling.* Here was a seemingly nice man, down on his luck and alone. But we were unsuspecting, and he was a crook. In the past, I might have pushed the whole thing out of my mind, but now I find I can't let it go. Is it the mystery I want to solve? Fate has a certain shadow of doubt that it drags along.

"I am famished," Millie whines. "I cannot do one more thing until I get something inside of my stomach. Hear it growling? You can try to convince me over dinner. What does that advertisement say?"

Resigned to appease her appetite before she believes my story, I read: "With our wide selection of dining options, we are sure to satisfy your taste buds. Offering an attractive and stylish getaway, the **Brass Lamp Steakhouse and Lounge** offers its expertise to rejuvenate your energy and satisfy your appetite. Begin your evening with a cocktail in our fireplace lounge, listening to American and International classics played on the baby grand piano. Once seated in our gorgeous dining room, peruse the menu and wine list for an experience to remember."

My stomach starts to growl, too. *You need fuel to solve a mystery, and puzzles can be worked on over dinner.*

Millie

Alva's mind is doing somersaults. Not in a good way. After dinner (it was a really wonderful dinner), we sat and listened to the piano player, but Alva was distracted. The Brass Lamp turned out to be a lovely old house set back in the Wisconsin woods that someone turned into a restaurant. Walls inside it were torn down so that the dining room and living room were just one big dining room with round oak tables sitting on old oriental rugs. A glass beaded chandelier cast soft light over the diners. The Fireplace Lounge was a tiny space that probably used to be the parlor. It was so cozy in there that we almost forgot the day's events. But I mistakenly talked Alva into having a small glass of sherry, and it got her back to talking. This whole story about the robbery seems farfetched. I mean, I didn't see anything. It could be true, but her visions have shed some doubt on her mental awareness. Alva argues that those visions, when she has them, come with sensations of being in a totally different place. "This robbery," she said agitatedly, "happened in the casino, and we were both right there. And you, Millie, are not that observant. Also, you are *never* in my visions."

I am not sure how to take that. I have been such a big part of Alva's life these last years. How is it that she is dreaming about going places without me? Needing some comfort of my own while Alva is still sipping her sherry, I walk to the restroom and call Sam. He sounds less concerned and more amused when I begin to tell him about Alva's heist theory. But he asks some good questions and starts to take it more seriously as I describe the scene. His voice is reassuring, and he asks if he should drive up to the Dells and lend a hand.

I'm not sure what to say to that. My mind thinks it over, and I realize that, on the one hand, I'd enjoy his company and his insight into Alva's stability, but in the end, I know it would be a disservice to my sister. She needs this adventure, and she needs to feel in control of whatever is happening. *Really,* I admonish myself, *is there ever a time when Alva doesn't know what she is talking about?* I assure Sam that we will be fine muddling away on our own and that I just need to know he hasn't forgotten us. I am certain I hear him smile on the other end.

Walking back to the lounge, I begin to take Alva's robbery theory seriously. *The quick end to my winning streak may have shocked me so that I didn't see what was right in front of me.* It is risky to ignore Alva. She has a way of always figuring things out. I resign myself to follow her intuition.

Alva

It did make the *Wisconsin Weekly* headlines the next day: "HO CHUNK CASINO WAS ROBBED." Lightning had done some damage several days ago, and the surveillance cameras were not working. "This is *not* Vegas," said a casino security guard in a surprisingly arrogant way. Almost $500 in chips disappeared off a table while people were waiting for paramedics. They weren't sure if they had been cashed in yet. Wasn't much of a crime.

"Hello, Precinct Five. Is this an emergency?"

"Officer, we know who took the money from the casino."

"Ma'am?"

"We saw a man pretend to have some heart trouble. He kind of fell, knocking the chips off the table, holding his chest, and while he was under the table, a big lady helped scoop those chips up."

"Are you talking about the robbery that was reported yesterday?"

"Yes, well, we weren't totally clear on the whole thing, but once we got back to our room, we talked it through. Millie believes me now."

"Okay . . . could you come down to the station and fill out a report?"

"We are starting out this morning to Niagara, but it shouldn't be hard for you to track that man down. He went in an ambulance to the hospital." I had been holding the phone up so that Millie could hear and then realized I could use the speakerphone feature. *So much easier!*

The pause was unmistakable. He heard my raspy old lady voice, and I knew he pictured some crazy old broad. "Ma'am, generally, when an ambulance takes a person to the hospital, the paramedics believe it is a health emergency. Do you think you might have gotten a little confused about what you saw?" I looked at Millie's grimace and touched the end call button.

Old people… Nowadays, everyone assumes that if we do or say anything unusual, we have Alzheimer's. I remember hearing a story where an elderly man was moved from his boyhood home to a nursing home. For eighty years, he lived in the house that his grandfather built for his family. He was a boy there; he was a father there. A widower there, too. So, the time came when his family was concerned with his ability to care for himself, all alone in that big house. They sold most of his belongings and got him situated in a "better place." Well, he stayed the first night in his new little room where nothing was familiar. He slept soundly like he always did, and he woke up to urinate, the same way he always did around three in the morning. He raised himself from the bed and slipped on his slippers. He shuffled sleepily out the door and headed left towards the bathroom. An orderly found him relieving himself in a hall closet. Thing was, almost every night for those eighty years in his old house, he turned left toward the bathroom. In the nursing home, the facilities were on the right. His family was alarmed at the morning report. The nursing home staff was alarmed at the mess. The advocate on his behalf believed that dementia was the obvious cause of the accident.

It wasn't that he was senile. He was just used to a pattern, one that changed overnight without anyone telling him. Medication muddled his brain, and after *that*, he *was* demented. *The end.*

Millie and I were breaking our pattern, and I may feel like a fish out of water, but I'll be damned if someone is going to convince me that I am off my rocker. "This needs an investigation, and if the police—"

And it was about that time that Millie lost it.

"I've got to go back to the casino!" she yells, knocking all the trappings off our tiny motel dresser as she snatches the keys from underneath the checkout information and a few postcards.

"What's the matter with you? Are you having some kind of medical emergency?" I am concerned.

"Oh," she moans, "Oh, I've left it."

"Left *what?*"

"With all the excitement yesterday, I must have left our coat in the casino. What was I thinking?"

She was out of breath, and I headed to the bathroom to get a cold washcloth.

"Oh . . . the sentimental value. I mean, Irvin *gave* that to *you*. And now he's dead, and I've been wearing it, and I was planning to give it back to you. People cannot, should not, go and lose memories."

"I won't miss it." *I might be lying,* I think. *I will.* "Lie down on the bed for a minute while I think. You cannot drive anywhere in your state. I put the washcloth over Millie's eyes and take a breath.

We stay that way for a very long minute, but Millie is hyper-focused on the mink. She jumps up and I follow her out the door, heading for the car at a pretty good clip, purses banging against our thighs. At the far end of the lot there is one of those big Winnebagos. Same name the girl at the casino mentioned, I note. *Is it the same one Millie saw before?* It has a poster taped inside one of the windows, but I can't make out what it says. "I think the circus is following us," I say. "Isn't that odd!" But Millie isn't listening. "Millie! Slow down!!"

It is a twenty-minute drive back, and it only took us twenty-one.

Millie

The coat isn't at the casino. The table upheaval seems to have more intrigue then. I try to think like Alva and piece things together slowly. *Pete in convulsions, poker chips gathered, a really big flowery woman, and Pete on a stretcher, wrapped in . . . wrapped in a fur blanket!* We decide to take matters into our own hands.

Like Alva said, it is too easy for people to believe that we are a "bit off," and at this revelation, it is too easy for us not to take advantage of it. And on top of that, it makes us mad that people always think the worst of us. "Let's pretend that we are his sisters and pay Pete a visit at that hospital."

"Millie, won't we have to show our IDs or something?"

"Nope, like you've been saying, no one is going to not believe us. We're *old*," I proclaim with a sense of entitlement and control.

I guess the adventure really begins then. Alva jumps behind the wheel (jumps" doesn't really do her justice; wriggles like a salmon struggling upstream with purpose?). And we take off for the hospital. It is a small rural clinic, not really a hospital, sturdily built with a whitewashed front and URGENT CARE in bright red letters on the signage. It was urgent that we find Pete.

We enter the building and go directly to the front desk and inquire breathlessly about "Our little brother Peter. Is he going to be okay? What the heck happened, eh?" For some reason, our pretending affected our diction, and we sound Canadian.

The young woman looks flushed. "I know that a man was brought here from the casino. I heard the driver talk about some hubbub over cards and money falling to the floor!" She checks her ancient computer monitor. "Do you know the last name?"

Which makes us smile later because if we were family, certainly we would know his last name. We go blank. "Smith," I stutter at about the same time as Alva whispers an unintelligible something that sounds to me like, "Smwilsonlund." The young woman, impatient at our confusion, just searches "Pete." It wouldn't occur to her to question our relationship or our sincerity. Why? Well, you already know the answer.

"His name is Pete Werner. Says here that he was examined by the intern and released."

"Oh no, where would he go?" we cry in unison.

She points at the screen. "Wouldn't he just head home? Norway? Norway, Wisconsin? Isn't that up near Wind Lake?"

So, back to the Buick we go. With the map on the front hood, Alva looks up Norway. He had a full day's start. Alva starts to get in the passenger door. It creaks with overuse, and a couple of old Kleenex fall to the parking lot. Alva doesn't like to litter. There is a plastic cup and an old newspaper on the ground, too, so she picks it all up and heads to a trash can near the front entrance.

"For goodness' sake, Alva, we are in a hurry! You don't need to clean up other people's messes. Don't waste our time with your conscience." I know my face gets all scrunched up when I'm angry. Alva used to say I reminded her of crab apples. When we were kids, we would carve faces on those little apples and let them dry in the sun, and they got more pinched and more troll-like till they completely rotted away.

Alva

She has a point, of course. In the past, my conscience has been a real hindrance. Especially when it came to Irvin. In 1948, when I was just 19, I left my home in Crookston, Minnesota, with my girlfriend Shirley. We were headed to the city because we wanted to find work, and she heard that Honeywell was hiring young women with no experience to work in their shipping department. We had just finished secretarial school, and I have to say I was a pretty good typist. I was better than Shirley, but I never would have said it. We took a ride on the Northern Pacific that lasted hours: it snaked slowly around Minnesota farmland and North Dakota cornfields. I remember being so scared leaving home that I was afraid I'd be sick. In the train car, I sat next to the window where the rain leaked from a small crack, and the rain poured down the whole trip, seeping in at that crack. We stopped briefly in Fargo, and I had to go to the bathroom something awful! But I was one of the last ones to get off, and there was a long line, and it was such a short stop. "All aboard!" they called before I reached the bathroom door. Back near the window, suffering in silence, I wet myself and prayed that people would think it was the rain that soaked my dress. I told Shirley about it finally several years ago, and I don't think she's ever looked at me the same again.

Once we got to our final destination, I was in a great big hurry to find our room and change clothes. It was a small boarding house several blocks away, and we had to hike with our bags. A young man saw me struggling and offered to help me carry my things the rest of the way. What a dilemma!! I didn't want him to notice anything unusual about my dress, but the rain really was coming down hard and I was soaked all over. And I did need help. Shirley was always one step ahead of me, striding confidently along with her suitcase.

He was good-looking, the young man, different from the ones I knew in Crookston. He was very tall, with dark hair (the rain made it look even darker) and puppy dog eyes. He was kind of cocky in the way he acted, like he had saved me from some kind of horrible fate. Turned out I had already seen him once before when we boarded the train that morning. He was an apprentice engineer. "A fireman!" he used to say, like he was saving people from a burning building. He wanted to eventually be a train conductor. He had been watching me.

He was quite the charmer. Long story short, we started dating. He would travel for a week or two at a time, and he always would pick me up and twirl me around when he came back. If you asked Irvin, he'd say that, at first, it worked great when he worked on the rail and saw me every week or two. The track was straight; his chums were strong; there were moose out the window, and they drank whiskey on the sly. But more and more, I knew he missed me. He said as much. "I missed my Alva, her wonderful smile. She wants me, and nothing more!" he'd proudly boast. I was never sure if I should have been offended.

But I really didn't want more. And that fur coat became my albatross.

Alva

I stop my reminiscing for a sec because Millie is on a mission. We are speeding off in the direction of I-94E toward Milwaukee. Her eyes stare fixedly at the road and her hands are tight on the wheel. It is like the time we went to our fiftieth-class reunion. Well, it was hers, but I'd come along because the school only had fifty or so people in the twelfth grade, the year Millie graduated, and about half of those were dead. She drove like she didn't want to miss it, like she was afraid if she didn't hurry, she would wind up one of the dead ones. She didn't get the irony. I felt like if she wasn't careful, we would both be on our way to heaven.

"Norway!" exclaims Millie. "Niagara is on hold again, but maybe there will still be time. It is kind of on the way," she says. "Should we really do it, Alva?"

I am watching the road with alarm instead of really listening. She yells, "*Alva!*?"

"I think it's a little crazy that you keep asking if we should, yet you are driving like a bat out of you-know-where to get there."

We have left the hospital and look at each other like sisters do. Not that we read each other's minds or anything, but we've always been close, and almost eighty years is a long time. What else are we going to do? We don't have a solid plan—just out trying to prove we aren't irrelevant, even if only to ourselves. I find a black fine-tipped permanent marker in the glove box, not just your ordinary pencil or pen, and map the route. There is no erasing, no turning back.

"Have you figured out how to get there yet? How long will I be on this Interstate?"

Back to the map I go. "It's probably about 160 miles to Norway, Wisconsin. Take us a little over five hours. We should stop when we get closer and find a place to stay and come up with a plan. You know, like having a home base when you're not home. That way we can do some reconnaissance." *I'm excited.*

I understood Millie's desire to find Pete: she wants to recover "our" coat. She doesn't ask why I am agreeable to the retrieval of something I am not fond of to begin with, but I guess she figures it is because we are on the right side of the law.

Alva

The trees rush past as the car barrels forward. I shut my eyes to try to calm my nerves and think back to my early married life with Irvin. Each time he went on a job, he came back with something for me. The first time, it was just a bouquet of wildflowers. The second was a bag of blackjack taffy; the third time was a carved box with my initials on it. The gifts got progressively more expensive. I told him to stop buying me things because I was worried that, as an apprentice, he didn't have any money. He assured me that he had put some cash away before getting interested in the train conductor business. "I put away a *mountain* of money from the packaging company job," he'd say with all the bravado of a Hollywood actor. I knew there wasn't a mountain of anything except for his tall tales piling high on top of each other.

But I loved him. His shoulders were broad, and like I said, he was tall. I was just a short gal (*I'm probably even shorter now*), and when he picked me up like that, I felt like I'd been to heaven and back. When he put me down, I could never figure out if I was just dizzy or if my legs wobbled because my whole body was swooning. He was both confident and tender, which seemed to be just the right combination. When I heard that train whistle blow as it came into town, my heart skipped two beats. I'd wait outside the depot on Hennepin Avenue, breathless, until he came out and took my hand. We'd wander across the stone bridge and down the streets of North Minneapolis until we reached the little clapboard, two-floored building that I called home. One night, my Ukrainian landlady saw us kissing on the steps, and she chased poor Irvin down the darkened street with a broom! Later that month, he came back from a trip to Sioux City with a tiny gold band. And a couple of months after that, he followed me up to Crookston to meet my parents. It was a quick romance and a quickly planned wedding. I wasn't pregnant, nothing tawdry was going on, but we just couldn't wait to live together.

Even after the wedding, the gifts kept coming. It was part of his character back then. He wanted to be the guy that all the other girls dreamed about. Not that there were any other girls, but, you know, he wanted to be the best. He knew those things were not important to me, but he couldn't help himself. With his apprenticeship over, we should have been saving all the money because we had a child on the way. I finally put my foot down, and that's when he told me that some of the stuff he'd acquired (perfume, earrings . . .) was from the train's Lost and Found. He said the guys would just divvy up what didn't get claimed. I begged him to stop because it felt like it was stealing, and he finally *did* stop on October 17, 1951. It was the night our son, Robert, was born. Irvin was so excited. I called him just before we left for the hospital (Millie had come down to help me and was driving kind of like she is now) and told him to hurry. He ran from the rail yard to the hospital with a large garbage bag in tow.

Well, I don't know what got into me that night. All kinds of emotions came pouring out at once: seeing my beautiful son after the anguish of childbirth; Millie saying, "Well, he's small and has kind of a pinched face," when I was so full of love over my beautiful baby; Irvin's huge smile, and him saying "You are the best in the whole world, Alvie," and the beautiful fur coat he held out to me while saying "You can snuggle up with Bobby and it will keep you both toasty warm all winter." And, I don't know; I'm sure I don't like to think of it myself, but I think it was the look of absolute jealousy on Millie's face that, well, it was so not like me, but I said, "Oh, Irvin, you are the *best* husband ever."

It wasn't until later that I discovered the truth. It was just as I'd feared. It was stealing. Yes, those presents came from the lost and found, but the time for finding had not expired. Irvin and his cronies had taken turns raiding the storage room, using the black plastic bags that they wrapped around their feet in the cold engine car to stuff the loot into.

As Irvin told it, the night of the coat theft, the new kid PJ got caught with some of the other stuff.

"It was the damn cinder dick," Irvin said bitterly.

"*Irvin,* I do not like when you use that language."

"Sweet Alva, that's what we call railroad detectives. It's not a bad word. There's always a checker for us ashcats."

"Huh?"

"Never mind. The fact is that they don't have any actual evidence against the rest of us, and 'lil PW isn't gonna tell. But they fired all of us. Said they needed a crew they could trust."

Sure, I was disappointed in him, but that got lost under all the love I had in my heart with a new child. I gave him some credit for not taking it any further. He talked about being a boomer, a drifter who was kind of a glorified hobo, one who would work odd railroad jobs when the seasonal demand got too great. But if that was in his heart, his head took over: *We were a family.*

Not more than a few years later, the last of the steam engines that he loved so much switched to diesel, and the firemen disappeared. Luckily, Irvin didn't have to watch the demise of his importance: he had already started working at the printing company, trading his ideas of heroism for being responsible for the news getting out on time.

And you know the rest. I finally let Millie take it from the garage sale after Irvin died because she loved it. I just couldn't look at it anymore. It *had* been stealing, and it was the one thing that tarnished my memories of my dead husband. I didn't want it. But I sure wasn't going to let anyone else have it.

Alva

The drive is now turning out to be a comedown from our hopes of high adventure. Halfway to Norway, we stop at a Mobile gas station.

"Alva," Millie starts in, "I don't want to drive anymore; my eyes are sleepy."

"What? You only just started driving thirty minutes ago, and you napped the hour before that. How can your eyes be sleepy?"

"I don't know, but I think it's because there is nothing to see out there. No elephants, no casinos, and it's starting to drizzle again. That's what made me want to pee, in case you are wondering."

"I wasn't wondering why you had to use the *facilities*."

"Why can't you just say 'bathroom?' That's what it is."

I'm exasperated. "A facility is a place that is necessary to do something. You have to do something. It makes just as much sense."

"Well, I don't *just* have to do that. I want something to chew on. Pretzels?"

"All right," I say. And I realize that now I *will* have to drive because Millie cannot manage both the steering wheel and the snacking. *I'll get that nice young man to help me put the gas in the car.* "Full-service gas stations are disappearing fast, but this little gem of a station has someone manning the pump." *It's not that I don't know how to do it, but I don't like having to get out and pay and then watch the numbers on the pump slow down when my purchase amount is pending. Makes me anxious.* I get out anyway, even though the young man washing my windshield seems perfectly capable. There is only one other vehicle on the other side of the station—a big camper with a tank that would take forever to fill—so it doesn't look to me like the attendant is too busy to answer a few questions.

"Excuse me," I say to him, "do you know of any motels up there toward Wind Lake? One that wouldn't be expensive but not too dirty?"

"No."

Not all that friendly. Probably doesn't like his job. I was going to ask him something else but decide against it.

I go around to the driver's seat and wait for Millie.

Flash! *I sit on the front porch of an old cabin, listening to wild pigs root around in the forest beyond. There was the sound of cicadas, too, counting off the seasons. I just about doze off when a boar charges at my rocking chair. He stops inches away, mesmerized by the methodical rocking. He waits for me to finish so he can eat me. I keep rocking. He falls asleep at my feet.*

Millie comes out of the station with a pleased look on her face. She plops down in the passenger seat with her Snyder's salty sticks.

She glances at me while tearing the bag of pretzels open with her teeth. "What's the matter with you?"

"I don't know Millie," I say with *absolute* surety. "It happened again. There was a wild pig." Millie waits in silence, as I close my eyes for a minute. I know she is worried about me, but she's giving me space. After another deep breath, I open them and look one more time at the camper at the adjacent pump. *Winnebagos are popular up here, but surely, they don't all have circus posters in the window.*

I drive for a couple more hours, I guess, and get us to unincorporated Chasten, bordering Wind Lake, and skimming the skirts of Norway. Luckily, it was still daylight, and the rain had stopped, revealing a narrow river and a little mist hovering after the downpour. Exiting the road, I cross over a decaying bridge and practically run into the Happy Family Motel. You could rent a room for the whole week for $195. Now *that's* happy.

Millie is the first out of the car because she has to shake all that salt from her black cotton pants. The air is cool but humid, and we both amble up the little cement pathway and into the overly air-conditioned office. Millie is barely through the door when she announces, "We don't want to stay for the whole week."

"You don't need to yell," I whisper. "We can walk up to the desk like everyone else."

"This place is only big enough for the desk, that magazine rack, and the two of us. And I didn't yell; I practically whispered."

The 60-ish woman is wearing a large hearing aid in her left ear, or maybe she is listening to the radio. She has an angry disposition to match her bloodred Christmas sweatshirt that says, *I'm getting blitzed with Blitzen.* It isn't close to Christmas. She hasn't heard Millie whispering or yelling.

"We just want to stay for one night," Millie tries again, separating each word with a tap on the counter.

The woman does not look in our direction, but she does yell. "Now what are you doing? Pounding on the desk like that?"

"Okay, *you* talk to her," Millie says. The woman is staring simultaneously at an instant lottery ticket and the numbers appearing on the small static-filled screen mounted in the corner. She is muttering a string of words that I cannot repeat.

"Ma'am?" I say in my most respectful voice while waving my arms up over my head.

She sees the movement and finally turns to look at us. She puts her lottery ticket down with a bang and says angrily, "Okay, I heard you. I am busy if you can't see. I have a worthless ex-husband who won't give me my due. Guess I still need other people's money; not getting rich tonight. So, you need a room for one night? Why not stay and enjoy our pretty little town for a bit longer? How about I charge you the week's rate tonight, and if you check out early, I can give you some of your money back?"

"There won't be any need for that," Millie says. "We are on a deadline and will need to leave right after breakfast."

"What's the hurry?" she demands. "Why is everyone in such a goddamn hurry?"

"*Ma'am!*" I practically shriek. "There is no reason for that kind of language. You are an inn proprietress. You should have more manners."

"An *inn proprietress*? What is that? An *inn proprietress*?" Strangely, she glares at Millie instead of me.

Millie shrugs. "See. You probably only want us to stay one night."

"Forty-nine, ninety-nine. For five bucks more, breakfast is included."

"We will stay for breakfast. It is the most important meal of the day and will give us the sustenance we need to further our journey," I say, handing her two twenty-dollar bills, a ten, and a five.

"Seriously, Alva?" mutters Millie. "Do you always have to make things worse?"

Alva

When we get into our little—and not very clean—room at Happy Family, I sit down in the one garish purple tweed armchair and sigh. I haven't had one of my visions for a while, and this last one has taken me by surprise.

"Millie, does the motel manager remind you of an angry boar? Is her bark worse than her bite?"

"You dreaming out loud again?"

"I'm just trying to make sense of a few things," I reply.

"I don't think anyone can make sense of the Blitzen lady," Millie chides. "But she probably isn't as dangerous as she is aggressive."

Unsettled, I convince Millie to take a walk and look for a sandwich and maybe a glass of milk. She is not so hungry because of all the snacks, but neither of us will make it to breakfast without something more in our stomachs, and since I have been so haughty to the front desk l-a-d-y, Millie is sure she is going to spit in our food.

We walk together up the virtually abandoned street. It is after 6 but still plenty light out. Where is everyone? It is a northern lake town: a tiny main street with clapboard houses, a few spidery alleys. Not that far north, but it is still Wisconsin, so it is going to get really cold in the next month or two. A few leaves are already turning yellow. I feel an undercurrent of unease here. It is like one of those towns where they tout themselves as ". . . the most beautiful small town in America," but when you really look, there are messy handwritten signs in private yards. *Solve the murders!* one might say. Or *Find Haley!* Ugly things happening under the surface.

Chasten Union Church sits stoically in the middle of the township, and a few people mingle outside. Putting my unsettling vision about a church aside, I think *Oh good! At least the Holy Spirit is home.* The people smile and, perhaps because we look like we are lost, wave us over. Because we have nowhere else to go, we inch forward. As we near, we can hear a choir practicing and the deep baritone of the soloist.

Inside, it is warm but shabby. The walls are whitewashed but need a new coat. The pews are few and are overshadowed by a hundred mismatched and misplaced folding chairs. The altar is a rectangular wooden box that, if you'd put it horizontally, may double for a casket should the need arise. I don't mean to insult these followers of God, but it isn't very nice. The whole place looks dilapidated and empty, save the folding chairs. The choir is singing about a plentiful bounty, but to be honest, they are a little off-key. The entire scene just seems sardonic. *I think the Holy Spirit might be on vacation.*

Millie and I are standing in the back, taking it all in, when a man introduces himself as George and immediately starts to apologize for the mess.

"We had some water damage a few months back. The river overflowed her banks, and well, we just haven't had the resources to put it back together. It's getting colder at night, so the choir has come back here to practice. In a week's time, I've got a Sunday school class to teach, so I thought I'd come over and see what all needs to be done."

I hear Millie whisper, "A lot," and I poke her in the ribs.

"Yes, um . . . Well, we've been meeting down by the river these last months. Not just for baptisms and all of that, but to share fellowship, you know? It's called Humility River. Got its name because it has a lot of current for a shallow river. I mean, it usually is shallow. People sometimes used to drown because they'd get overconfident in navigating the waters and end up getting their boats speared right through by an errant log. It's a logging river."

"So, you are turning the other cheek?" I think this is a very amusing way to put it. "The river destroyed your church, but you are down there on its banks as an act of forgiveness?"

"Not exactly," says George, sounding very serious. He didn't get my joke. "But Pastor Francis says, cuz of its name and its wildness, God put it there to keep us humble. So, I guess you are kind of right."

"Seems like that river is not anything to be messing with," says Millie, and I poke her again.

George changes the subject. "Are you relocating to this area or just passing through? Would you like to meet Pastor Francis?"

"Actually, the latter," I say. And then, for no reason, I decide to add, "We are heading up to visit a friend of ours. Pete Werner."

"Pete? My goodness, I *know* Pete! He comes down from Norway every now and again to help us with construction. He's a pretty good fundraiser, too, for the cause. He is one of Pastor Francis's special parishioners."

I am confused. "A special—"

"What? You know Pete! Alva, he knows Pete!" Millie is bubbling with excitement. I am still trying to grasp the coincidence.

"One of the men who gives and gives some more. And he's not even a full-time member," George continues.

"He is a giver?" I ask.

"He is a taker. That's what he is." Millie is on it like a hound dog.

"Goodness no. Not the Pete I know! He doesn't take anything except for donations!"

"Wait, what cause are we talking about?" I ask warily. *I don't see how the stealing of a coat could be a misunderstanding about charitable giving.*

George says, "Let's sit down." The sun is setting; its orange hue seeps through the purple of the one stained glass window and casts us in a muddy glow.

We reposition a few of the folding chairs into a circle, and all of a sudden, I am part of some conspiracy. It's the way he talks, in a whispered excitement, his shoulders hunched and his rosy cheeks getting rosier. *What is he saying?* I listen harder. *He is talking about building a farm for the E-L-D-E-R-L-Y!*

"They will eat and pray together, and we will have a doctor who will live on the property—a group home with health care. Pastor

Francis's mother already lives there, and he says she is the happiest she has ever been."

The more George talks, the more it sounds like one of those places described in science fiction novels where there is a Sandman, and he puts the old people down. Does he read my mind?

"No," he continues, "more like a commune for people like Pastor and Pete's mothers or my dad. He's still with us, thank the Lord, and me, too, eventually, when it all gets up and running, a place where we can go together and not have to give all our money to the government. We are going to grow our own food and be caretakers. A lot of us around here are struggling, the kids have moved away . . ."

"Commune?" I close my eyes and think about the Babayagas. *A very long time ago, I sat in my son's home on the gray-blue sofa. So calm. My granddaughter sat squished in the corner next to me. I always remember that. It was a long couch, and we sat at the far end, packed like sardines without a tin. She was about nine and was reading to me a book she found in the library about a ferocious forest creature (Baba Yaga) who only wanted to be a grandmother—a babushka. She saves a little boy from a pack of wolves, and the town finally realizes she is kind and good. I loved that story about a kind, fiercely loving grandmother. I hoped that was how she saw me. And then, just a few months ago, I received a letter from her that included a little newspaper clipping. She must have thought about me when she saw the title:* The Babayagas House. *It was the story of a couple of elderly women in France who had started their own housing development. Just a building in the center of Paris, where around twenty old women shared a philosophy of growing old and staying active. I remembered the catch line. "Growing old well means keeping the gray matter going." Wish I would have written that.* When I open my eyes, I realize George is still talking.

"Actually, Pete and I, and a couple of the others, are going with Pastor Francis tomorrow afternoon to visit an assisted living home over in Plymouth. There are a few of the residents there that we think might want to hear about an alternative, a place where you work with others until you aren't able, and then a place where people don't just watch you die but care for you and prepare you for life everlasting. Pastor says it's the hardest work, preparing the aged for the hands of God."

"I don't need any help preparing; it comes naturally," says Millie, a little too defiantly. Then she lowers her voice so that only I can hear. "What I need is to find my coat."

"What kind of preparing can you offer?" I ask.

"Oh, you know! Prayer . . . Letting go of the material world and relinquishing control of the here and now. Showing them God's bounty."

What are they? Pirates? But I don't ask it aloud.

"Pastor says we need to convince more people to join us on the farm. He's calling it *Eden*. We need a lot of people who are willing to share all our resources like God wants."

First off, could they not come up with something more original than Eden? *The coat theft is just the start of the appropriation.*

"Who will manage all of the finances, that material stuff?" *I think I already know the answer. Pete.*

I am even more intrigued when he says, "Pastor Francis, of course. You should definitely see it for yourselves. So, meet here tomorrow? Around noon?"

I agree and start back to the motel. Millie walks behind me and pulls out her phone. *We have agreed not to call our kids, so who is she talking to?* "Millie, who's that?"

Millie covers the little machine with her hand and mouths, "Sam."

"Why are you acting like he's a secret? What does he want?"

She speaks quickly into the phone and then puts it back in her pocket. "Alva," Millie sighs, "I just wanted to let him know where we were. I don't know. Isn't that okay? I already told him about the casino theft. He wanted me to keep him posted, so I left a message."

"We don't need a babysitter." I am angry that she feels a need to check in with anybody, much less a man we met a couple of days ago. She catches up with me and puts an arm around my shoulder.

"Alva, you never know. What if we are poking a bear? Maybe no one needs a mink coat except for the mink?"

She is always mixing her metaphors.

Alva

We had to settle for the McDonald's on the outskirts of town for dinner and then, this morning, the motel continental breakfast. Cereal and milk, and orange juice in a box.

This whole thing, organized care for the elderly, I know is a trend. There are more of those buildings popping up in Crystal, Minnesota, than bunnies. It's just, by the look of their church's disrepair, I am not sure I think Chasten Union Church and its clergy are up for the task. I can't shake the feeling that Pastor Francis and his pal Pete care more about profit than prayer, but maybe I'm just being ornery. Seriously, I'm sure a leader of a congregation could not possibly be part of such a scheme, but I decide that what we need is a little background information about this town and the church. We should know things before confronting Pete. So, Millie and I go to the library. Small towns always have a church and a library. It's not a very big one, but it has plenty of microfiche of old papers and such.

I read with amazement. As it turns out, there are some groups that specialize in victimizing old people. Many of their prey are lonely, maybe suffering from dementia, usually retired with a nest egg. Sometimes there are even more dastardly consequences. I guess it's not a new problem but one that not many people associate with the elderly, more like the Manson girls. There really have been churches that purchase big swaths of property and then do heavy recruiting from senior citizen centers and the like. Some of the biggest scams are out of Miami. *Churches!* My Lord, is nothing sacred?

I read aloud to Millie. "They get older people to give up their life savings and sign deeds for church projects . . . prevent them from giving money to their children and *invite* them to live in *special* communities. Oh, and look here, Millie, there is something called the People's Temple, and they were supposed to provide apartments for old people, and then they were exposed for starving those poor people and stealing their social security checks. Then there's Church Universal and Triumphant." *Boy, do they have an ego.* "And some guy named Wierwille in Indiana . . . it says here that some of these places were more like concentration camps!"

"Aren't you being a little dramatic, Alva? And why are you so interested in all this cult stuff anyway? I thought we were looking for information about Norway and Chasten, not the Universal Church of whatever. We don't live here. It is not my problem that some folks in Wisconsin decide to invest in senior care. Lots of investments are bad ones." Millie is reading something off the shelf about the sociology of church etiquette.

I toss a book in her direction because I don't know how else to get her attention. "I want you to sit down and listen to this," I demand, and point to a table and two chairs in the corner.

Millie glowers in disdain at me above her glasses.

"Okay. Here's one about a niece whose old, widowed aunt refused to leave her apartment. Turns out the old lady was approached by a small religious group in her neighborhood who convinced her to give up all her stuff, including some valuable antiques. *Millie!* It says she was just crying in the middle of an empty apartment when they found her. Hadn't eaten in *days.* Some state assemblyman says it happens all the time: elderly people turning over thousands of dollars to these so-called good Christians. Most of them are too embarrassed to tell anybody they fell for the scams." I am angry. "If they don't tell anybody, those crooks get off scot-free! I don't know what's going on here, but Millie, I feel like we're meant to be here. We are meant to put a stop to it." I have raised my voice beyond library decorum. Behind me, I hear, "Shhhhhh."

"Are you about done, Alva?"

"Don't you see how important this is? Maybe Pete is involved in one of these kinds of scams? I don't know if he is or isn't, but there is a time when you just have to put your foot down." There is a thrumming in the pit of my stomach.

"You mean put your foot in your mouth? Again, this is *not* New York, or Miami, or even Indiana. I don't see any valuable antiques stacked up anywhere, much less a concentration camp. You are jumping to conclusions. You know what you are doing? You are projecting. Isn't that what they call it when you take something someone else is doing and make it apply to you? Or is it the other way around? Not everybody is jumping in on the "take advantage of seniors" bandwagon. These are good, prayerful people in Badger country. What if Chasten Union Church is not at all what you think? Maybe Pastor Francis really is trying to help."

"I've just got an inkling." My eyes dart around the shelves. "All of a sudden, I do feel like Agatha's Miss Marple. I've always wanted to be a sleuth."

"Alva, I have actually never heard you say that you've wanted to be anything besides what you already are."

I turn and stare at her for a long minute. "Millie, for some reason, you are reminding me a lot of Irwin right now."

Millie

Since Alva will not let me leave the library, I do some pleasure reading of my own. I find a letter that makes me almost wet myself. Laughing so hard I almost double over, I pull Alva over and point out some of the more outrageous statements. *Who knew Wisconsin was such a fiendish state?*

"Look here, Alva, a pastor wrote all this stuff. It is alarming if true, I guess, but it does sound a bit conspiratorial, don't you think?"

I read aloud:

"I have been a Lutheran pastor here in Taylor County for more than forty years and feel that with my background in theology, and as a student of cult activity, I must bring to the forefront my fears about our state of Wisconsin as a whole. We are being overtaken by Satanic cults which now number in the hundreds, with almost ten thousand members circulating in our midst."

"Hmm," says Alva, with a slight grin. "I don't remember reading anything about this in the papers. Surely, if the state has gone to hell, some other people would've noticed."

Alva grabs the letter from my hand. "Let me read the rest…

More than any other state, we have areas so filled with Satanists that even the animals of the forests chatter about pending danger. They are frightened of being sacrificed by the disturbed, the pedophiles, the psychopaths. Pockets of Nazis and the Ku Klux Klan wreak havoc on the small communities isolated in our vast territory. Especially dangerous are the foreigners who are the ones secretly supporting these devil worshippers. They cut 666 into the trunks of trees and print articles that glorify serial killers like Dahmer and Manson.

The diabolic non-believers are in charge of all the media, too, and in charge of the courts. They dismiss cases of violent aggressors, allow offenders to walk among us and force us to watch their pornography. Instead of flocking back to the church, our poor citizens are being lured away to belief systems like Atheism and Islam. Our fellow Lutherans are being taught about science and evolution and trips to the moon, which our Bible has disproved time and time again. This is nothing but Halloween doctrine, make-believe of the most egregious kind. We cannot let outsiders continue their genocide of our values. We need to rid ourselves of such drama, using lobotomies if necessary. We need to get the devils out of our schools. They influenced Stalin. Do not let them get their claws into you. Protect Wisconsin from the occult.

The Lord be with you,

Pastor Bunderson

"Well?" I say.

"Lobotomies. Wow. That is one crazy Lutheran!" Alva says and giggles.

"Cults seem to be of the utmost significance in Wisconsin," I say.

"Sounds to me that no one is beyond suspicion."

"Satan abounds."

"Some people fear everything." Alva stops her laughter and gets serious. "Or they pretend to see demons everywhere to get other people afraid enough to listen to them. In our case, we don't know anything about Pastor Francis. This Bunderson is obviously off his rocker."

At that point, I am nodding. "Okay, but I am starting to get an uncomfortable feeling too. This whole place is giving me the willies. So, you think Pastor Francis may not be on the up and up. And Pete is helping him do extra fundraising with casino chips and our fur coat?"

"Or the other way around. Maybe. I don't know all of it, but my insides are all wound up. Something doesn't smell right." Alva sniffs the air to prove a point.

"What should we do?" I ask, even though I know Alva, so I know the answer.

"We go with George, meet up with Pete, and see what his reaction is when he sees us. Maybe he comes clean about the coat. Maybe he really has good intentions and a better explanation." Alva is a planner.

"Okay, but what if he thinks we are going to turn him in to the police? Pulls out a gun or something?"

"That's when we say we want to join the commune," my sly sister says, and winks at me.

"I want to go home," I say.

A chill runs down the length of me. Alva is already pacing ahead of me, moving to the exit of the library and then toward the church with resolve. I follow with less enthusiasm.

Alva

Breakfast had been terrible, and the hour at the library made me ill at ease. I was trying to understand how people could be taken advantage of with these schemes. *Old people. What do we find so enticing? Is it the company? The promise of community warmth in the darkest of days? Salvation?* As I leave the library, I am thinking I might need to head back to the motel for another morning constitutional, but I force myself to walk toward the house of worship.

My mind continues to go around in circles. *Am I being outlandish with all my suspicions? Why would Chasten Union Church make promises that they cannot keep?* We just arrived in this town, but I can't shake a sense of foreboding. *Is the whole congregation privy to the underpinnings of Eden? Why do you have to give away all your belongings before you die? What's wrong with letting the relatives fight over them like they've always done? My own grandmother solved all that bickering by writing names on all her possessions. I used to go to her home and pick up a candlestick or toothpick holder or whatever, turn it over, and check if it was going to be mine someday. It was a great game.*

Millie seems to read my mind. "Remind me to write names on the back of my good dishes when I get home."

"Do you think that Pete has already cashed in our mink coat?" I ask. I am getting used to saying "our" because we are in this thing together. "And what about that big lady at the casino? Is she his partner?"

"I guess we should just come out and ask him," snorts Millie. "Maybe the coat was a down payment for a little spot in heaven. Seriously, I am distraught that I talked to him in the first place. I am usually a pretty good judge of character."

"You couldn't have known. A lonely man in Wisconsin wouldn't really raise any red flags," I say sincerely. *I am questioning the statement as I am saying it. Didn't Dillinger and Al Capone call Wisconsin home? Do I sound like that Pastor Bunderson?*

"I don't know if he is really all that lonely. Alva, I just assumed, the way he was talking, that he was a widower. Do you remember? He just said his wife "used to" like lacy things. He never said she was dead. Maybe he's stuck her in a closet somewhere. Or maybe the luau woman was his wife!"

I can't help but smile at her description of the big lady in the floral getup. "I don't think so. I think that maybe she was just an accomplice. Or maybe she was the congregational gang leader who was assigned to watch over his winnings?"

"Is there such a thing as a congregational gang leader?"

"I think the Jehovah's Witnesses have them."

"You know a lot of interesting things, Alva."

"Okay," I say, standing up with resolve. "Let's head over to the church. George said they were meeting there at 10:30 to drive over to the assisted living place. Let's go see your Pete and get some of our questions answered."

"Not *my* Pete."

"What? Oh. I'm sorry," I say, and mean it. "In a way, I am very glad that you spoke to him. He has brought new significance to our adventure. A real turning point in our travel story."

We stop back in our motel room to get Millie's scarf, and to eat a quick snack, and then we march out of the motel door and join arms as if comrades heading to battle. Millie lets out a little "Whoop!" as we cross the empty parking lot and head up the main street toward the chapel.

"Stop right there this minute!" a woman behind us shouts for all she is worth. "Stop, I say!"

The stocky, angry woman from the front desk is barreling up the road, waving her hands over her head.

We stop and turn. Millie looks at me. "What'd we do?"

I shrug. "No idea." Closer to us now, the woman is panting.

"You said *one* night. Checkout was three minutes ago: at *10*. You are still here, and you have not paid, and now you are on the run. I'm calling the cops!"

Millie looks down at her feet and rolls her eyes. "Neither of us is running anywhere."

"Now Millie," I say, trying to tamp down the situation. "She . . . I'm sorry, what is your name?"

"Bertha. Bertha McDowell!"

"Of course it's Bertha," Millie snorts.

Bertha moves quickly and is standing nose-to-nose with Millie before I can get out my next words.

Millie giggles. "Back up, *Bertha*."

Millie can be a daredevil and just so *sure* of herself. Had the church bells not started chiming at that very instant, I fear there would have been a fight. That "heading into battle" routine wasn't meant to justify any conflict except for our beef with Pete. *Millie's testosterone levels might be a little high. I read an article about testosterone levels in elderly women, and it turns out that women around 80 have almost ten percent more testosterone than women in their 70s. It might mean our bodies are just trying hard to survive, or maybe we should drop the age limits for boxing in the Olympics.*

Anyway, I start to hum "Amazing Grace" along with the bells, and both women turn to me with shocked looks on their faces like I'd grown a second head.

"Okay, okay," Millie says to Bertha. "But you could've just asked us for the money. You didn't have to threaten us. It looks like we have more business in Chasten than we would have liked. We will pay you for another night."

"No you don't." Bertha is not letting up. "You are going to pay me for the whole week. How do I know you won't do the same thing tomorrow? Just walk away owing me money?"

"Our belongings are still in the room!! Our car is out in front, you old bat!" Millie's temper is back. "I was the one on your side when this one"—she points to me— "started talking about *sustenance*. Do you remember that? Why are you so mad? Lose another dollar on the lottery?"

"This is silly," I say, reaching into my purse. "You said it was forty-nine ninety-nine a night, including breakfast. Well, I am not sure what we had this morning was anything passing as breakfast, but we will pay you in advance for three more nights." I fish out a one-hundred-dollar bill and a fifty and place them in her outstretched hand. "You owe me three cents."

"Forty-nine ninety-nine is the day rate if you are going to stay all week. This is still not enough!" But she stuffs the bill into her pocket.

"Three more nights in this place?" Millie groans. "Seriously, Alva, I don't think that will be necessary."

"Worst case scenario," I say. "Now let's hurry to the church."

"Why do you want to go to that church?" Bertha demands.

"We know some people over there," Millie says dismissively. "Why do you care?"

"Figures." Bertha turns and starts to walk away. "I don't trust those fools, and I don't trust you."

We watch her move away from us without a word. Such a disagreeable person, and then she tosses in a bit of shared sentiment.

"Well. I might have to reconsider my opinion," Millie says.

"We don't know what she knows. Let's go find out for ourselves," I say, and we walk down the tree-lined street.

When we reach the door, we can hear a man preaching with fervor. It still isn't Sunday, but nevertheless, I feel like a heathen in my travel slacks. I was not expecting a service. "Millie, they are holding some kind of meeting! Let's just stand over there by that tree near the steps. When people come out, we will sneak in and find our man."

"You mean a 'meet our maker' meeting?" Millie says sarcastically. "I'm just kidding. I know what you meant."

"We need to find all *three* of our men, but not the biblical ones. George first, Pastor Francis second, and then the most elusive: Pete."

We stand (or rather hide) behind an old pine tree, as spindly as the clapboard siding, until the doors creak open. A small crowd, dressed in their Sunday finest even though it is Saturday, come out nodding their heads in unison, praising their good fortune to have been able to listen to their leader for what might have been hours. Like fish heading upstream, we move back toward the door, heads down, in our most furtive fashion.

"Hullo, oh hullo!!" George spies us on the second step, and we lift our eyes to his beaming face.

"So glad that you came. So glad! Come with me. I've told Pastor Francis about our run-in yesterday evening, and he is anxious to meet you. Pete is already here and pulling the car around. What an exciting day!"

"Is it?" Millie mutters under her breath. We both feel a little hesitant now that we are about to have a confrontation. Her hand reaches out for mine and squeezes it hard. Our hearts are beating in unison. I know this because I can feel her pulse through her fingers and because that's how Millie and I are. We're sisters.

George hands us some literature and waves his hand with a flourish, indicating that we should take a seat. He swooshes away to pull Pastor Francis from his handshaking and guides him toward us before we have a chance to run. As I sit there in one of only two pews, with the slippery new varnish, I take in the tall man with the long, dingy white robe. I don't mean to glare. Millie notices and gives me a little shove. A turn of events, surely, since I am the one who usually has to reel *her* in.

Pastor Francis takes three steps down the aisle toward us, wiping his brow as he approaches. (I think he thinks it gives the impression of self-effacement.) He stands before us with a soft, composed expression, presumably waiting for George to make the introductions. His quietness unnerves me since I'd heard his bellowing from behind the doors just moments before. *An actor,* I think.

I set the bulletin on my seat, take a quick little breath, and stand up, softening my expression as well.

"Pastor Francis," George says quite formally, "this is Miss Millie and Miss Alva." And then, looking awkward, says, "I am so sorry, I didn't get your last names."

Pastor Francis, obviously not interested in surnames, clasps my hand and then Millie's with a bobbing-of-the-head motion seemingly adopted by the entire organization. "Very pleased to meet you both. Very."

With effort we smile, as amicably as is possible.

Alva

After the niceties are done, we all walk out of the ramshackle church. Pastor Francis has his arm wrapped around my shoulder, and is leading me to the dusty parking lot, and Millie is following helplessly behind us with George. Only now does it occur to me that they are expecting us to get in the car with them. I thought maybe they'd just give us directions or have us follow them. I have no intention of being an enabler, but my curiosity holds fast. *What can I do?* I am physically shaking, which I am sure is taken as a sign of rapture. I spy Pete in the driver's seat, a silly wide-brimmed sun hat covering much of his face.

Pastor Francis lets go of me and turns his attention back to the small crowd that has gathered at the foot of the church steps. "We are heading to Mercy's Milestone this morning, folks! Pray that there are souls there who are waiting to be delivered into our hands."

I see people putting their palms together and hear the murmuring of prayer. Praying mantises. And another silly name!! Mercy's Milestone? I guess death could be considered a milestone.

"George told me of your interest in our community," the good pastor is speaking to me again. "I am so beholden to you for wishing to accompany us this afternoon. You can see firsthand the joy we give to people. Perhaps I'll have Peter drive us over to the construction site after our stop. Yes? You will see the beginnings of our Eden!" This last part sounds disingenuous.

Right now, all I focus on is Pete. The car he drives pulls in front of us, and I will Millie to keep quiet. Leaning close, I whisper, "Remember, he doesn't know that we think he has the coat."

It's an old Pontiac sedan that Pete's driving, green with a little rust on the lower panel. George opens the door and ushers us into the back seat. It smells of smoke, but there is a little cardboard tree hanging from the rearview mirror, emitting a faint evergreen fragrance. My blood is pumping fast, and I hope I won't have a heart attack before the adventure is over. Pete turns around in his seat then and grins broadly. "Well, I'll be a monkey's uncle! The ladies from the Dells!" He eyes the pastor, who has gotten in the front seat. "What a wonderful surprise!"

"Be cool," I hiss. I squeeze Millie's hand again, and she grits her teeth behind narrowed lips.

"Yes!" cries George. "They said that they knew you and were coming to see you. What a surprise indeed!"

"Coming to see me! Imagine. I hadn't known I had made that kind of impression," he chuckles conspiratorially.

"Oh, I thought you were old friends. Marvelous. New friends!" George babbles on as Pete steers the car out of the drive.

"We were so worried about you," Millie chimes in. "We stopped by the hospital, and they told us you were already on your way home to Norway. Well, we were heading in the same general direction, so here we are. And then we met George, and well, here we are." I think, *Now who is babbling?*

George looks alarmed. "Pete, I didn't know you were in the hospital! Goodness me, why didn't you call me? What happened?"

I see Pete's eyes shooting darts at us from the rearview mirror. Then he smiles and says offhandedly, "It was nothing, George. Had a little bit of heartburn and some nice folks thought I should get it checked out."

"My ass," Millie mutters, but luckily Pete has turned to pay attention to the road. I kick Millie harder than I mean to, and she goes quiet.

"Thank God it wasn't something serious," George is saying.

I am grateful that, after a moment, Pete turns his attention to Pastor Francis. Their conversation has drifted to their mission at hand. I catch Pete's eyes in the mirror, sneaking quick peeks at us, puzzling something out. George is repeating everything he told us yesterday.

I try to make out their words over George's chatter. Pastor Francis is talking in a hushed tone. "So, like I've stressed . . . will have to invest . . . money to complete the . . . the brochure is top-notch, don't you think? Just came in. I did it in Milwaukee along with a friend who is really an architect . . . the soon-to-be continuum of care facility. . . it really looks comfortable, meditative . . . that feel. . . says we will have an office . . . for medical. . . a garden space. That said, we market it like long term . . . Applicants need to . . . their finances over with the peace of . . . their needs will . . . good faith."

It appears that George is oblivious to any details, though the guileless are not always the guiltless. Pete and Francis are perhaps into something nefarious, but I don't want to jump to conclusions. I may be projecting, like Millie says. What it sounds like is once they have all the nest eggs of the unsuspecting residents securely in hand, the divvying-up process will begin. They probably just stole enough money from casinos and such to do the advertising; just enough money put in to make it appear legitimate. Again, how terribly *not* original. How will they run it? A few hundred passed to the retired physician? Enough groceries to keep people fed but not necessarily nourished? They'd have to pay a heating bill but might not keep the rooms toasty in the Wisconsin winter. A request for church volunteers? *Bare bones. No frills. Just enough to keep people alive and in the giving spirit,* I think. I don't know. *How could they get away with all of that without the parishioners suspecting foul play?*

George is *still* explaining his understanding of the mission. Glancing at both of us, he suddenly seems genuinely concerned that our hearing may be impaired. We haven't really been listening. His voice gets louder. "Pastor Francis says we need to have more start-up money. People need to know that we are working very hard on their behalf: we have a few units erected already. And a small chapel. Need to do some plowing and get more water piped up from Humility. It really will be idyllic. I can see the whole thing in my mind. I see you two there, too! You should join us. You would be such assets to our community!"

"I don't want to be an *ass. . .et*," Millie retorts, trying to make light of a situation that keeps growing darker. Then she realizes she was profane again and starts over.

"Aren't you a dear!" she exclaims in a tone drenched with sarcasm. "Did you all say something about money? Do you take other donations as well? Say, maybe good furniture or fur coats?" After that, there is a long period of silence. Again, through the rear mirror, I see Pete's eyes narrow at Millie. It is stuffy in the car, and I rest my head against the window.

Flash! I am sitting in a pew near the front of the church. The pastor says, "Bow your heads," and I do. My eyes are open, trying to read the prayer, but a thin layer of dust settles around me, and I see roaches on the floor. Roaches, by the thousands, swarm, mate, conduct wars. They forage for food. Something has spoiled in the church, and I can smell its offensive odor. Toxic spiritual residue has accumulated and rotted. Moving to the baptismal font, I tip it over. It should cleanse, shouldn't it? I need more water.

I raise my head wildly. Millie looks at me uneasily. I am very worried that the car has child locks, and I am claustrophobic. We exchange glances, and then I try to open the back passenger door.

"Miss Alva!" George squeals as the door swings open, and I nearly fall out on the pavement. "What are you doing? The car is moving!" He reaches quickly over my lap and grabs the handle, pulling the door shut before I tumble to my demise. "Oh my!" I exclaim, catching my breath. "Oh my!"

Pete moves the car onto the shoulder and then stops abruptly. "What the hell?" he says, turning around in his seat, truly baffled as to my motive. I am baffled, too. In shock, kind of, because I don't have a death wish.

"Alva, you frightened me out of my wits!" exclaimed Millie. The rest were all just staring at me.

"It was an impulse move," I say, brushing the beads of sweat off my face.

"An impulse move?" questions Pastor Francis. "Do you have some sort of condition? Seizures? Tics?"

"Did you take a walk in the woods?" George chimed in, his face full of concern.

That one took me a minute. *Oh. Tics. Ticks.* "No, I don't have any kind of motor disorder," I say. "I just got very warm, and I thought I was rolling down the window instead of opening the door."

Millie doesn't look convinced. "Alva let's take a little walk. Do you mind, fellas?" She actually purrs like she is a saucy Southern Belle.

Everyone gets out of the car. The men lean against it, shaking their heads, while Millie and I stroll down the gravel shoulder.

"Seriously, Alva, what happened back there?"

"I really don't know. I had one of my visions. It was crazy, Millie, a million roaches were infesting the church and . . . and, oh, I drowned them with blessed water. Then I realized I was back in the car, and it was kind of airless in there. I felt like I needed to escape. Right that minute."

"Save that thought," says Millie. George has poured a cup of water from the thermos they had in the car and is coming toward us.

"Please drink some water," offers George politely. He really is a dear, and maybe even innocent. The paper cup is flimsy and filmy, but I take a sip. It would be rude not to.

"Thank you," I say, and when I don't say any more, he wanders back to the two other men.

I empty the paper cup in the little rocks under my feet and scrunch it up in my fist. I take a deep breath and try to steady my nerves. "I don't know, Millie. I feel like I *know* that we are heading into a perilous situation. No one knows where we are. What if these men really do try to kidnap us or something? Drug us and force us to hand over our life savings? Oh no! What was in that little cup that I just drank? It tasted funny."

"Probably some of that river water. It can't be pure water; nothing innocent around here," says Millie, only half mocking.

"I am *serious*!!"

"I know. Okay. But maybe your blood sugar is high." Millie is digging into her purse for I don't know what.

"I don't have diabetes, Millie. Or at least I didn't." My breathing comes back to normal, and I stare over her shoulder at the men watching us by the car. "I'm better."

"So what do you want to do? We can't ask them to drop us off here."

"No. I'm telling you I am better. Need to use my brain instead of letting my emotions get all whacky. We'll go back and say that I am just a little tired. Maybe we are not in immediate danger, but I think Pete knows we are suspicious of something. Why did you have to mention the fur coat?"

Millie smiles. "Just checking for a reaction. Got it, too. I'm telling you: we are not in danger because they haven't got us to sign away our life savings. We are not much good to them already dead. And remember, I left word with Sam, so someone does know where we are. I am sure their endgame is money, not manslaughter. If there even is an endgame. Are we both making something out of nothing?"

"Hmph. My imagination is admittedly in overdrive, but my intuition smells a rat—or *rats*. Let's not make them too nervous." I fiddle with my hair and smile back at the men. Give them a little wave. "We need to let them think we are two frail old ladies and not threats. And then *whammo!*" I whisper that last part.

"Yes," Millie concurs, "we play dumb until we show them we're not."

I lean against Millie, feigning weakness, and we amble back to the car. I will tell them I want to go back to the motel, and then we will figure out our next steps. The day is getting warmer, and I sure wish I didn't have my navy cardigan on over this paisley dress, but I don't want them to think I am being flirty, so I keep it on.

Alva

We rejoin the men. Pete is drawing deep pulls on a cigarette. His worn khaki dress pants are wrinkled, and he has sweat stains under his arms. The pineapples on his Hawaiian shirt look like they've spoiled. George, also wearing a big hat like Pete, has rosy cheeks blossoming under it because of the warm temperature or because he is a gullible St. Nick. He has a cherub quality to him that, no doubt, Pastor Francis flaunts to reassure the doubtful. I'm leaning toward him as the top banana. Pastor Francis is wary, a look of feigned distraught tugging his lips downward. He has unrobed in the car's stifling heat and is wearing a button-down shirt with stains under his arms, too. His clerical collar is still in place, looking slimy with perspiration.

"I hope you are feeling better, Miss Alva," he clucks. "You gave us quite a scare."

His *tsk-tsking* sounds like that Dr. Baker on a *Little House on the Prairie* episode. I have watched all the reruns. For some reason, that image gets me chuckling inside. I relax.

"I'm doing *much* better, kind sir." (Just like what they say on *Little House on the Prairie:* they were so polite.) And then I imagine him with his collar but wearing only his underwear because that's what you do when you are nervous. "But I think I might need to go back to the motel. I might throw up."

"Yes," says Millie. "I think we need to go back."

"Well, ladies," Pastor is back to being impatient. "The thing is, we are more than halfway to our destination. It would be better if you just came along to the home. You will be able to rest there and get your second wind."

What's the name for kidnapping old women, granny-napping?

I look at Millie. I don't know what the right decision is. I could continue to pretend to have an upset stomach and force them to take us back. But maybe going along with this show-and-tell will be more eye-opening. What about the *whammo* I have planned? "Well, okay," I finally say. But I do it with a kind of hiccup and cough. I want to keep them on their toes.

We all climb back into the ugly green sedan and drive in silence for a while. Then Pastor Francis resumes his marketing spiel. Every now and again, he turns around and looks at us, making sure we are appreciating his zeal. He continues about Chasten Church and its mission of saving the souls of the elderly. He equates himself to a prophet, saying, "I heard the Lord calling me specifically to be a spiritual liaison for that population: people who have worked their whole lives to protect their country, their church, and their culture. People like you ladies. You know what I'm talking about, right?"

We look at each other and then nod, simulating interest in his shenanigans.

"People like me. We need to believe in miracles and embrace the supernatural, which is God. We need to get back to our conservative values and trust the Lord instead of all these government services that are not looking out for our best interests. The Lord has shown me that we need to take the last years of our lives and invest in our transition to heavenly bliss, not pour our hard-earned dollars into assisted living homes that only serve to make the corporate owners wealthy while we rot in the black hole of the unfaithful. Our Eden will be a sanctuary."

"He's one of those Medicine Men." Millie coughs in my direction. Did she guess that I, too, just conjured up a TV show with covered wagons? We are so sympatico.

"What we offer," Pastor Francis continued, "is solace and comfort not available in mainstream America. There is an anti-Christ sentiment that has settled over our country, and we must reconnect with Jesus. Adult children are worried about their parents, but most of the time they just don't understand their true needs. Our elderly want to live in a community where worship is paramount, not conducted in small chapels in Senior Memory Care centers where there is no full-time clergy. I will be there for them twenty-four seven. I will live amongst them and bring them peace."

"He's the one drinking the river water," noted Millie, her mouth close to my ear.

This 50-something white man in shoddy black dress pants and graying white button-down, with that damned collar, is a pessimist. The worst thing to be. How dare he talk about the world and its anti-Christ spirit when all I've known is goodness? Maybe I haven't had the experiences others have, but I know what I know.

"Pastor Francis," I interrupt, "you seem to have little faith in people."

"Alva! I thought you said to go slow!" Millie says in a low voice.

"I think many have lost their way," he says sternly. "People don't go to church like they used to. They leave the elderly in the care of institutions instead of family. They forget that the devil is real, and we have to do everything in our power to enter God's Kingdom with a clean heart. Do you question that, Miss Alva?"

"Well, I just want to tell you that I have many friends who have moved into very pleasant, assisted living facilities. They get to play Bingo and go to Walmart. *And* they go to church. And they have services for all denominations and respect everyone. I have a friend, Nancy; she is 88, and she just moved to the Palms. They don't have a beach or anything, but they have a swimming pool in the center of a nice courtyard. She has a little balcony, and she grows petunias. Oh, and they have a communal garden. She grows carrots with her friend Jean. There is a step-down program where you get more care when you need it. I know another lady there, too. She may not recognize me, but we used to do sewing class together at the Rec Center. Every time I see her, she is sitting in her wheelchair and smiling. I just don't know why you think that your 'garden' is better than that." With that, I close my mouth and stare straight ahead.

Pastor Francis is now turned around in the front seat, facing me. His mouth twitches and his eyes go a little cold for just a second. But with a deep breath, his face relaxes, and he considers me. I don't know if he is coming to some kind of conclusion or not. Are we worth putting up with if we fall victim to his scheming? Do we have money? Do we know that Pete stole our coat? Maybe he thinks he can sway us with his charm. Maybe he thinks he should tread lightly in case we become a problem. Maybe he really does believe that he is doing good, like some of those decent right-wing Republicans. In the end, I think he settles on the first scenario, which is we are not clever enough to worry about, and puts that fake smile back in place. He talks to me like a child. I hate that.

"Alva, Alva, Alva," he croons. "I see where you are coming from. Yes, I do. I know that there are perhaps places for seniors where care appears appropriate. Maybe for a time, it is. But what we are envisioning is so much more. Take your friend in the wheelchair. She is smiling, you say? But what is making her smile? Her comfort? Her friends? Or only her failing mind? She is precisely who we wish to help. She needs to be surrounded by prayer. Our constant presence will tend to her spiritual consciousness. She will be enveloped in God's love and will feel his forgiveness as she is welcomed into his home on high."

I think, *What a bunch of nonsense.* People with dementia will understand people praying over them about as much as people singing to them. Actually, I've heard that music can provide emotional support for Alzheimer's patients, so that might be more meaningful. The car is slowing down in front of Mercy's Milestone, so all I say is, "Hmmm."

Millie

Alva knows she has said too much, so she keeps her head down and gets out of the car, not making eye contact with the other passengers. Her little episode in the car has me more frightened than I've let on. Like I've said, my sister survived a stroke, but I am not sure that she will survive a devil in Wisconsin. I'm really fond of the state myself, and I hate that this situation is tainting my view. We used to have a friend with a cabin in the north woods, a couple of hours from here: canoe rides, swimming in that midnight-blue lake, accompanying ourselves on the autoharp— all are such great memories. I think of the time I waded into the shallows, and when I came out, my leg was covered with leeches. Not wanting to scare me, my mother said, "Oh, Millie! Look, you found all the water puppies!!" I tried to pet them as she pulled them from my flesh, none the wiser. I confronted her when we were older, and Alva and my mom laughed and laughed. "It's all in the interpretation," she said.

Pastor Francis gives Alva and me the once-over before opening the car door with an uncalled-for big yank. He and Pete immediately go to the trunk and start hauling out equipment. *What?* I am flabbergasted by all the stuff they unload. There is a large, rolled screen, certainly an antique, a computer monitor, probably dated as well, but I don't really keep up with that sort of thing. There are two big speakers. I guess they think that the old people will need some serious amplifying apparatus to hear the message. There is even a guitar in an old beat-up case that Pete pushes toward George. *How'd they get all that stuff in the trunk? They are ridiculous.*

We are in a small parking lot abutting the faded bricks of Mercy's Milestone. I guess it's more of a loading zone. The place is bigger than I thought it would be, which turns out to have fifty-six units, not half of them occupied. Not much to look at, with its slanted rooftop and peeling white pillars at the entrance, but it looks clean, and the grass is cut. A sign out front says they treat their residents with *Dignity, Respect, Compassion, and Loving Care.* Well, that sounds good. Why would anyone want to leave? We enter a side door into a room that looks like it might be used as a dining hall. The floors are linoleum, and there are empty buffet tables sitting at one end and a small, raised platform in front that sports a microphone and a stool. Large windows let in the sun and a good deal of heat, which contributes to the oily smell. I crinkle my nose, and so does Alva, in total denial, I suppose, that that smell doesn't linger in our own homes. We looked it up once, something about omega-seven fatty acids and weakened skin and oxidation as we age. Old skin does take on an odor of its own. Oh, just one more thing to deal with.

There are about forty folding chairs set in a semicircle in front of the "stage." A stooped-over custodian in dusty overalls moves about setting the chairs just right. I think he must have one of the compulsive obsessive disorders you hear about these days. After each row, he steps back to appreciate his work and then goes back, moving each chair an inch to the right or left. Seems unnecessary since most of the people probably won't even know where they are. *Oh, my goodness, did I think that? How truly awful am I getting, probably from hanging around these sordid sorts?*

Alva and I sidle to the back and watch without speaking. The men are assembling the equipment with fluid motions. They have certainly done this before. The screen is set, and the computer, I guess, begins to project images of happy old people and Bible verses and wildflowers. The pictures are grainy, giving them almost an ephemeral quality, time passing with each click, kind of like those View-Master things Alva is always talking about. The people get older and older, the Bible verses head toward Revelations, and the wildflowers now cover gravesites. And then the slideshow repeats. It is subliminal. Hypnotic.

Then George, sweet George (I'm going to call him that because I think his heart is in the right place and he is being bamboozled), pulls out the old guitar, sits down on the stool, and starts to sing about a gentle guitar weeping over love's lost potential, as the strummer grows old. Seems fitting somehow.

Alva

George has such a tender voice that I am transported. I look at Millie and know she is thinking the same. He stops and starts a song over and over while Pastor Francis is up at the mic again, readying to speak and saying, "Testing. . .testing." *Be quiet,* I internally beg the Pastor. *Please be quiet.* I cannot believe that George's voice is so beautiful. I know why the other devils keep him around. He sings like an angel. He will draw people to their cause without even realizing that he's the pied piper.

A stunning African American woman comes out to greet Pastor Francis and the rest. Her smile doesn't really seem that welcoming, though. I think she is rather dubious of the good pastor's intentions, but how can you refuse to let a man of the cloth speak to the residents who want to listen? She is wearing the most beautiful shawl I've ever seen, gorgeous swirling colors wrapped around her shoulders. *It is prettier than our fur coat,* I think. *She better not put it down anywhere, or that Pete will be all over it.*

"Testing…testing," Pastor Francis again addresses the microphone. And then he turns to meet Ms. Vivian Reynolds. There is animosity in the air; I feel it way over here in the corner.

"Ms. Reynolds! It is so wonderful to see you again. I cannot thank you enough for your continued hospitality," exclaims Pastor Francis.

Ms. Reynolds gives him a curt nod. "Pastor."

He crosses to her and attempts to grasp her hand, which she quickly uses to adjust her scarf. He becomes a bit more subdued, more reverential. "You are, as always, so gracious for allowing us to be here.

Your kindness, your generosity to your patrons and your staff, well . . . it is no wonder that you have their absolute devotion."

Ms. Reynolds nods again, even more curtly, and checks her watch. "I'm sorry, Pastor, but you will only be able to speak for forty-five minutes today. We have jewelry-making scheduled in this room at 11."

"That is just fine," he says, but his demeanor has changed again. Pastor Francis pulls his robe from a duffle bag and dons it with an air of importance. He looks so much like a magician putting on his cape before he makes people disappear or even cuts them in half! Millie squeezes my hand, and I know she is thinking the same. It is performance art, but people will believe his message. They will want to believe; it will be a suspension of reality in their lonely lives.

More people start to arrive. They've missed the musical intro but made it for the second act. I don't think they mean to be rude; it is just that it takes a while for these people to get moving, not so different from Millie and me. There are a few that walk in unassisted. Then there are the women and men with canes, walkers, and those electric scooters that seem all the rage in grocery stores (*not just for the old people, if you know what I'm saying*). Many more come in wheelchairs pushed by younger staff with pleasant smiles. The fastidious arrangement of the chairs is desecrated in minutes. An ornery man dressed in blue plaid flannel pajama bottoms and a white undershirt that was not really that white is causing a stir because he wants a place in front, and his lady wheelchair driver has pulled up in the second row.

"Dammit, Carol. Up there! Up THERE!"

"Mr. Gomez, you will be in Ms. Collyn's way. She won't be able to see."

"Just stay back there, you old coot," chirps Ms. Collyn.

"You can't see a lick anyway," retorts Mr. Gomez. "You can't hear anything either. Why do you even come to these things?"

"I need to pray for your soul, you nasty old man."

"Fuck you," said Mr. Gomez in a fairly polite tone.

"See! See!" Ms. Collyn's voice was reaching a crescendo. "Nasty, *nasty* old man."

And it went on and on for a while until Ms. Vivian Reynolds inserted her authority, and the room settled into silence. I, for one, was a little upset with the whole exchange. He did have a nasty mouth. But no one else in the room seemed to be perturbed. They stare straight ahead, anxiously awaiting the words of Pastor Francis.

The lights dim (Pete is back there controlling the ambiance), and a woman in the front—her name tag says *June*—starts to giggle. The projector hums and the screen once more comes to life, the white light illuminating the pastor for pure effect. He moves to the side, to the podium, but Pete is having a hard time rewinding the video. The blank screen holds our attention, and then June gives a little scream. Her short gray hair stands on end, her wrinkles so deep it's hard to determine facial features, but she has a twinkle in her eyes. She waves her hands up in the air, casting shadows in the light. "Ooh," she cries. "Look at me!"

"Put your hands down, dear," says a woman next to her.

"Who let her come anyway?" says Mr. Gomez. "It's not like she doesn't do this every single time."

"Ooh la la," June replies in a singsong voice. She wiggles her fingers in Mr. Gomez's direction. His nostrils flare. His cheeks get red.

And then Millie guffaws. She always laughs first. I have more discipline. It breaks the tension, and now I'm belly laughing along with her. The others turn and stare at us newcomers. Just as quickly, they lose interest.

"Sorry," says Millie, wiping her eyes with the back of her hand. "It was just so funny!"

I'm still chuckling. I am about to open my mouth and agree with her when Pastor Francis sucks all the air out of the room.

He preaches and cajoles while George hands out more literature and lots of little pledge cards. Pastor Francis spins a tale Disney-worthy where Eden is ". . .perfect in every way." By the end, everyone in the room wants to die there.

"Amen," he says.

"Amen," the group mimics.

"Well, sign me up!" shouts Mr. Gomez. "Anything to get me away from the nuts in here!"

"Take him," says Ms. Collyn. "I'll go, too, but you have to keep him in the hospice wing. You do *have* a hospice wing? He's close to death. Just look at him."

Mr. Gomez shoves his middle finger up in the air.

"I will stop by each of your rooms before I leave." Pastor Francis is panting. Is he tired? Or is he on the prowl?

"Time to go to bed!" yells June. It is only 10:57 in the morning, but there is no use pointing it out to her. The young woman behind her pats her head like she would a favorite pet and wheels her away.

The whole lot starts shuffling about. Tables are set up for the jewelry-making class, and the compulsive custodian is asleep on a folding chair, his legs propped up on another folding chair. Those two chairs are the only ones left in a straight line. Ms. Vivian is pushing the haphazardly vacated chairs around the tables. Millie and I help.

Millie

Alva stands in a corner, and I watch her eyes take in the room, now successfully transformed from a pulpit to an arts and crafts studio. People, mostly women, move back and forth between tables, selecting pretty colored beads. I wonder if she's having another one of her visions where she feels displaced. She is very still. I feel a little disorientated myself.

A kind of shadow envelopes me. It has been a long morning, and I worry that the afternoon will be longer. It's hard to think clearly after a thorough brainwashing session. Pastor Francis, with his words, showering us with compliments, lying, attacking. He is a pretty good manipulator. I go over his sermon again, how important we are, that God wants us, that we deserve better, all the while making empty promises about the kind of assisted living he offers. Heck, didn't he tell us that the place is still under construction? Alva whispered something about him "attacking the government funding and our complacency while extolling the virtue of our 'agency' in our own physical and mental decline." I might not have put it so smartly, but I knew what she meant. My old friend, Alice, was married to a man for years who was abusive. Not until her kids had some kind of intervention did she agree to leave him. Pastor Francis reminds me of that rotten bastard (sometimes you just have to say it). He never hit her, but he might as well have. He never told the truth about anything. He made her feel like everything she did was wrong.

Francis is like that. I'm not going to call him Pastor anymore. I'm pretty sure he implied to all of us in the room that it would be our fault if we rotted away in diapers, that we could choose hell or his Eden. If we were willing to give up financial control and housing security, he would personally deliver us to God. And sure, it sounds ridiculous to me and Alva and anybody else with a working brain. But what about those who aren't using theirs?

I look over as Alva straightens a little, and I get the feeling she has figured out something.

Alva

My eyes inspect the scene in front of me. Something more is wrong here. Why in the world would an assisted living facility allow a pastor to come in and recruit their paying customers? I can tell that Ms. Reynolds didn't like the man, so why allow his nonsense in her building? I find her gliding around the tables, nodding to some residents, stopping to praise a certain bracelet or necklace. Really, I think many of these people are very creative. I would wear some of them. The bracelets, not the people. I need to practice clarifying my thoughts.

There is another skirmish readying at the glass bead table, and I get distracted.

"Ms. Reynolds! Elsa took that green one, and it was the one I needed to finish this." The speaker's name tag reads *Althea*, a short, squat woman of about 80. My age, but she looks older. One of the creative ones, I suspect, noting her black velvet jogging suit with the constellations embroidered over her rather large chest. Stars erupt from her ears as well: crazy earrings that bob when her head moves. She has long, white hair pinned in a bun and round, tortoiseshell glasses, too big for her face. One of those characters, you would say, is "larger than life." She is holding a surprisingly delicate string of beads, alternating stones of blue and green.

"I already lay claim on it; it's in my bowl," says the instigator. Elsa is very tall, with dyed blond hair that can't possibly disguise the all-over gray, dressed in a pristine purple pantsuit. She is not a sharer. Each person had been given paper soup bowls to collect their beads, and Elsa's bowl is overflowing. She collected much more than she should have and can't possibly use them all. For that matter, there are most likely twenty identical green beads buried deep among them. She is probably Finnish, I decide, because she's tall and has good posture. Also, because I never believed in all that stuff about how the Finns are the most honest people on the planet.

"You took too many!" counters Althea. "You always think that you deserve more than anyone else. Well, let me tell you something. The universe will get you in the end. You are probably going to be reincarnated as a ferret." Althea isn't messing around with her threats. She might not be one of Pastor Francis's sure things.

There is a tussle when Althea tries to grab the green bead from Elsa's stash. The unsteady vessel tips over, and the tiny globules scatter across the linoleum. I personally see three beads matching the description darting between the chairs. No one moves. Not a surprise because of the mobile disadvantages of most of the people here. Elsa raises her cane in the direction of Althea.

"Look what you've done!" she screams. "Now what am I going to do? I needed all of those!"

"You are a damn fool, Elsa. You would have to string one hundred necklaces if you were to use all of those. Lift your foot, I think I see the one I need."

"This is all the farther my foot goes," Elsa replies, with a sly smile, moving her foot up about half an inch despite walking in here with just a little help from her cane. "I don't want to trip on any of them. Your eyesight isn't that good anyway. You couldn't have seen that little bead land under my foot."

Althea doesn't get up but drags her chair closer and starts to kick Elsa in the shins. It doesn't appear that she is doing much damage because she didn't scoot her seat far enough. Her toes barely glance off Elsa's pant legs. But you wouldn't know that for all of the shouts of hysteria. *Oww! Stop it!! Stop it!! You witch!!*

Ms. Reynolds is moving swiftly, already with a broom in hand. "Ladies! This is no way to act in front of our guests!" She points in my direction. I'm not sure either woman knows or cares if I am a guest or not. Althea makes a grab for the broom, and for a minute I think there will be a curious sword fight, broom against cane, but the director manages to yank the broom back with one hand and catch the swinging cane in the other. "It's almost lunchtime. Both of you head to the cafeteria this minute. I will clean up this mess."

"But I'm not done!" wails Althea. "I just need that one bead!"

Ms. Reynolds sighs, bends down, and rescues the green one from under Elsa's foot, and then pushes Althea's chair, with her in it, across the room to an empty table. She picks up the nearly-done necklace and sets it and the bead in front of her. "Finish it. Now." Then she sweeps up the rest of the beads and, with a flourish, dumps them back into Elsa's bowl. "I will get you another bowl, and I want you to only put half of those beads in it. I will put your name on the new one and you can resume your work tomorrow."

"But—" Elsa starts.

"Half." Ms. Reynolds turns then and starts to corral the rest of the seniors out of the room and into the dining hall. She's a force to be reckoned with.

Flash! *In a field, the birdlike old women flutter their skinny arms and shout epithets at one another. Their gray plumages bob in time, accentuating the words. I walk through the long grasses, the disarray of memories, and gently tug them back in order. "No, I say. This is how it happened." I sing a lullaby.*

I am leaning against the wall, sitting on the linoleum, humming. I don't know if I just slid down the wall or what. I'm not explaining these episodes well at all, to myself or to Millie. My mind took me to that field, but my body felt present there as well, a mix of grasses and wildflowers at my feet. It didn't smell at all like the disinfectant and incontinence that surrounds me now that I am back. At least this vision isn't so confusing. There are plenty of old women here that need saving.

After a minute I follow them to the dining hall, which turns out to be a little more formal than where the pastor spoke. Here, the ceilings are higher, there is green carpet resembling artificial turf, and the walls are painted a cheery yellow. Some of the residents are sitting at four top tables, others standing in line with their plates, waiting patiently for servers to plunk down some casserole that I can't identify, but it smells pretty good. *What was I going to say? Oh yes, I need to ask Ms. Reynolds why she'd let that repulsive pastor speak to her residents. It isn't right.*

Now there is the possibility that they are working together, the Mercy's Milestone director and the church. "Excuse me, Ms. Reynolds." She is monitoring the line. "May I ask you a few questions?"

She turns her lovely face to me, her scarf floating. *Kind, not a wicked bone in her body,* I decide. She nods her head, and I continue. "Maybe somewhere in private?" Now she looks on edge.

"Certainly, Ms. Alva. My office is just there. That is your name, am I right? You are one of Pastor Francis's entourage?"

"*No!*" I say with obvious distaste, so I recant a little. "No, my sister and I were sort of talked into going on this little expedition. It's a long story. We aren't members of Chasten. We were visiting someone there, and all of a sudden, we were visiting here. I am just trying to understand this whole thing."

"What thing, exactly?"

"Well, this care home, Mercy's Milestone. Who runs it? Doesn't it bother you that Pastor Francis is trying to get some of your paying customers to leave and join his community continuum place?"

"It does bother me. *Immensely.*" She leads me down the short corridor to a small office with a tidy desk and a nameplate listing her as the occupant. There is a cheap wood bookcase drowning in books and two chairs covered in some kind of olive-green velvet in front of the desk. Ms. Reynolds turns one chair to face the other and ushers me to sit down.

"It looks like you read a lot," I say because now I feel like I'm intruding. "I read, too, all the time. Unless I am doing something else."

"Are you doing something else now?" she asks politely.

"Right. Well, yes, I am." I am trying to get some answers, and I'm not sure how to go about it. "Does it bother you that some of your residents want to leave this place? It seems all right to me."

"It is more than all right. We are still up to code, and I try to make it feel like home. As you can see, there are lots of activities, and my staff are kind—"

"So why?" Then I think back on some of the conversations that were going on between the seniors. Some of them were pretty cantankerous. Maybe she just wants to get rid of those people. "Do you not like some of them?"

"I don't *love* some of them, but that is not why. I actually will hate to see them go."

"Then why?"

Ms. Reynolds looks around and seems to be debating talking to me. Maybe my nice face wins her over. Or maybe she just needed someone to listen. "We are closing. I can't believe I'm saying it out loud. I have been here for nine years. These people. . . These people are my family. I've lost some, sure, and it is so hard. But losing them this way? Because of money problems? I never would have believed the management company would do this to the residents. Displacing people like Helen over there?" She points through her office window at a diminutive figure, smiling vacantly. A heavyset man in his 20s pushes her along and carries on a one-way conversation. The director shakes her head in disgust. "Helen is 99. She has been here for five years. She only remembers bits and pieces of things. I know she needs memory care, but we don't have it. She exhausted her savings years ago and, at that time, expected Medicaid to cover her after that. But everyone participating in Medicaid's Family Care Program is screwed. Mr. Berg, the owner of this place, isn't accepting Medicaid anymore. I didn't even know you could do that. And I sure don't think the good pastor can provide what she needs."

She pulls a box of Kleenex out of the drawer but doesn't grab one. "I've seen the brochures but don't know if his 'Eden' is ready to provide for all the residents. We have just thirty-four people here. Small potatoes, really, but they will all need to find a place to go. I have to let him speak because if it becomes a reality, it is going to be one of very few options. There are just not any places around here for these people to go. We are a rural community. We don't have enough skilled nurses; the medications have gotten more complicated; we don't have memory care. It is almost impossible to keep going. So, it's a corporate deal. We are done. I have thirty days after I present the residents with the impending closure to help them find substitute care. For most, that means they go back to live with their kids. And the kids don't want them. Certainly, they can't care for them." She is tearing up. "I have to let them all know by the end of the month, and honestly, I don't know if many of them will understand. I just don't know how…"

"How many other facilities does this corporation own? Can't they move them somewhere else, so, even if they don't live in the same community, they'd be safe? You can't just throw people away." I have tears in my own eyes.

"There are five other ones left in Wisconsin. But the Skylight Corporation is out of funds for all five. They are under investigation for Medicare fraud and neglect. The founder and CEO, Mr. Berg, is just in it for the money. He's been moving money around, not paying bills, and, I'm sure, siphoning off the profits. Rumor has it that he has *also* been defrauding Wisconsin Medicaid by charging them for 'worthless services'—services the residents never see—like good, clean sheets. I know because I've been taking sheets and washing them at home, so have some other care workers. People are dying in those other homes, with bedsores and maggots. Without good management, there is no money for staffing. I'm pretty much it as far as day-to-day operations, but without me? Our residents would not be safe in any of them. I've done the best I can. Sometimes I use my own money, like for the beads and for toilet paper."

"Oh dear." I am truly at a loss for words.

Now reaching for a Kleenex, she continues. "We've moved eight people over to the 'GARDEN' a few weeks ago. They were all Medicaid recipients; most of ours are. Haven't heard anything from their families, but that isn't unusual. A son or daughter, or a brother, comes over and packs up their meager belongings, and they are gone. Two more people left us early last week. One was that Pete Werner's old mother. Her name is Patty. Did you know his mother used to be a resident here? Well, I suppose not. She is almost 90 but suffered a great bout of depression when her husband passed away. I am not sure that she was even aware that Pete intended to move her out. She didn't socialize very much, but she had made one dear friend, Harriet. Harriet went with her."

"And they took them to 'Eden?'" I ask incredulously. "Your worries are justified. When we spoke with George, he also made it sound like they were only in the early stages of construction."

"I just don't know," the tired director sighs. "I tried to go out there one evening after work. There was a gate across the entry road, and I really couldn't see beyond it. It's spooky, way out there in the woods. There was a tractor and a few small buildings, and I thought I saw a light by the old chapel. When I asked Pete how they were doing, he said that they had hired their second onsite health companion to oversee his mom's and Harriet's needs, and they have a full-time nurse on site. They say they have already secured a cook and a maintenance man. How can they pay for all of that when *we* are struggling? Medicaid pays out managed care organizations, which are supposed to evaluate the needs of enrolled members and pay for those services. It's a monthly rate which is used to pay a reimbursement rate to service providers. But they froze the rates, and we can't cover the costs. How can Pastor Francis cover them?"

My eyes are glazing over with all the details, which is a shame since I will be in the same position in the near future. *I need to look over my policies.*

Ms. Reynolds continues, "I know Pastor Francis's mom lives on the property, or at least she did. Haven't seen her in almost a year. Pete said Pastor Francis was available to all the residents all day, every day. That's obviously a lie since they're there and he's here. And then I got a letter."

"A letter from?" *This gets stranger and stranger,* I thought.

"Harriet. Ms. Harriet Olson. Patty's best friend. She used to be a big deal around here from way back. Before my time, really. But I've heard the stories. She had the biggest house off Main Street and lived there with her husband and daughter. One night, that beauty of a house went up in flames. She survived but no one else did. The word is that she doesn't even like to be reminded of her last name. She is only

'Harriet' now, and she lived the rest of her life in a small bungalow on some old family property outside of town. Until she couldn't take care of herself, and she came here. She has lots of money to pay for home healthcare, but she paid out of pocket for this place: could really go anywhere for her long-term care, but she decided, after all of those years alone, that she wanted some peers to talk to. She didn't make a lot of friends here, but she did have one."

I wince at the thought of all that money and my imaginings of Pastor Francis's proclivities.

"She considers Ms. Werner her best friend. When Pete moved his mom, Harriet signed the papers right then, authorizing Chasten Union Church to act as guardian for her estate. Pastor Frank had a moving truck here in no time. Took the few things she had brought with her: an antique dresser, a small nightstand. She had some nice art that she kept in her room closet that never got hung. She told me that she hated to leave, but she was afraid that Patty wouldn't be okay without her. It doesn't sound right, does it?" Ms. Reynold's eyes plead for me to make sense of it all. I sense it; I can't prove it.

"Wait," I say. "What about that letter?"

She stands up, not so poised now. Wearily, she pulls that shawl tighter around her now-slumped shoulders as she continues. "Oh, okay, I received a lovely letter from Harriet about four days ago." She rifles through the neat stack of papers on her desk, leaving them uncharacteristically disordered. "Here." She looks it over thoughtfully. "It is addressed to me, Ms. Reynolds. She thanks me for the excellent care she received here at Mercy's Milestone and signs it Ms. Olson."

I get up, too, when she pauses. Since she looks uncertain whether to continue, I reach out for the letter. I skim it quickly. There is nothing unusual about the thank you. Harriet describes her new home as very pleasant and writes that she is quite happy to share a room with Patty Werner. She mentions the chapel and how Pastor Francis is so kind. I glance back at Ms. Vivian, who is shaking her head back and forth.

"It sounds as though she is doing well," I offer.

"Yes . . . it does, doesn't it? But I don't think she wrote it."

I grimace. "Why would you think she didn't write it?"

Staring hard at me, Ms. Reynolds replies, "Because she'd call me Viv. When she came here, and I told her my name was Vivian Reynolds, she said that she knew this was going to be a good home for her. Said her daughter's name had been Vivian, but she called her Viv. She asked me if she could call me Viv, too." Taking the letter back from me and staring at the words, she went on. "She would have said, 'Dear Viv,' and she wouldn't have signed it 'Ms. Olson.' She was just Harriet to all of us. On top of that, I don't think that is her handwriting."

We stare at each other, both lost in thought. Then she gives me her card and I mutter that I will call her if I can think of anything to do that will protect her wards. She smiles wanly and heads back to the cafeteria. *Me? I'm going to go visit Eden come hell or high water.*

Millie

I see Alva disappear down the hall with the director, so I stay and survey the lunch crowd. I find a table unoccupied at the back, offering a dandy view of the room. Relishing my alone time, I blink my eyes against the mind-numbing florescent lights and ponder the absurdity of our situation. A kind cafeteria helper asks me if I want a cup of coffee. Caffeine is not my friend, but I think I'll be plenty tired when my head hits the pillow tonight, regardless of how many cups she pours. She points to the line, worming its way to the buffet table, but I am content to just sit here. A married couple joins me. They are large people, overdressed compared to the rest, who are mostly in rumpled loungewear. The woman wears an ill-fitting blue, wool, crepe dress, her hair in a bun that looks like she slept on it. Too much blue eye shadow, too. The man wears a suit, ill-fitting as well. While her frock is baggy, this suit is way too tight around the middle. They motor to the table in matching fancy wheelchair things, putting them in forward and then reverse gear over and over until their pairs of legs disappear under the table.

"Just a little back," the man sings to his wife.

"And just a little forward," she trills back to him.

And again, I take the Lord's name in vein under my breath. I'm sure it's still a sin, no matter how quiet I say it. The lunch trays are balanced on their laps, and I wonder how in the heck they can do all that maneuvering without dropping the food everywhere. Or maybe they don't. They grin from ear to ear when they see me noticing their wheels.

"Yessir, these are the latest models! Pride Mobility's 'Jazzy Model Number Two!'"

"Wow, jazzy!" I say absolutely without any enthusiasm.

Their name tags read *Jon* and *Gladys Hansen*. I can't figure out if the name tags are for the benefit of staff and visitors or because the individuals may need to remind themselves. I must have questioned this out loud because Gladys informs me that on days when they have special events—Francis being the special event—they are supposed to wear them so the speaker can address the residents appropriately if they were to ask a question.

Jon makes a big deal reaching for his napkin and wiping off a little corn kernel from Gladys's rather hairy underlip. "I dislike the name tags," he says haughtily. "Sometimes I find a bit of adhesive has remained on my suitcoat. I like to dress for a meal and for any special occasion. We get so few of them around here. Occasions, not meals." He smiles at Gladys. "We do like the food. Some people complain, but the food is fine."

Gladys, in turn, brushes a bit of green bean from his tie. "We have listened to Pastor Francis each time he's visited. We look forward to it. Such a fine man." Gladys turns and beams at someone behind me and slowly begins to move around in her seat excitedly. I turn to see what has the woman gyrating. Like a specter, Francis appears to my right and sits down in the fourth unoccupied chair. I shudder a little, but I can't exactly tell Gladys and Jon about our suspicions. So I remain while Francis sets his sights on the prey.

"Miss Gladys. Mr. Hansen!" Francis begins. A misogynist right off the bat, I notice. "It is wonderful to see you both! I saw how attentive you were to my words today. May I ask you a few questions?"

"We are eating, Francis," I say dismissively (even though I am not). I can tell he doesn't like that I called him Francis, but I am not backing down. He is no pastor.

Nonplussed, he continues, "What a beautiful shade of blue you are wearing, Gladys! It is the color of God's sky above Eden. Or is it azure? And isn't that a beautiful word? Oh my, and your lovely necklace! Are those pearls a family heirloom? They look stunning on you. What a vision. A lucky man, Jon. My goodness, you are a fortunate man!"

Interesting how he notices her jewelry. They are probably the two most stylish seniors in the home despite the food stains, and I'm sure that's why he's singled (well. . . coupled) them out. There's not a lot of monied people in this place, and I am betting that they are better off than most.

"I am fortunate to still be alive, still more to have Gladys at my side," Jon agrees with a big hearty laugh. "Yes, we were intrigued by your words today, Pastor. Gladys and I have been thinking about making a change. Mercy's Milestone has its niceties, but we are part of only a handful of people in this place who aren't widows or widowers. Do you have a plan for married people in your Eden? Double the down payment, don't you know!"

A big smile crosses Francis's face. I get chill bumps.

Gladys continues, "I worry about our souls. I also worry about our Fefe. God made the animals, too, right, Pastor? Our rooms here—and I say *rooms* because we have several: two bedrooms, two baths, a kitchenette, and a living area—are quite comfortable. Not to brag, but it's the biggest in the place. The problem is our neighbors on either side of the hall make complaints all the time about our Fefe. They say she yips. She *certainly* does not."

"I'm surprised your neighbors could hear the dog," I say with a hint of my own sarcasm, but then continue, "I think, surely most people appreciate that dogs are allowed here. Gives the place a homey feel. I bet they would be heartbroken to see you leave." My inner voice says, *Don't go anywhere with this man,* even though I don't really care where they go. They are not particularly likable.

Francis ignores me and regards them thoughtfully, nodding, "Of course we take in couples of faith. And your little dog too."

"Christ," I say before I can stop myself. And six eyes glare at me. "Sorry, I am so sorry, I didn't mean to say that. I *never* say that—like that. I pray, of course. It's just that it felt for a moment that I was in a movie in Oklahoma somewhere. The strangest thing—I adore dogs. I used to have a poodle. . ." I'm glaring right back at Francis.

I believe he smirks. Moving his chair closer to the Hansen's in a gesture of mock intimacy: "I think that I have overwhelmed poor Millie here. We had a long drive over here. Overexcited, maybe?" He pats my arm.

I pull my arm from his reach. "Overexcited?" I say in disbelief. The audacity.

Placating now but still addressing his potential acquisitions: "Millie is one of our newest supporters, and this is the first time she has seen the true need of our work."

"I don't know if I support—"

He cuts me off midsentence. "You two are just the kind of people we have in mind for Eden. I can assure you that you would be even more comfortable with us. We will have cottages on the property that will stand alone. You will not have immediate neighbors on either side. I can begin to draw up some papers. There will, of course, be a place for Fefe."

"In the ground," I say, and then instantly regret my words. Too harsh. Now who is being scary?

"What?" stammers Gladys. She is staring at me with eyes wide as saucers.

"I mean, when they break ground on the new 'cottages.'" And now I do sound like a supporter.

Alva

"Millie! Over here!" Millie has just gotten up from a table in the dining hall, and I pull her into the hall as soon as she gets within reach. She almost falls over an exuberant scooter driver, who misses taking her down by inches.

"Dammit!" she squeaks, and then, "I have never cursed so many times in one day. I will probably go to hell now, and—"

"No one is going to hell. Or at least we're not."

"Alva let's just get out of here. We can call a taxi. Get back to the motel and our own car. We can head any direction you like."

"I don't think we can, Millie. The plot has thickened." We walk slowly and notice the pastor slip into one of the residents' rooms. "See there? More recruiting." I grimace.

"I see that little weasel. He was sweet-talking the Hansens, too. Said he had room for their dog. And he called me 'overexcited.'"

"Why did he call you that?"

"I don't know," Millie says stubbornly. "He was schmoozing, and I was getting in the way, I guess."

"Right. So, let me tell you about the conversation I had with Vivian Reynolds. She thinks something is rotten in Denmark, too. Pastor Francis and—"

"Stop calling him Pastor," Millie says angrily. "I made a mental note to just call him Francis."

"Okay, excellent idea. Francis and Pete have already transferred ten people, including Pete's mom and a lady named Harriet, to Eden. Vivian doesn't know if they are safe. She got a letter from Harriet that says everything is fine, but she thinks the letter was forged."

Millie's voice was a whisper. "You think they are being held against their will?"

"If they have a will."

"Oh, Alva!"

"Millie, let me finish. What I found out was that all of these nice old people and even the staff here at Mercy's Milestone are going to be kicked out on their fannies. Ms. Reynolds has been told that she has to give them a verbal eviction notice by the end of this week."

Millie is shaking her head. "Not possible, Alva. You can't just go kicking 90-year-old people on their butts. Who told Ms. Reynolds she had to do that?"

"The head honchos. The corporate owners of this place. And they are making her do it instead of taking any responsibility. She said that many of the residents have paid in advance for their stay here. Up to a year."

"How are they going to get their money back?" Millie is flushed with anger.

"I don't know all of that yet. And she said that Francis has been coming around ever since she found out about the dislodgments. So maybe he's got some partnership going with them."

Millie is taking big gulps of air. Fishlike. I pull her into the ladies' room and sit her down on the toilet. "I don't have to go."

"Just rest for a minute. Your face is getting all blotchy."

"This is giving me a giant headache. I'm so mad. I don't have the stomach for all this cruelty, Alva. I thought I was the strong one, but you are handling this situation much better than I am."

I watch Millie struggle to unwind some uncooperative toilet paper and pat her face. It's a little bathroom, and I'm holding the door open. We both look out toward the mirror and see our reflections, all old and indignant. Holding out my hand, she takes it, and we stand at the sink. The sink and counters are flesh-colored, the walls gray, and the lights overhead are unkind. We blend in. Staring at each other in the mirror, we recognize us as what we aren't. Superheroes.

"I have underestimated you for years, Alva. You have more gumption than I thought. Me? I don't know how much fight I have in me," Millie says.

"But, if not us?" I say.

Alva

We wash our hands because if you are in a bathroom, you should always wash your hands. I guide Millie back out toward the dining hall, deftly dodging a second senior stampede. "Millie, I think we need to gird our loins for the long game." I am focused now, despite the pounding of walkers hitting the hallway tile and scooters bumping into walls as people head to their rooms and nap time. A long time passes before the dispersal is complete, and I can resume our conversation. Millie is looking at me warily. "One of us, and I think it should be me, should start acting like we may need Francis's services after all. But first, I think we should see the property ourselves, not with Pete and Francis. They won't show us anything unsavory."

"I don't like where this is going," Millie says angrily. "How did we get into this mess anyway? I just gambled a little and lost our coat and here we are, characters in some kind of awful crime novel. And we don't have *time*, Alva. How can we bring down a villainous group in a week or two? That's all the time we have before our children will start to look for us. And what about our travel adventure? Coming to this town doesn't qualify as *traveling*."

"I'm going to map it all out. It's hard for me to think in this place, but once we get back to the motel, we can put things into motion. There are a lot of pieces. We need to find out if Francis has any association with the corporate heads of Mercy's Milestone. I was thinking, if that place is going under, could it be that they are somehow paying Francis to take old people off their hands? Maybe they wouldn't get such bad press for shutting down if there was an alternative place for the residents to go. You know, like the kind of place Evy was in back in Crookston?

Remember how Connie, down the street from the old house, started taking in older people like her, who needed more services than they could get at home? I don't know, Millie, there has got to be some kind of scheme happening and we just have to figure it out. If we get in over our heads, we will just call the police."

"Why would the police believe us?" Millie asks.

"I'm working on that. Maybe I'll pretend to get sick and ask to spend a few nights at Eden to get a good rest before we go on our way. Oh, and then you could sneak around, pretending to visit, all the while taking pictures of the place. And then I can look for files and such at night. We will put together a real case for the authorities."

Millie rolls her eyes. "Alva, you've put together quite a tall tale. While you're at it, why don't we hire a private detective like Columbo to help us?"

"I'm a Telly Savalas fan still to this day. It was his shiny head. But I don't think either of those types would want to work for free. We don't have enough money for that. So, help me think through it all. We will make a list of dos."

"We need to get out of here first, Alva. We should have never left our car at the Happy Family. That front desk lady has probably sold it for parts. I don't trust her."

"Just one more person to keep our eyes on," I say, and mean it. "Let's see if we can round up the three Samaritans and be on our way: get them to drop us off, not go out to the Eden site. I'm not sure they really want us out there and am quite sure they won't show us anything we want to see. Then we can go buy flashlights and such in order to explore it all tonight. Columbo has nothing on me."

"Give up the secret-agent stuff, Alva. I think you are right about doing reconnaissance at Eden, without any tour guides. But what we need is our own car and better shoes."

"How are we going to get them to just take us back to our motel?" I say dubiously.

"Leave it to me," says Millie. "I'll come up with something."

We leave the dining hall and try to find the pastor—or Francis, I mean. Walking down the corridor, I feel a little dizzy. The carpet is made up of brown- and sage-green squares and the walls are covered in yellow stripes with little flowers stenciled in. Don't really know what look they were going for, but I am sure they hadn't met with success. Knowing about the imminent closing of the place makes me take notice of the little things: the dusty plastic plants, the torn vinyl shades in rooms that we pass, the peeling paint. The whole place seems to be sagging, stooping under the weight of the future. We hear laughter coming through the thin doors of some units and sadness seeping out of the doors of others. Many of the doors lining the hallway have yellowing wreaths of flowers, and some are covered with handmade watercolors, done in the art classes on Thursdays. There is light *and* darkness.

The third door on the right is wide open, and Millie shoves me in before her. The entry space inside is tiny, with a hall closet on one side and a bathroom on the other. I don't like being shoved, so I shimmy back a little and try to push her forward. It goes on and on like this until I finally give up, and we both stumble into Helen's bedroom. We enter to see a tableau of Francis, Pete, George, and a tiny nonagenarian lying still on a bed rimmed with metal bars. The able stand in a row at the foot of the old woman's bed, with somber expressions. Francis has a sympathetic smile plastered on his pasty face. I move closer, firstly because I want to make sure the woman is breathing and second, to help her stay that way. Francis is in mid-sentence.

"Miss Helen, I am so full of love, so pleased that you have decided to join us."

The woman stares straight ahead and right through Francis. Her hand twitches a little when Pete puts a pen between her fingers.

"It's a big decision, I know," Francis continues.

"Come now," coaxes Pete, "this decision will be a new beginning. And you can see my mom. Remember Patty? And Harriet Olsen? Two of the nicest women in the world. They can show you the ropes, tell you about the peace they feel."

"Ropes?" Helen peeps.

Roped in is what she is. Helen is so small, swathed in a faded pink blanket, and surrounded by deceptive shepherds. She is incapable of making this decision on her own. Where are her children? Doesn't she have an advocate? I feel so helpless because, of course, I can't be that advocate. I am a stranger. I remember the dire picture Vivian Reynolds had painted. The children don't want caretaking responsibilities, and there is nowhere else for her to go. Small towns, limited options. My blood pressure is building. I look at Millie, and her mouth is hanging open again; she is making strange throaty noises.

I don't think Millie can speak, but then she yelps instead. The noise shocks everyone except for Miss Helen, who does not react at all. She shrieks again, and at the same time, Millie wrenches me to the floor. I land hard on my rump with my feet outstretched in the air, and everyone probably has a decent view of my girdle.

Millie

"Oh no!" I scream again. "Alva, are you okay?"

Alva is gawking at me in astonishment. All the men in the room get a quick peek at her girdle. I try to shush her, but she is sputtering with fury. George rushes over and tries to pick her up by her armpits. Alva stops her guttural stammering, only to start slapping George away, and he drops her down on the floor again. His cheeks are flushing with embarrassment because he had struggled to get her partially standing, only to witness another flash of undergarments. The action quite successfully interrupts the little gathering in Helen's claustrophobic space. With some hesitation, Francis and Pete move in our direction. They move slowly; I'm sure they don't want the ancient cash cow to fall asleep before signing the contract, and we are again an unwelcome distraction.

"Well, my goodness, she has done it again! These fainting spells are so unusual for Alva. Oh, Alva!" I say with visible concern. Not that I think that Alva is hurt, but I am concerned that she will not speak to me for a week for this latest subterfuge. My eyes plead with her to go on with my impromptu ruse. "Gentlemen, I fear that we really must be on our way. *Right away.* I need to get my sister back to the motel. She just isn't feeling right."

Good ol' George regains his composure enough to try again to right Alva. This time she manages to stand. They are both red-faced and damp with perspiration. Anger and embarrassment make them look like a pair of baboon butts. The image is more than I can take, and I put my hands over my face and pretend to cry. I needed a laugh. After a few steadying breaths, I peer between my fingers and see Alva. The color is draining from her cheeks and is being replaced by what I hope to be a calm understanding. She's still mad, but it will be okay.

Director Reynolds also has heard the commotion and steps in to take control. I think that she bonded with Alva during that talk they had, and she is not taking any chances with her new friend. She places her hand on Francis's shoulder and guides him toward the door.

"Please, Pastor," she says firmly, "you must take Alva back to Chasten immediately. You are more than welcome to come back tomorrow and bully Miss Helen." She chuckles and pats his arm like it was a funny joke between the two of them. Francis doesn't laugh. He only gestures reluctantly at his cohorts, and we all move out of the room. I take another look at Miss Helen. She is still staring at nothing but, with difficulty, eradicates one frail arm from its swaddling and waves goodbye to the wall.

Alva

I give Millie a little push out the door, so she knows I am still perturbed, but then we start walking slowly just to annoy Pete. He's the one that seems the most easily provoked. He is cursing under his breath while collecting the last of the equipment left by the door.

"If we have to go, then let's go." Pete is fuming but trying to hide it. "You two are slowing up this whole operation."

"Operation?" questions Millie.

"The business of soul saving," Pete rephrases. "I meant we are in the soul-saving business."

"There are so many souls that need it," says Millie sarcastically while shooting daggers at him with her eyes. "So, when you were at the casino, were you not really gambling? Just finding souls to save?"

"You have to be in tune with people in order to teach them," scoffs Pete. "Everyone knows that."

"Everyone? Oh." Millie is exasperated.

I squeeze a little harder to remind her that we shouldn't argue with him. He might be our biggest hurdle. Even after mentioning the fur coat, there is a chance we can convince him we are easy marks instead of threats, but it'll be the hardest part. I squeeze one more time, pinching her to make sure she knows I'm still miffed about the doorway stunt.

Millie has her arm around my waist, ignoring my stiff posture, and pretends that she is pulling me along. Yep, the push and pull of relationships. I don't like that she just took it upon herself to cut short the recruitment ceremony. I could have used a heads-up before being shoved on the linoleum. But it was, I admit only to myself, effective. Pete has reached the back door. He has a box of pamphlets in his right hand.

The microphone is in his left hand, and brandishing it like a sword, he stabs at the door. George runs to his rescue and turns the knob. I look around and don't see the third mangy musketeer. Now that we are alone, I admonish Millie.

"Why didn't *you* pretend to faint?"

"You have a history going."

She is not one bit sorry. "Millie, didn't you think that Pete would probably catch on? He's the one that invented that little skit."

"What?"

"Millie, remember, that's how we got here! Pete pretended to fall under that table at the casino. So stereotypical. And now you make me fall down on purpose. It's the same kind of thing."

"What about you falling out of the car, Alva? What about that?"

"That act had a little more finesse. And I wasn't even trying," I say haughtily.

"I think that people have been doing it all the time as a distraction in all kinds of situations. It's comedic," Millie says. "And Alva, if you are going to make a pun about falling from grace, just know I already thought of it."

"That would be an idiom, not a pun." I know the difference.

We pick up the pace and follow Pete out to the car.

Alva

We ride back in silence. Francis and Pete are sullen, and George looks just plain tired. He had done most of the work, packing up the car, and it was so hot. George is sweaty and doesn't smell very good. The air conditioning isn't working well, so all four windows are at half-mast, and even Millie's coarse, curly gray hair is cavorting with the warm wind. I reach into my canvas tote bag (I have always thought a purse was too small for a long trip) and pull out my ball cap. It was Irvin's, and it is one of my favorite possessions. Definitely vintage Minnesota Twins. My granddaughter laughs every time she sees me wearing it. "You look like a kid, Gram," she says even though we both know that I surely do not.

I loved the Minnesota Twins, our home team, even in the years when they were horrible. Oh gosh, Irvin and I used to sit and watch those games from March to October. He would whoop and holler at every hit, at every error. "Who's on first?" Irvin would start dramatically. We knew that Abbott and Costello skit better than the Nicene Creed. It would go on and on until I finally squealed, "I don't care!" and Irvin would yell, "He's our shortstop!!" And we would both dissolve into laughter.

After the World Series had come and gone each year, we would just sit and stare at the TV like it had taken away our firstborn. And now, I have to say that I don't watch baseball that much anymore. I plunk that hat on my head all the same, and I feel better about our predicament. My fine wisps of gray hair are still. "It's my thinking cap," I whisper to Millie. She puts one hand over mine. The other hand goes over her nose.

"I don't have anything to put over my nose," I whisper again and gesture to George, who is sitting on Millie's left. She picked the middle to make up for throwing me to the floor, but now I know she regrets it. George's head is resting on the window now, and his eyes are shut. His odor is suffocating.

"I can hardly stand it," hisses Millie. She digs her hanky out of her sleeve and covers her nose. "Don't know why you don't carry one of these. You sure you don't have something in that bag of yours?"

"Everything but," I sigh. This is the first time I can remember wanting a mucus-laced square of fabric stored up my sleeve. I try to breathe in and out through my mouth. It must sound like I am gagging because Pete turns his eyes away from the road and back to me.

"Do not be sick in the car," he threatens. "It is bad enough in here as is."

"I am not going to be sick," I say, "but I really wish that pine tree thing on your mirror was a little more fragrant."

Francis has his head almost fully out of the window, his slimy hair the only thing not moving in the wind. His eyes are also closed, and he is mumbling to himself. I think he wants us to believe he is praying. George farts.

Francis yanks his head back in to yell, "Goddamn it, George!"

Oops, I think. "What did you say, Francis?" I say sweetly, only to annoy him.

"Never mind," he replies gruffly.

More silence. Millie and I exchange little smiles and then stare out the window, willing the familiar sights of Chasten to come into view. We pass a few townships, each of them seeing better days. People just don't want to settle in small places anymore. I see a sign that says Chasten is eleven miles ahead and heave another big sigh—of relief this time. *Another few minutes,* I think, *and I can get the heck out of this car.* I didn't notice right away that we were coming in from a different direction, the small downtown seems bigger from this vantage point. There is a feed store, a few boarded-up buildings, and a dilapidated gas station touting the best ribs this side of Detroit, on my right. There are a few men standing around the pumps and off to the side, a picnic table with a harried-looking mom and her two sons eating the advertised Doc's Barbeque out of foil-lined plastic containers. Millie is looking out the left window where there is more of an assortment of businesses. A hardware store, a café, and then Millie grabs my knee with such force I almost hit my head on the car roof.

"Over there, over *there*!" she is trying to whisper and shout at the same time, teeth clenched, head bobbing wildly toward her window, eyes looking past George to a small, white-bricked building. The neon sign barely blinking in the sun reads PAWNSHOP. Pete had just then slowed the car at the only red light in town. I have no idea what is happening.

I speak softly. "Millie, are you having some kind of tremor?"

She focuses again outside the window on the other side of George, and then turns and glares meaningfully into my eyes.

I look, as best I can, past Millie and George into the grimy window of the pawnshop. "Oh! Oh! Millie! I see it!!" I say with Millie's same forced whisper. And then, thinking quickly, I point out my side of the car and direct Millie's attention to the gas station. Loudly, I say, "Those ribs smell wonderful! Maybe we should stop?"

I slap a hand over Millie's mouth before she can say, "It's our fur coat!"

"Don't tell me how bad ribs are for me, Millie, I didn't get lunch," I whine in my most loud and obnoxious voice. I do not want Pete to know we saw the coat. Thank goodness she gets my meaning. She starts to complain loudly so that the men in the car are too distracted to note our discovery.

"But Alva," she begs.

Pete stomps on the gas as soon as the light turns green. "No! I can drop you two off at your motel or at the church. We have meetings to get to."

"But—" Millie continues with the charade.

"No," Francis joins in. "I am sorry, ladies. We have had to take this detour to get Alva some needed rest, but I need to be on my way to Eden, and then I intend to resume my work at Mercy's Milestone."

"Well, I am so sorry to have ruined your plans," I say but not in a kind voice. Then I remember myself, realizing that we have to keep our enemies closer. "Yes, I know you need to check on Ms. Werner and Harriet. How's your own mother, by the way? Perhaps tomorrow I will feel well enough to take that tour with you."

"Pastor's mom hasn't been feeling well for a while now. But he prays with her every day, right?" George is trying to get back on Francis's good side but is babbling. "Do you think I should pick her some flowers? I really want to visit; she should know there are people here that care for her."

Francis's mouth puckers in a tight line. "She isn't up to visitors."

"I get it," I say. "I know how it is to want to be left alone when I am not up to snuff." But I don't really get it. I have to think more about Francis's mother.

Francis just nods. The car swings into the Happy Family Motel, and none of the men offer to open our doors. I pull Millie out my door and quickly close it behind us. They drive off. They don't spin out the tires or anything like that, but they obviously are glad to get rid of us.

Millie

I am no fan of this motel, but standing in its virtually empty parking lot gives me a sense of peace I haven't felt all morning. Alva and I head to the blue door with the number six on it, our car parked in front looking no worse for wear. Walking inside, we are greeted with the hum of the air conditioner wall unit, and we collapse onto our respective full-size beds. I pull my purse to me from the nightstand and empty it out. I find some saltines and some peanuts and hand half over to Alva. A few bites later and I am exhausted, but my mind is racing. "I am going to close my eyes."

"Permanently?" asks Alva. It's one of those end-of-life jokes we are so used to saying to one another. It's a little morbid, but going to sleep gets riskier and riskier at our age.

"Take a nap, Alva," I say.

"We both need to put our feet up, but we haven't even talked about the coat yet! I'm so impressed you saw it there!" Alva tries to work up some excitement, but truth be told, she looks exhausted.

"It won't disappear during our naptime. We need to just breathe for a moment. Maybe take a bath?" I feign stretching and yawning for good measure.

"Okay," Alva relents. "Gosh, I feel like it's about midnight, but I know it's just a little past one. What a terribly long morning. We will give it an hour. Then we will drive down to that little café and get some real food in our systems, and then head to the pawnshop. It said it was open until 5. Oh, but Millie. . ."

Alva tries to fight off the sleep for about two more minutes and then I hear soft little snores. I want to close my eyes; my body is heavy, but my brain won't turn off. An hour passes. I peek over at my sister. She is flat on her back with that Twins cap at a forty-five-degree angle. Her fine, gray hair is longer than it usually is, and it sticks out from beneath the cap in all directions, spidering across the pillowcase. Her skin has always been beautiful. Maybe because she's plump and has more fat padding that hides the wrinkles. She hates it when I say that. But more likely, since Alva isn't an outdoorsy type, her cheeks remain creamy. Now they have the soft, dewy fuzz that comes with less estrogen. (Just another one of those things people don't tell you about getting old.) Laugh lines at the corners of her eyes only enhance the hazel twinkle, now quieted by heavy lids. My sister is lovely in my eyes.

I get up and fight the urge to brush my hand on her cheek. I don't know exactly where all the tenderness is coming from except that I worry this running around is too much for her. *I'll be damned if her sense of honor, and her newly found independence, jeopardizes her health.* Sure, we can see if crimes against the elderly are being committed, but Alva does not need to fall victim to Francis and his cronies to prove a point. *Let her sleep,* I think. I need to go get that coat and then we can leave this awful place.

My heart starts to pound after I sneak out of the motel room. I thought Alva heard me when the keys jangled in my pocket, so I listen intently at the door before making any further move. Then, looking at the Buick, I decide that starting it would surely equal an alarm clock going off, so I head for the sidewalk. *I'm just going to go buy that coat back, no matter what the price is, and be done with this mess. We can let people know our suspicions when we get home. If I remember right that pawnshop is not more than a couple of blocks down.*

It's further than that.

Dripping from the heat, I plod on down Main Street. I wish I would have worn my paisley dress like Alva did today. It only now occurs to me that walking back to the motel carrying a mink coat on such a hot day will be problematic. *Oh well, let the residents of Chasten think I'm off my rocker.* I have my black slacks on and a three-quarter-length sleeved white blouse with a scalloped collar. *Thank the Lord I put my feet into my cushy tennis shoes.* I nod to a young couple who pass me on the sidewalk. They are looking at me with a kind of pity, or maybe they're just hot too. I just can't understand how it can be this steamy in Wisconsin. I stop for a minute under an elm tree, the last corner before the "Downtown District." I've not rested for more than a minute when I look down to see a mosquito bloated with my blood attached to my forearm. *Dammit. Just Dammit!* I smack the little thing so hard that a little red spurts on my white blouse. I take out my hanky and spit on it, trying to rub the spot out, but it just makes it worse.

Frustration at an all-time high, I pick up the pace for another two blocks until I am standing in front of the pawnshop. There is a sign in the doorway saying, *Be Back Soon.*

What is soon?? I stare incredulously at the sign and then start knocking on the door. *Maybe they forgot to take down the sign. Maybe they are having a late lunch.* Exasperated, I keep knocking and peering into the door until the young man who had passed me on the sidewalk and who is now sitting outside the café one door up with his girl says in a loud voice, "I don't think they are in there."

The girl smiles sweetly and adds, "I think they will be right back." They both hold up their cups of coffee like they are toasting my stupidity.

Embarrassed now, I say, "Oh." And then ask, "Are they eating in there?" pointing to the café door.

"We don't know. We don't know them. We just saw the sign," they reply, trying to be polite, but I know they are laughing at old me.

I wave a little thanks, then, embarrassed, walk toward the parking spaces in the back, trying to get out of sight. There are a few cars in the lot, but I don't pay attention because all I'm thinking about is getting that coat and getting the hell out of Dodge. I stand against the building where there is a small patch of shade and wonder if I have time to wait before Alva wakes up, or even better, if I have time to run over to that little café and get a sandwich because I didn't have much of an appetite at Mercy's Milestone, as well as time to wait before Alva wakes up. I do not want her worried. This was only supposed to take fifteen minutes or so. I pray silently that she is really snoozing. There is a little window in the back door of the pawnshop, so I stand on my tippy-toes and try to peek in. I think I see someone in there. Then the door swings open so violently that I am knocked into the grass. Someone puts a hand over my mouth, and I am shoved into a car. Even when they take their hand away, I cannot scream. I have no breath.

Alva

Whooee, did I fall hard asleep! Dark and dreamless. You know when you are so tired you just collapse and don't remember even putting your head on the pillow, much less taking off your shoes? I wrote my own haiku about it once. Let's see. . .

Less dead to the world,
Revitalized by darkness
My soul is ready.

That was it. I have so many haikus written in journals from over the years. Some pretty good starts to quirky murder mysteries, too. Always thought maybe I'd put them into a book for my granddaughter. It's something to revisit when we get back.

I am still pondering poetry.

Flash! *The bumbling man is like a bull in a China shop. I watch him from my place at the register as he knocks over displays and awkwardly resets them. He is on an errand for his boss. "What are you to buy?" I say.*

"I am to buy his explanation," he says slowly. I want to comfort this man. Protect him. And just then, a shot rings out, and pieces of the man fly into the sky, and his blood coats the stars.

And as quick as it appeared, the images are gone, like a camera when someone covers the lens. My sleep was dreamless, and now here I am, awake and haunted. Looking around, I feel lost or like I've failed to do something. My journal sits on the bedside table, and I sit down and start to write, absorbed in the absurdity of my visions: a fur, snakes, deer, a wild pig, teeming roaches, and old women. Now a bull. When I finish, I take note of the quietness.

The room is dark, those blackout motel curtains drawn. I look anxiously around but don't see Millie. The bathroom door is closed, so I get up and start to pound. "Millie! I think I slept too long! Let's go to the pawnshop! Millie? Millie!!!"

I give the door a push and see it's empty. Throwing aside the shower curtain, no Millie. I don't know why she would be standing in the shower without the water running, but that is how uneasy I feel (and I think I saw that scene in a TV movie). Now the pounding is in my head, and I hurry back into the little room with its two beds and note that the bedspread on Millie's has not been wrinkled by sleep. I draw the dark curtains open, and I see it is late afternoon, the sun still high in the sky. The Buick is parked right in front, the gold-and-pink-colored rays bouncing off the hood in a spectacular prism. I move to the door and find it unlatched, although I am positive I had secured the chain. The car keys are not on the dresser. *Why would Millie take the keys and not the car? Maybe she went to the front office for some ice. Or for some, something. Gosh, how long had I slept? Several hours?* The pounding has moved down my forehead and lodged directly behind my eyes. I need my glasses and my shoes and, more specifically, some answers.

Surely, there is a fine reason for Millie to be absent. She does get hungry much more quickly than I do. It's her metabolism. And, come to think of it, neither one of us ate a lot at lunch. Those saltines won't hold her! But couldn't she have waited for me? I take calming breaths and convince myself that nothing dreadful has happened to my sister. I have to get down on all fours to find my shoes, and when that doesn't work, I finally figure out that I wore my shoes to bed and that they are tangled in the sheets at the bottom. My glasses are, thankfully, not hiding. Donning my sweater and picking up my purse, I take the motel key card from the dresser and head outside. Hopefully Millie took her motel key with her wherever she's gone. It would be awful to miss her and have her get back to the room and find it locked. Visualizing that, before closing the door, I reach back inside and unlock it from the inside. There isn't a robber in the world that wants to steal denture cases or granny panties. *Let's throw caution to the wind.*

Stepping out into the parking lot from the dimly lit motel, my eyes had to adjust to the brilliance of the day. The sun is in high spirits, giving me a little bit of optimism about this latest predicament. Something catches my attention from across the street: a gleam of silver that seems out of place against the backdrop of the plain, stoic Church of Chasten. A metallic-colored pickup truck, like a shimmering mirage, is parked next to the side door of the chapel. It would have been in the shadows had that one ray of sun not slid through the pines. Probably belongs to one of the construction workers because it's filled with building supplies. Otherwise, the parking lot is empty. I remember the men talking about taking Francis out to Eden. Maybe Millie found a way to get out there? She could have taken it upon herself to do some exploring on the sly, but she'd know that it would anger me to no end if she embarked on a plan that wasn't mine. Isn't that the whole point of this trip? Perhaps she's sitting in one of the pews at Chasten saying a prayer for our continued well-being.

I go to the church, to the big front door. The thing is locked. *Aren't churches always supposed to be open? A refuge for the grieving, a respite for the anxious?* Just one more example of why this town's religious piety, or lack thereof, is unnerving. Regardless, Millie doesn't seem to be here. Wandering behind the church, I find a path skirting the river and think maybe it's just the sort of place that would grab Millie's attention. She's always loved to walk. It feels very fortuitous coming upon such a trail, and in my gut, I feel its significance. *Millie is out for a walk, waiting for me to wake up. Of course she is.*

More serene, my footsteps sync in time with the song sparrows, and I follow the river downstream. A little rowboat rests, tied loosely to an old dock, rocking softly to the gurgling of the water. Millie probably felt the calming effect of nature, too, after the sickening day we've had and needed to recharge her outlook on the goodness of people despite the rottenness of people willing to throw old people out on their rears. When we were little, we loved to head to the park in Crookston. Just a wide-open area with picnic tables and grills, lots of paths to take winding through the woods, and lots of places to skip stones into the river. I remember my own dad showing me a mark so high up on a tree. "Look, Alva," he said, "when the river flooded, the water came all the way up to there." Shoot. It was as high as the top of the slide. "The power of nature," he'd say and nod his head.

I nod my head now, too. The sense of panic from my earlier "blood and stars" vision dissipates. *The power of nature to destroy and heal, to rejuvenate.* I breathe in deep and keep walking, determined to intercept my sister and pack up for Niagara and its violent falls. *Better than a sadistic pastor. Screw the fur coat.* And I mean it. Not a smart word, but an appropriate one. Our present predicament is one of our own choosing. When we get back to the motel, I am going to look up some newspapers and the like. I'll make a few calls and get the story out about Mercy's Milestone having to close. I want to crack the case, but I don't want Millie or my head being cracked while investigating.

The bird songs slip inside me, and I listen for meaning. One day, when I was about 13 or so, I remember playing ball outside with my brothers. They always made fun of me because I really wasn't very coordinated. I was up to bat and there was this robin atop the fence. Just staring at me. In my head, I believed it was my grandma, newly dead. When I swung and missed, it laughed. Clear as day. I scowled at it. Then I heard it tut and warble, "Hit it harder." And, just that one time, I did.

The path curves left away from the river and, turns out, keeps going in a long, easy circle back to the motel. It must have been almost a mile and still, I haven't seen Millie. Suddenly, in a mysterious twist, those darn birds who had, until this moment, been singing an upbeat chorus of "Chattanooga Choo Choo" hit a minor key, and a cacophony of squawks set my pulse racing. "What?!" I shake my fist at the nearest tree branch. Bird poop nearly misses my elbow and lands with a splat near my big toe. Our relationship no longer harmonious, I take it as an omen that my peaceful walk has now turned portentous. I really had lost all sense of time. How long had I been walking? My shadow is longer. I'm less round and more angular. Everything is.

Millie

I don't know where I am, and my head hurts. I don't think I ever lost total consciousness, but I feel woozy. It was Pete. Pete took me. I had been looking in the back window of the pawnshop, when he pushed the door open so violently I was caught off guard. Almost toppled down the stairs head first! Lucky for me, I have pretty good balance and managed to hold on to the railing till the last minute. But, what do they say during the Olympics? I didn't stick the landing. Before I could get up, Pete moved with surprising speed, and clamped a hand over my mouth. He shoved me into the back seat and slammed the door. I tried to scream, but nobody was in the parking lot to hear me. Pete jumped in the driver's seat, and we were off.

I didn't go quietly into the night. Or afternoon. "Pete," I bellowed, "take me back to the hotel this instant." And, "I want to see my sister." And, "This is *my coat! Mine and Alva's!!*" The fur was sitting on the seat next to me, looking every bit like a dead animal. My ranting was in vain. I started pounding on the back of his seat.

"Stop it and shut up, Millie. Or, I'll tie your hands and find a bag to put over your head," he said.

The *nerve*! But it gave me an idea. I threw the fur over his head, blinding him. The car swerved wildly as Pete tried to pull it away from his eyes. In retrospect, I probably should have thought that through. He shook free before we ended up in a ditch. That's when I must have hit my head. He hadn't actually meant to slam my head against that car door. The little lock button may have made a permanent dent over my right ear, but I don't feel blood running down anywhere.

Curled up on a couch, I have that tickly feeling when you know someone is watching you. Someone strikes a match and lights a cigarette, and I figure it must be Pete standing over me. No way I am opening my eyes yet. Maybe he will just leave me alone, and I'll be able to just walk out of here. He does just that. I hear a door creak open and slam shut, and the smoke dissipates a little. Pulling myself up to a sitting position, I take stock of my surroundings. A trailer. Dingy lighting, peeling wallpaper, and this old pleather sofa I'm on with ripped and stained cushions. I am sure the cockroaches have gay old parties here every time the sun sets. There is an aluminum door, and though the tiny window is covered with a soiled blanket and duct tape, thankfully, there is still a small sliver of light peeking through at the bottom where the hinges don't quite match up. It's not dark yet, so I haven't been gone very long. I swing my legs to the ground and am about to stand when I hear the unmistakable growl of Francis's voice. He's not in this room, but he's on the phone, and he's close. I lay back down and shut my eyes, and I listen.

"Yes, sir, I get it. I know you need to get out before the state looks too closely at your profit margin. And I appreciate the kickbacks for this little operation. That bitch at the nursing home can't stop us. Close it down as planned. Bring the old farts here, keep 'em sedated and transfer them out in batches."

Batches? What are we? Cookies? But Alva was right: Ms. Reynolds is between a rock and a hard place. Who is he talking to? Francis must've moved further into the trailer. I strain to hear, but I can't make everything out. Something about delivering us from evil, or delivering us to a pharmaceutical company maybe? And somebody's daughter, named Bonnie, is stealing medicine from tigers!

There is more to this scheme then we originally thought. I hear Francis' footsteps move further away. Needing to understand the whole of their plan, I dare to get up from the couch and tiptoe towards the back of the trailer. I am crouching down as far as my knees will let me, when I realize, if he comes back quickly, he will be able to see me just as easily as if I were standing. And my knees hurt. I rise and flatten myself against the wall.

A single lightbulb hanging from the ceiling of the hallway, casts jagged shadows across the cramped interior. Alva knows I get claustrophobic, but she is not here to help me. My breathing comes fast and shallow. Thankfully, Francis must be wearing heavy boots, because I hear them thudding against the linoleum floor. His clumping about, and his vulgarity, masks my panting. The way he talks makes my skin crawl.

"So, see, everyone benefits from me taking these useless old sacks off their hands. Picked up the cash from Phitech myself. Hope they don't send any back this time; I'm not fond of digging graves." He chuckles, sharp and mean.

My ears are buzzing. There is a sound of dishes banging around. He must be in a kitchenette. Then the sound of a cigarette lighter again. A plume of smoke curls around the corner toward the stained ceiling; wispy vapors head my way. It's too much. More than just woozy now, I think I'm going to be sick. I practically run back to the couch, putting my sweaty cheek against the cracked vinyl. It doesn't help much, but at least I am lying down. Can you faint if you are already reclining? My heart is hammering in my chest.

Just breathe, Millie. I conjure up the image of those people doing the Thai Chi in the television ads. In and out. In and out. Focusing on my breath, I don't hear Francis come back into the room until he starts rifling through a drawer, muttering to himself about "logistics."

I play dead, thinking of the residents back at Mercy Milestone—their predicament, and their fate. And what about my fate? *Did he say something about digging graves??*

"Aha!" Francis cries. He must have found what he was looking for. I hear the click of a slide being pulled back and released, followed by a metallic snap of a magazine being loaded.

God Almighty.

Alva

She's still not back in the room. The motel office has large, mucky, glass plate windows and is situated in the center of the motel, the guest rooms forming Ls to the right and left. Big Brother—I mean, Big Bertha— could see anything going on from that viewpoint. I'm desperate, so I hurry to confront the lady Grinch. The humidity has been increasing exponentially as the sun starts to sink, and the air feels heavy with the promise of rain. Reaching the office, sticky with sweat, I feel an overwhelming sense of trepidation. The timer on the sign above the motel suddenly starts to flicker and hum intermittently. It is unnerving.

"Millie?! Millie?!!" My eyes dart between cars, and then I burst through the lobby door.

"Excuse me? My sister is missing."

No answer.

"Excuse me. Have you seen my Millie?!"

"Madame!" The mean woman comes through a door in the back and strolls to the desk. "As your inn proprietress, I do not condone your bellowing." I swear she's been practicing that line for hours.

Reining in my anger, I retort, "As an inn proprietress, you should always be attentive to your guests' concerns and be willing to lend an immediate hand when needs arise."

"I don't give one damn about where your sister run off to. Probably needed a little break from you." She plops down into the desk chair.

It doesn't take her long to resort to her old, barely literate self. "She could have been taken!!" I am panicky.

Her eyes open wide, and then she sputters, a little chewing tobacco running down her chin. "Taken?" she cackles. "Who is crazy enough to nab a coffin dodger?"

"A wh—" Never mind. "Seriously, has my sister come in here in the last couple of hours?"

"Nope. She knows I don't like her."

"It doesn't matter if you like her. She may really be in danger."

"Listen, lady, from the moment you two came in here, my luck has been running low. I don't know what it is, but you got some no-good juju following you around. Maybe you only want to stay two nights—I'll get you your money back and everything. When can you check out?'

"Well, not before I find her. Obviously."

Bertha nods to herself then hoists herself out of the desk chair. She moves toward me, placing her elbows on the counter. "Putting it that way. When did *you* see her last?"

"Around 1, I think. I fell asleep, and when I got up, she had vanished."

"Very dramatic. Maybe she just went to the laundromat next door. Put in a pair of panties or something."

"Nice alliteration," I say without meaning to, in the same way I know she didn't mean to use a literary device. "Did she come in for some coffee?"

Sputtering again, with gusto: "No way I'd call that stuff coffee. Made it myself!" She finds this hilarious, even though the joke is on her.

"Bertha, *think*! Did you see her at all this afternoon? Do you ever pay attention to anything that goes on in this place?" I've lost my ability to be diplomatic and am close to tears.

Bertha comes around the counter and pours some of the black liquid into a little Styrofoam cup. She doesn't break eye contact with me, which is completely unnerving. I don't know how she didn't pour it all over her fingers. "Okay," she says wearily. "Just in order to get you out of here at your earliest convenience." She bows down a little, pretending I am acting like royalty. "I may have seen that sister of yours coming out of your room around one-thirty-ish, maybe a little after, and heading that way." She points in the direction of downtown.

"She was walking?"

"More like huffing and puffing. Like a dragon." Bertha roars with laughter. "Looked like she wanted to burn someone alive!"

"Walking toward . . . *there*?!" I don't understand why she would've left me in the room. "Is there a grocery that way? Or an ice cream shop?" But it had to be what? Hours ago? Even if she went to get food, she'd be back by now. And why would she be mad at ice cream?

"That's all I know, and I only know it because it's pretty damn boring sitting here all day watching the cars go by. Seen my ex go back and forth. Seen that big-ass trailer with the circus poster go back and forth." Bertha downs the coffee in one gulp. It must have been lukewarm. "All I know. Hope you find her so that you can check out! Oh, there is one more thing. There was this man who jumped in his car and may have followed her. I don't know how she could have not noticed him. Good-looking guy."

"What man?" Now I am shrieking. "A strange man was following my sister, and you didn't think to call the police?"

Bertha matches my outrage. "I didn't say he was a strange man. I said he was a good-looking man. Guy checked in late last night before you two got back."

I shuddered with anger. "What if he has done something to her?"

Bertha calms down and winks at me. "She should be that lucky."

I am so full of rage that I stride toward her and stick my finger in her gut. "You will march yourself back behind that counter and get me that man's name."

"I will n—" She sees I'm about to explode, and I poke her again and again until she stumbles back. I take her arm and pull her toward the front desk. I'm not strong enough to have much effect, but Bertha, who is now back to laughing, decides the whole thing is a good joke. "Okay, okay, I'll tell you the Romeo's name. Maybe it *is* Romeo. *So dramatic.*" She squeals in delight.

We look through the two names on the ledger. One was Sam. "That one." Bertha points.

Sam? Sam from Eau Claire? I don't get it. Why is he here?

I feel a little calmer. Maybe Millie isn't taken. Maybe she is just spending time with her new friend without me. I still don't like it. Hours have passed, and she would have surely told me if she were going to be out for the evening.

Bertha is looking at me curiously. "Anyway, she ain't back, but neither is he. He left not too long after you two were already up and gone. He looked a little mad, too, like he missed you last night, and then he missed you this morning. I've seen him driving around in circles all day, almost ran into a bus, and then, like I said, he must have spotted that sister of yours when she headed out without you. Maybe they both were taken." The bells on the church ring four times. We both count them in our heads. She smiles amicably and then adds almost conspiratorially, "Maybe them church folk got 'em."

I take a minute and look at her quizzically. "What do you know about those church people?"

"Church folk," she clarifies. "That's what I said."

I wait.

"Them *church folk* and I am talking mainly about the pastor and my ex, have some land near my trailer. If you have to know, they say they are building some kind of weird building, or maybe it is a park, for *God.* I have no idea what they are talking about, but I don't hear much building. I hear crying sometimes."

"What?" I say incredulously. "*What?*"

"Do not yell at me," Bertha says with a grunt.

"I am yelling *with you!*" I yell.

"What? I'm not yelling! I'm telling!" Bertha is vexed.

I think for only a minute. "I am speaking loudly to show that I have concerns about those church 'folk' as well. I think they may be holding some elderly women there without their permission."

"Nope." Bertha shakes her head firmly. "I asked them about it. They said the crying was just one person, one of their mothers, probably my ex-mother-in-law, now that I think about it, and she was sad because she lost her husband and hasn't gotten over it. I don't know. I'm not that cold where I would be listening to my mama cry and not try to help. My ex-mother-in-law is a whole 'nother story, so just maybe I let her cry. But I wonder why I don't ever see the old coot. I only see that pastor man and Pete. Oh, and some really fat woman. And the place is an eyesore. Why would anyone stay there?"

For a woman who was not willing to talk to me a second ago, she has become a fountain of information. Then I stop. "Your ex-mother-in-law? Your ex-mother-in-law is Pete's *mother*? Did you used to like lacy things?"

"I still do. You have a problem with that?" she snarls.

Millie

I was thinking that I had to make a run for it, no matter what, when I hear the trailer door open again. Someone is back in the room with me, and I hear Francis join them. I try my best to look unconscious.

Pete stammers, "I didn't hurt her."

"How come she's unconscious?"

"I just put my hand over her mouth and shoved her in the car. She was absolutely fine the whole way here. Once she recovered from the shock, she didn't stop yelling for a second, even though I threatened to put a bag over her head. Guess I gave her an idea, she threw the coat over my head, while I was driving. I swear to God, Francis, I wanted to kill her. Almost ran us off the road. I had to jerk the wheel to avoid the ditch, and the old bag slammed against the door. So yeah, maybe she hit her head, but I personally didn't do it. I carried her in here and put her on the couch. She was moaning, even tried to stand up before you came in, then she just fainted or something. Just like that sister of hers."

"She's got blood on her sleeve. Why did you feel it necessary to do anything with her at all?"

I can feel their eyes staring at me, and I'm nothing to them, just the old lady curled on the brown vinyl couch.

Francis adds nonchalantly, "You should've probably killed her. Put her in the family cemetery."

I hear Francis say it, and all I can think of is that I'll never see Alva again.

"I told you there's an old family cemetery on this land. Remember, we're going to call it 'the Garden?' My mother's grandparents are buried out there."

"Jesus, Francis. Where'd you pick up that preacher license again?"

"I told you. Online. Wisconsin doesn't require state registration, and you know Chasten's churchgoers were desperate for new leadership. All they had to do was like me." Francis sneers, "And they do."

My stomach twists, anger rising like the tide, ready to spill over. I fight to keep my face slack, and my lips parted. *No one likes you, you snake!* I scream on the inside.

"Now what are we going to do? Why are you sure she was on to us? And if she is, what about the sister? I bet she'll get the police involved if this old bat doesn't go back to the motel. What the hell, Pete? What made you take her?"

"She was peeking into that pawnshop."

"So what?" I can hear the anger in his voice, and I wonder why even Pete puts up with him.

"The pawnshop, Francis. That's where the coat was. I got $600 for it! Told you it was worth something. We've got to cover costs, Francis, and we promised those guys we'd have a building ready for inspection."

"A fake inspection with a fake inspector, Pete. Weren't you listening?"

"But she recognized the coat. I was working on the finance part. I got a good deal on the coat, but when we drove back through town, I realized that some fool at the pawnshop put the damn thing in the window. They heard me say to keep it in the back, but Andy, or his brother, must have thought it was worth something more. They put the prettiest stuff in the window, like as if it was women who come in to shop. It's a cover. Everyone knows they make the real money from the guns in back—"

"This story is about as long and tedious as the Old Testament, Pete."

"I didn't want Millie and Alva to see it. The Carter brothers are such idiots that they left the door unlocked. I went in, took the coat, and planned to hightail it out the back. There she was, peeking in the window. She saw me steal it this time. I couldn't let it go."

"On top of that, Pete, I told you that nothing gets stolen or sold anywhere near here. No shitting in the town where we eat," Francis says.

"What the hell is that supposed to mean? Speaking of eating, my mom needs food. Bonnie said we were running low on groceries. Ma isn't supposed to suffer. Just be a way to get Harriet to invest her fortune. She doesn't require much, but she does need to eat. I'm in this for the money, Francis. I don't want nothing to do with hurrying death."

"You never liked your ma, and she doesn't even recognize you. Old people die all the time, Pete," Francis says without sympathy. What a scallywag he is. Makes me want to slap his face. Then he seems to reconsider his tone. "Listen, as soon as we get this project fully financed, you can move your mom anywhere you want. Right now, we've got this problem." I'm worried he means me, and I can't help but try to peek just a little.

I think my eyelids must flutter. They go silent for a minute, and I wonder if they know I have been listening. But another minute passes, and they continue.

"Get out of here, Pete." Francis almost growls it. "I'll take care of this myself. I want to be able to trust you. You need to go back and cover your tracks. Anybody see you go into that pawnshop?"

"No, Francis. I'm not stupid."

"Huh. Convince me. Get rid of that damn coat. Go clean up your mess. Come up with a story."

There is a long pause. The room goes dead silent. Is it one of those Mexican standoff scenarios? Nope, that would mean that neither of the parties has a measurable advantage. My gut tells me that Francis still holds all the cards.

Pete slams the door. I say a prayer, and, focusing on the memory of my sister's face, send it out into the ether. *Are you listening, Alva?*

Alva

Bertha has unknowingly given me confirmation of all our fears.

"Bertha, listen to me. Millie and I have really good reason to believe that pastor and his cohorts are up to no good. I'm going to go out *again* and look for Millie, but if I don't come back, will you call the police?"

"The *police?*" she sniggers. "I was kidding about them before. First off, we only have one guy that patrols around here, and he is from Steven's Point. You get county police in Chasten, and you don't get 'em too often. And second," she is counting on her tobacco-stained fingers as if she really needs help keeping up to only number two, "no one is going to believe me if I say that pastor is a murderer."

"*Murderer?!*" I cry. "I didn't say *murderer*! No one is going to murder Millie!" I wasn't thinking murder. I just think that they are keeping old people alive in poor conditions. Isn't that what I've been thinking? "It just might be a hostage situation. If I don't come back, just call that police person and tell them to come out to that property you just described."

"For a hostage situation," Bertha replies nonchalantly, "you will need SWAT."

"Do you have a SWAT team in Chasten?" I wring my hands and take deep breaths.

"No way!" Bertha hoots. "If you find her and they've got her, will they kill you both, *you think?*"

"You'll never get your money then." I try to match her daft logic in hopes of roping in an ally. I'm desperate.

Bertha considers. "Okay. Go find your sister. She's probably bothering some other poor business owner down the street. Or making kissy noises with that Sam man. But if you don't come back, say, in a few days, I'll call the po-po."

"Bertha, if I don't come back tonight, call the 'po-po.' I mean it!"

She stares at me dubiously.

"I'll buy you ten lottery tickets."

Her face lights up like Christmas. "Okay! I don't forget a promise like *that*."

And then I get a better idea. I search my pocket and find Vivian Reynolds's card. Grabbing a pen off the counter, I scribble her name and number on the reservation's list. "If I'm not back, call the po-po *and* this lady. Tell her what has happened."

Bertha looks put upon.

"Twenty lottery tickets," I say.

She does a little twirl.

Millie

I squint and see Francis's profile, his sharp nose with a bead of sweat threatening to drip I don't know where. *Please, God,* I think, *not on me!* But he is shaking his head so violently as Pete turns that I think it lands on the dank paneling across the room. And then Pete is out the door again, and I am alone with the villain. His eyes convey a callousness so intense; I pee a little bit and he sniggers to himself like he knows.

I squeeze my eyes shut again, hoping maybe he will just go away. I know everything I need to know, and I can't wait to tell Alva. It smells like broccoli in here, so that bastard (yes, it's come to that) might go finish his dinner, and then I can run for the door. Listening, I still hear his breathing and some shuffling about. I sneak another look, Francis rifling through my handbag. I forgot I had taken it with me. Pete must've thrown it in the car at the same time he threw me in there. I'd had enough.

Pushing myself to sitting, I conjure up Alva and admonish him in my most severe voice. "It is incredibly improper for a man to look into a lady's purse unless he's her husband, which you certainly are *not* and will never be." I'm a little dizzy sitting up so fast like that, but his broccoli breath acts like a handful of smelling salts, and my head clears. He ignores me and continues to rummage through my personal items, I assume to steal my money or check my insurance card. He pockets my cell phone. "I have Medicare just like all those other old people that are always dying."

"Have you been listening?" He smirks, tosses the bag on the floor, and looks at me in a most patronizing way. "Millie. Do you know why you are here?"

"Do *you* know why I am here?" I retort.

"From what I can ascertain, Pete had some misgivings about selling a coat that may or may not have belonged to you. Although, I am sure he had no idea at the time. You were upset with him, and it was hot, and to get you out of the heat and move us all toward an understanding, he brought you here."

"I understood before he pushed me headfirst into his car." I sit up straighter on the sticky couch and glare at him. "He stole our coat. And now he stole *me*."

"Millie, that is a pretty brash accusation," he says gently. I do think Pete was right to bring you to me. I think you have a little heatstroke, maybe? I'll get you a glass of water."

"No, sir. Just give me a ride back to town." I say it clearly so there can be no mistake as to my wishes. But Francis is already heading down the little hallway, muttering into his phone, and then I hear tap water running. I jump up and go for the door, but before I reach the knob, he is back and blocking my exit.

He grimaces at my feeble attempt to escape. "Drink this, Millie."

I wish I wasn't so thirsty, but I am, so I take the glass and take a few sips. The water tastes vaguely like sulfur, and I hand the glass back quickly. I should have thrown it in his face. This whole place feels infected: the peeling wallpaper a yellowing puss color, the paneled wainscoting is separating from the sheetrock, the carpet soiled and threadbare. He is looking at me the same way I am taking in my surroundings. I guess we are both disgusted.

He tries once more to cajole me. "Seriously, Millie, I do think you need to rest. I've called our nurse, and she will be right over." He moves to stand so close to me that I retreat to the couch, but I don't sit on it.

"Nurse!" I choke. "Like this place is a hospital! I do want to know exactly where I am. Is this pleasant area the lobby of your Eden? 'Cause you are way off the mark—"

"*Millie.*" Francis's voice has gotten low and menacing. "Sit down and shut up."

I suck in a deep breath and sit. Francis probably does mean to kill me. I try and manage to sound contrite. "Alva will come get me. Let me just call my sister, and we will both get out of your hair." I take another deep breath and try to remain calm.

He ignores me and paces back and forth, trying to work something out. My destiny, I'd guess. His long fingers wave through the stale air like he is conducting a symphony of ideas buzzing around his head. It is clear he doesn't have a good one as to what to do with me. I can almost hear him contemplating burying me in the "Garden." A laugh rattles his chest as a sizeable silhouette blocks the door and any light filtering in from outside. She seems a little out of breath, like he snapped his fingers, and she came running.

"Where have you been, Bonnie, taking a nap with the old-timers? I called you thirty minutes ago."

A woman steps in and pauses. The dim room seems to swim, and I remember I am still holding my breath. I put my hands to my temples and squint at a chubby face. She looks like she just lost her best friend. More than that, and maybe I am delirious, but she looks familiar.

Francis continues to berate Bonnie. "Take care of this. I need some praying time." He gestures at me. "Millie is overexcited. Did you bring something to calm her nerves?"

"Oh no, you don't!" I scream. "I am *not* overexcited!" Bonnie moves toward me with a syringe of clear liquid. And I *know* her. She is sweaty and has on that same flowery getup she had at the casino. She is one big garden and Pete's casino sidekick. She cranes her massive neck in my direction.

She looks disdainfully at me. "Her again?"

"Don't you come near me," I hiss. "And don't you ever change clothes? Really, that thing is dirty and wet. Those flowers are drooping under your armpits."

"You and Pete have made a mess of things. She's *your* problem." Francis picks up a plastic clerical collar from a basket on the counter. "I have to get back to the old folks home."

They pass responsibility for me like I was KP duty. I gather my wits and lunge for the water glass on the coffee table. With all my might, I throw it in Bonnie's face. It bounces right off her jowl and crashes to the floor. Blinking at me curiously, she muscles me backwards with a mere twist of my forearm, her huge mitt of a hand dwarfing my entire limb.

"You are freakish!" I cry. "Let me go, you circus clown!"

I immediately remember the clowns in Baraboo and feel bad that I've made such a horrid comparison. Nothing funny about *her*. Then I remember the motorhome with horses housing the World's Fattest Woman, and I have an aha moment! Bonnie *is* the Fattest Woman!

"Wait, wait!" I scream. "You are the world's fattest woman!"

"Are you making fun of me?" She is very threatening.

"No, you are making fun of you! You have your picture on a poster for the circus. And really, you are not fat; you are big-boned, sure. And very tall. You are lying about being the fattest, and I think you lie about all kinds of things." I'm panting.

Her trailer had the poster tacked up with her name on it. But the characters were so faded. All we could make out was the capital B. We'd guessed Bellini, maybe like someone was trying to be funny because, literally, that would be "little beautiful one," and she certainly wasn't advertised as "little." Or maybe Baby? But it was Bonnie. She's Pete's accomplice! It seems impossible that this is all tied together. I try to scramble away, but she holds fast, uncapping the syringe with her teeth.

Bonnie sighs, and then addresses me, enunciating her words as if I were a child. "This is called xylazine. We use it for the tigers. Don't want restless tigers. Heh heh heh. I diluted it some. Won't hurt at all."

A petunia blurs. I drift off, contemplating why so many unpleasant women's names begin with a B.

Alva

Driving would, of course, make more sense, but Millie has the keys. I don't know where I'm going now, but it's in the general direction of Millie's last sighting, according to the newly-vigilant Bertha. Our adventure, at my bidding, seems to have taken another turn. I remember to pick up my feet so I don't shuffle; I'm in too much of a hurry, and I don't want to fall on my face. And I have to admit I'm getting a little tired after walking the river path, even though I rested on a bench from time to time. My estimate, including my nap time and the time it took me to traverse the mile of river path between the church and motel, and my conversation with Bertha, Millie has been missing for about four hours now, give or take.

Scanning ahead, the street is unnervingly empty. The church is omnipresent but currently forsaken. The gas station has no cars at the pumps, no families picnicking under the waning afternoon sun. The smell of barbecue lingers, but it is wasted: no noses turned up in the wind. It is so desolate around here I expect to find tumbleweeds dancing down Main Street, like in an old Western. Millie had to have gone to the pawnshop or to the coffee shop. It's too late for coffee, so the pawnshop. It must be almost ready to close! The air is so muggy that my sweater feels heavy around my shoulders. The idea of that damn fur coat makes me hotter. Millie must have gone to get it; it's the only thing that makes sense. Surely, she wouldn't have gone off with Sam. Would she? It bothers me a little bit to know he's here. We don't need to be looked after if that is his intention. If he has intentions toward Millie, I'd just as soon he wait until our trip is over before letting her know. Plenty of time for canoodling when we return to Eau Claire.

I gaze into the distance, and tears come unbidden to my eyes. How would I feel if Millie found a new relationship this late in our game? For the past decades, we have been inseparable: two sisters standing up to the forces of change. And by change, I mean all the newfangled ideas creating navigational nightmares for people after retirement age. It's hard enough managing new aches, new medicines, new country, sushi. Well, those last two are things my granddaughter mentions more than I experience. Point being that just when you think that you have been alive for so long that you have seen it all, the layers of newness increase a hundredfold. *I need my sister by my side to survive.*

This trip, spurred by my visions, was a chance to embrace a little bit of the exhilaration everyone in the TV pharmaceutical commercials experiences. I want to dance again, do some yoga, climb a mountain. It's clear that our current adventure is trivial compared to the aspirations of *National Geographic* photographers or astronauts. I just had hoped that at least once in my life I would feel less inconsequential. But would it matter if Millie wasn't here to witness my growth? If a tree fell in the woods. . . if Alva did something important…

Oh, for goodness' sake, I'm having a pity party. If Millie and Sam decide to have a torrid love story, we'd still talk all the time. The focus must be to find Millie so that we have a future.

Walking in the direction of the pawnshop, I peek into backyards. There is more life going on behind the homes than in the front. A few moms sweep up patio stairs; children with the odd doll or truck are making up pretend stories. A tire swing sways, the feet of a little girl sticking out and giving the ground a shove. A few charcoal grills are being fired up for tonight's dinner. A tiny boy whines that it *isn't time* to start washing up. I'm tempted to ask each and every one if they've seen my sister, but I am hesitant to interrupt evening rituals. Besides, if Millie had come unannounced to any of these homes, surely they would have helped her back to our room. A light breeze comes out of nowhere, and garden fragrances and the smell of freshly grown grass work like essential oils to calm my nerves. When Millie and I get home I am going to soak in a tub filled with lavender.

An old bloodhound sits on the front porch of a little yellow house. He watches me, his body never moving, following my progress toward the small-town center. *What are you thinking?* I wonder. He closes his eyes, not ready for an interrogation. A car or two pass me, and a pickup truck. The same truck I saw at the church earlier. What had I been thinking? Oh, it was like a mirage. That's it. My visions are like mirages, excited to have a label that makes sense. I see things that are right there in front of me, so clear, but they fade when I get close enough to touch them.

Finding Jim and Dan Carter's pawnshop is a waste of time because the place is locked up tight. I don't have to go all the way up to the door: there is a padlock, and a menacing *Do not trespass* sign on the front door. The little diner next door has a few outside tables, and I sit down to take a load off my feet, as they say. The day is drawing to a close, but the sign on the door says the summer hours are from 8 to 6. A young woman is wiping down the tables and stacking the chairs.

"Closing in fifteen minutes. You want anything? I mean, the kitchen is closed, but I can get you a drink," she offers politely.

"You are open, but the kitchen is closed?" I ask, not trying to be difficult, but everything seems confusing at this point.

"Coca-Cola? Iced tea?" she replies without really hearing me. Invisible again, I sigh and ask for the iced tea. I've run out of the motel without my purse and have only two dollars in the pocket of my dress. She brings it out right away so she can continue to shut the place down. It's my chance.

"I'm wondering"—or praying— "have you by any chance seen an older woman like me here this afternoon? A little taller?" My eyes plead.

She nods unexpectedly. "Saw a lady over there looking in the pawnshop about, I don't know, four or five hours ago? I was just coming on shift. She didn't eat here, though."

"White blouse? Black trousers?"

"Sounds right. Short, curly hair. Gray." *Obviously*. The woman is muscling the other two tables closer under the awning.

I down the iced tea, feeling the cold and caffeine surge through my tired body. She kindly offers to refill my glass, and I eagerly accept. A Millie sighting is so reassuring that I take a little time to breathe. Finally, reaching for my cash, I stand up readying myself for the walk back to the Happy Family. *Millie is probably already back and waiting for me. Bet that Bertha wouldn't even say I was looking for her.* Handing the waitress the two dollars, I head to the sidewalk. An ambulance sneaks up on me. Just as it is passing me, he turns on the siren and lights, the blast echoing in the silence. I nearly jump out of my skin. The world spins. Millie?!

Oh my God, ambulances are never good. I hope nothing has happened to Millie. Where did that ambulance come from? Where is my sister? I look around frantically, acknowledging the stillness, like the quiet I feel before my flashes. Movement from my periphery, back down towards our motel. No, past that. I turn and hurryingly retrace my steps, trying to notice anything out of the ordinary, anything that Millie might have seen or anybody that might have seen Millie. The wind picks up, and the pine tree branches seem to point in the direction of the church. The steeple shadow is a block long, and I step in, drawn to the allegory but not feeling any comfort.

The flashing lights are coming directly from behind the church, near the bank of Humility. *Is it Millie? Is it Millie?* I scream and scream. No one hears me as I push through the small group of onlookers. There are a few cars parked on the grass, and their headlights illuminate the darkening sky, now fat with potential rain, focusing on the gentle bank where a few people stare, their fists in their mouths. The paramedics are wrestling with a body, partly submerged, blue-faced, and bloated. I see legs, legs wearing . . . khaki trousers. Not Millie, and I cry with relief. One medic is pulling the legs while another is unceremoniously untwining reeds wrapped around his throat and shoulders. They should be taking care instead of yanking whomever out through the dirt and weeds. This, I think, is a crime scene. There are just too many odd things going on at this church. The body will have bruises now, and we will have no way of knowing if they happened before the body got there or after they moved him. My mind reels with every TV crime drama scene I've watched. I wonder who it is. What poor soul lost his life today? I dare myself to move closer and closer, then I see his swollen lips, his dead eyes, and gasp. An angel is heading to heaven.

Oh, dear George. Of all the people in this town, it is George whose hands are pale and wrinkled and who has a contusion on the side of his head the size of a baseball. I see a hint of a bloodstain at his temple, but I guess the water leached away most of the evidence. It could be that he had one of those brain bleeds where you don't know for sure you are dying until it's too late. But I think it's more nefarious than that. George. I sit down hard on patchy grass and put my head in my hands. The river baptized George in the saddest of ways. I draw a cross in the dirt with my fingertip. Looking around listlessly, I see baseball-sized rocks along the riverbank. A crime of opportunity? Of passion? I don't think the last one sounds right, but you never know.

I am so relieved that the body is not Millie that I almost forget that she is still out there, *somewhere*. I see Francis standing at the back entrance of the church, his hands folded in prayer, his lips forming words of comfort to a few of his flock before him. I watch Pete in the parking lot, pacing around his car, his head shaking in disbelief. Then, surprisingly, I see Bertha lumbering up the road, her hand firmly grasping the forearm of a man, dragging him along with her. She seems pleased with herself despite the somberness of the moment. A policeman gets out of a car looking forlorn, maybe because he is missing supper.

And then they start toward me, talking all at once. First to reach me was Sam.

"I didn't see you until just now. What in the world has happened? This not-so-ladylike lady saw me come back to my room and accosted me before I could get my key out." Sam was trying to wrestle his arm from Bertha.

"I was calling his name—Romeo, Romeo—but he didn't answer. I was investigating your sister's disappearance is what I told him when he finally stopped squirming away from me," Bertha says loud and indignant. She still holds his arm in case he makes a run for it.

"Why are you still grabbing at me? Why don't you just say, 'Excuse me, sir, may I have a word with you?'" Sam says.

Despite all the dire circumstances, I smile a little bit. "Sam," I said, "this is Bertha. She doesn't have a filter."

"What is *that* supposed to mean, huh?" demands Bertha.

"You are not very subtle."

"I know what I want," she says.

"What? And you want me? Is that why you won't let go of my arm?" Sam is trying to shake off Bertha's death grip.

From out of nowhere, Pete appears and punches Sam in the nose.

"Fight, fight!" cheers Bertha. And then stops when she recognizes that it is Pete who threw the punch. It happened so fast that she didn't have time to register it. Bertha immediately drops Sam's arm. Blood is dripping from his nose, and his eye is swelling, but he is in a fighter's stance and dancing around his opponent. The policeman looks at the scene by the river and the scene over here and ambles towards us.

"I still love you, Bertha. You can't love this guy more than me," Pete is pleading with his ex but keeping his fists up, eyes focused on Sam's potential left hook.

"She doesn't love me!" Sam cries. "She doesn't even know me!"

"Gentlemen." The police officer moves into the path of potential swinging fists.

"Pete, stop acting like an idiot. We are divorced; you can't go and tell me who I can love." Bertha is caught up in the moment as well and not making much sense.

"I heard you call him Romeo. You were holding his hand. I still love you, Bertha!" There is such sadness in his eyes that Sam puts his hands down at his sides.

Bertha herself is temporarily appeased. "Petey, you promised me you were done gambling. You know I can't stand you going down to the casino and losing all our money. You are not a winner." She shakes her head sadly. "I said, 'Just one more time and we are done,' and didn't you go right behind my back and race off to Ho-Chunk? All the ladies at

Bingo said you were a regular there this summer, said you'd been lying to me. You left me no choice, *Petey*."

I believe that the intimacy with which she says his name means she might still love him, too. Bertha's eyes are a little moist and she wipes her nose with her sleeve. This from a foul-mouthed motel clerk who plays the lottery every night and apparently some Bingo. She sees me looking at her with a bit of kindness and rolls her eyes. The moment is over.

"Hey Po-Po," she bellows at the officer, "you can go."

He looks at Bertha sternly but swaggers off to save the day down at the water's edge.

I've got to stop all this right now. I speak loudly, "While you three stand here acting like fools, George is dead, and Millie is missing. I need to find my sister before someone else dies."

I have Sam's attention, but Bertha and Pete seem oblivious to everyone but themselves. Sam doesn't understand the whole of it, but he is worried. I wonder if Pete knocked the sense out of him.

"I've been looking all over for Millie," Sam reveals. "I checked in late last night and didn't want to knock on your door, but you were gone before I got up this morning. Then, this afternoon, I did knock. Your car was at the motel, but then I thought I saw Millie walking, so I jumped back in my car to follow her. Then—she just disappeared! Oh, and I thought I saw another suspicious person in a silver truck. Looked really familiar. What the hell is going on? Where were you all day without your car? Were you with Millie? I got back just after six without ever seeing her again, and then this crazy battle-ax says you were looking for her too." He is rambling, but he understands Bertha better than I thought.

"It's a long story, Sam." I want to ask why he's even here, but it doesn't matter now; I need help finding Millie. "I will explain it all later, but right now I am very afraid that Millie is in danger. Why don't you go get cleaned up? You have blood all over your shirt. I'll meet you back at the motel. We can come up with a plan."

"Where are we going? I've combed this whole town." Sam rubs his eyes with the hand that is holding his nose. Blood blurs his vision. He is anxious but without direction.

"You need to tell me where you have been all afternoon, but first I have some questions for the man over there, the one that looks like a pastor." Sam glances in the direction of the church, but his right eye is one bulging purple bruise and I doubt he is seeing anything clearly.

"Hurry," Sam whispers to me. "I don't want to find Millie in the river, too."

I stare after him.

Flash! *I am in the heart of a neglected cemetery, the garden wildly overgrown. Among the twisted vines, thorns reach out like tiny teeth, ready to tear at my flesh. I am searching for the gravestone that holds the answers, but the thorns guard, like sentinels, the forgotten stories buried here. The horse nettles are toxic, I know. I put on my gloves and get ready to prune.*

I'm back sitting in the grass. I had turned to face Francis, but George's death temporarily shattered my doggedness. For a moment I am stuck between vision and reality. The dirt beneath me feels like it is swallowing me up. No. Not yet. I need answers.

Bertha and Pete are standing over me.

Alva

I watch Sam as he heads back to the Happy Family, holding his nose with a kerchief. Once I get up, Bertha and Pete lose interest in me and turn on each other. Pete looks miserable while Bertha berates him over his past behavior. Pete is a criminal, of that I am certain, but how felonious? Right now, he looks like a sad puppy. Is he behind Millie's disappearance? He keeps sneaking imploring looks at me during Bertha's tirade, but I can't tell if he is asking for help or wanting to tell me something.

"Fess up to it!" Bertha yells, "you are guilty of lying about your trips to the casino."

"I was guilty in the past," Pete says as tears drip down his cheeks. "But I've changed. I want you back, *Bertha Bear.*"

"You don't have to cry. You've never cried before; what is the matter with you?" Bertha is confused and softening a little.

"It's you," chokes Pete, "and it's George!"

I move closer to their conversation.

"George?" Bertha seems to finally understand that there has been a tragedy here. She turned to see the EMTs standing over George's still body. "Well shit, Pete, did someone die?"

"George is dead!" Pete's is doubled over, and his sobs are getting louder. "I found him, Bertha Bear. I found him in the water. Everything is out of control. He wasn't a bad guy, really, he wasn't! He didn't smell that good sometimes, but he had a heart. A heart, Bertha. Fuck, I've lost you, I've lost my heart, and George's too."

Bertha, not knowing what to do, pats him on the head.

"Pete!" I am not gentle or hesitant. I jump right in. Pete looks up at me and tries to regain his composure. "Who killed George?"

Pete stands slowly with a confused expression. "Nobody *killed* him!"

"Where have you been all afternoon?"

With built-up frustration and sadness, Pete spews an itinerary. "I was angry that we had to take you back to the motel. You know that part. I took George back to the church to put all that stuff away. I took the pastor over to Eden so he could get his truck. I came back to help George put the sound equipment in the office closet. George got a bee in his bonnet about something, and I decided to let him be. I came back a couple hours later, and no one was inside the church. So, I walked around to burn off some steam. Guess I walked around for a long time; I might have taken a bit of a nap on the bench down there. Then, I headed back toward here, and that's when I saw something tangled in the reeds. In the water! George was dead in the river! I don't know why he was near the banks, but he must've fallen in? His body was turned funny." Pete took a shaky breath. "I didn't know what to do, so I called the police, and then I saw Pastor Francis up at the church and yelled for him to come help me."

It was odd that Pete had seemingly worked out his story before I asked the question. "George has been hit on the side of his head. That is what killed him," I say with all kinds of Telly Savalas confidence.

Pete stares at me wide-eyed. "Why would anyone kill George? George? Maybe he slipped on something and fell on a rock and then slid down the bank?"

Pete looked so distressed that I changed tactics. "I thought you were all going to your Eden after you dropped Millie and me back at the motel?"

"I only took Francis to the site. George stayed back at the church to unload the equipment. Really, what are you implying?"

"When was the last time you saw George, before . . . now?" I glance uncomfortably at the ambulance, the siren quiet but the red lights pulsing in the parking lot.

"I told you. George got out of the car at the church. We unloaded our stuff at the front, and he said he was going to put everything away in the office. I took Pastor Francis over to Eden, then came back here. I helped for a while, but George said he could do it by himself. He was really quiet. Just sort of bumbling around. I had some errands to run. Told him I'd catch up with him later. That was this afternoon at one, right? Last time I saw him alive." Another sob escapes from Pete's mouth, but he disguises it as a cough.

"I thought you just said that you needed to take a walk. You didn't say you had errands to run?"

"No, the errands were earlier. I took a walk later this afternoon when I came back to the church. No one was inside, so I just walked," Pete says firmly, and, for good measure, repeats it all again. "I dropped George at the church, then left the pastor at Eden, returned to help George, who didn't want me there. Then I ran my errands. I came back to the church around five o'clock, maybe. It was a long day, and I was mad that my . . . errands . . . well, it was just a long day. I was going to go into the church like I said, but I was frustrated about some things . . . like with Bertha and me!" He adds it in like he was thrown a lifeline. "Yes, I was remembering about how much I missed her, so I thought I'd go do some soul searching down by the river. It's peaceful down there, you know? I just walked, maybe dozed off. And then, it was getting late and so I headed back, and that's when I saw something in the water."

Bertha kept her mouth closed during our exchange. She was staring at Pete now, trying to work something out. "Was one of your 'errands' going down to the Texaco? I know they've got them slot machines in the back."

Pete eyes her suspiciously, fiddling with his sweaty collar. The pawnshop is right across the street from the Texaco. Had she seen him drive over there? He had parked in the back.

"I swear, sweetie, I did *not* go into the Texaco."

"I'm pretty sure I saw your car zooming past the motel, coming from that direction earlier this afternoon." Bertha pointed down the street. "I was thinking, 'There goes Pete, probably he's upset those machines stole his money.'"

"I have stopped gambling, Bertha. I promise." Pete crosses his heart and probably his fingers. He reaches into his jacket and holds out a silver band with a barely-there diamond. "I'm sorry for everything. Take me back, please."

He is a liar, and I can't stand liars. "Bertha, you shouldn't listen to him. Millie and I saw him down at the Ho-Chunk just yesterday." I didn't really mean to get in the middle of an ex-marital dispute, but the truth should prevail.

Bertha looks from me to Pete and back to me. "What were you two doing at the Ho-Chunk? I knew you two were hussies from the beginning! You stir up trouble wherever you go. And Pete, go shove it where the sun don't shine."

With that, Bertha stomps away, following in Sam's footsteps. Just to anger Pete, she hollers, "Romeo, wait for me!"

Alva

I watched Pete slink back toward his car. I didn't believe his story, or not all of it. He's a gambler and a liar, and he stole my coat. You can't wholly trust a man like that, no matter how many times they apologize. I march up to Francis. "Where is Millie?"

"Alva, my dear," he sighs with empathy, or impatience. It's the same noise with him. "Let's find you a chair. This is such a terrible twist of fate, George taken too soon to sit with our Lord. There must, of course, be a purpose for him in the ever after."

"Francis, fate and foul play are not in the same ballpark. What happened to George is a matter for the police. But the more immediate question is, where is my sister?"

"The police?! Alva! Are you accusing one of our parishioners or a stranger of purposely hurting George? His unfortunate demise looks to be an accident, plain and simple. In times like these, our faith becomes our anchor. I am so glad that his heart was unfettered and that his faith was true." Francis's head is bobbing again. Up and down, wanting me to mimic his nod. I won't.

"In times like these," I blurt out, "the homicide investigation team would be out securing the crime scene. And yes, I'm aware that there isn't one of those around here. But I am going to talk to the lone officer in town and communicate my thoughts on the murder of poor George and the missing person who is Millie."

"Whoa." Francis stops bobbing and reaches for my elbow. "George fell down and drowned, and I don't know anything about your sister going missing."

I jerk away from him. "Why do people say things like that, like she 'went missing.' She just is 'missing,' there is no 'going missing' because that implies that she was trying to go somewhere and just got lost. I am sure that wasn't her intention at all. Millie is gone. When is the last time you saw her?"

"Alva, I have not seen your sister since lunchtime when we dropped you both off at the motel."

"What did you do after you dropped us off?" I sense unease in him, and it makes me accusatory.

His hand is back at my elbow now, his breath near my ear as he guides me further away from the milling crowd. There is such a dampness in the air, the darkening clouds tugging at the lights in the church, the mugginess worming its way through my thoughts. His touch is heavy, and his words barely register. "Alva," he whispers, "God always has a plan."

"What is the plan here? To kill off George? To hide my sister? I'll ask you again: What did you do after leaving us at the motel?"

"Your curiosity is misplaced, my dear. I have been delivering spiritual guidance to those at Mercy's Milestone all afternoon. I arrived here to prepare my sermon this evening and was confined to my office until I heard Pete's cries. Excuse me now, I see the coroner has arrived." He turns quickly away from me and takes long strides back toward the river.

I follow Francis over to a man getting out of a black sedan. Dressed in a pretty suit rather than any kind of uniform, the coroner is a slick, attractive man with an unmistakable sense of self-importance. They shake hands and smile like old friends. Francis looks over his shoulder, recognizes that I am not going anywhere, and, with a disparaging look, introduces me. "Alva, this is the coroner, Stanley Hansen. Stanley, this is Alva, a very concerned newcomer to our area."

"Sorry for your loss, Miss Alva," he mimes, tipping a hat, but he's not wearing one.

"I didn't know him that well, but he was a kind soul." I mean it.

The coroner moves around me and speaks quietly to the singular officer. I hear them detail the time of death and a few brief descriptors of the body as it was found. "Looks to be an unfortunate accident," he says without pause. "Take him over to Gunderson's mortuary and let his family know."

"What?" I say incredulously. "This man was murdered!" He chuckles, and I want to murder him too. "What about that wound on the side of his head? Blunt head trauma, right? Someone hit him hard."

The coroner sighs and speaks to me like I'm a child. "There are lots of rocks down there. When he slipped, he must've hit his head."

"What if he was hit over the head and then pushed into the river?" I counter. "When will the autopsy take place? Where is the medical examiner?"

"We don't have a medical examiner here in Chasten," tuts Francis. "Stanley is the coroner, and he is the one who determines cause of death in this county."

"Not much of a doctor," I say angrily.

"No, Ms. Alva," Francis replies. "Not a doctor at all. Coroners are elected officials in Wisconsin. And his decision is the one we trust."

"So, anybody can just say this looks like an accident, and a murderer walks free?" I cannot believe it.

"Not just anybody." Is Francis enjoying my frustration? "Has to be an elected official, one with a high school diploma, over 18, who lives here."

"George drowned in Humility. An accidental death. A terrible shame." Stanley has the decency to look doleful.

It's more than I can handle. "There is more than enough shame here to go around," I say with an even voice, barely controlling the vitriol that is bubbling within me. I don't look into the eyes of the devils but turn to follow Bertha and Sam. *Oh God, Millie.*

Alva

All my life I feel like I've been ignored. The realization smacks me on the head again, just like the rock that must've smacked George. *Even the kind people, my family and such,* now that I am thinking back, *didn't put much stock in my ideas.* They loved me, but that's not the same thing, is it? Maybe the stroke jostled my passivity, because I sure have been speaking my mind as of late. But, still, speaking and doing are different things too. I know the words because I do watch the news. Ageism and sexism, and I'm sure a lot more 'isms, are in play. Funny that I never thought about those things applying to me. They sound so political.

Back at the Happy Family, I find Bertha trying to administer first aid to an uncooperative Sam. It is dark when I cross the street, but only one room has the light on and the door opens to the parking lot. Sam's room is two doors down from ours and Bertha's voice carries.

"You are dripping blood on the carpet and I'm going to have to charge you for that," she admonishes.

"If you would just get away from me for one minute. I want to lie down on the bed, and I don't want you in it." Sam is trying to stretch out, kicking Bertha in the process, who doesn't get up and instead tries to straddle him.

"You need to keep this ice bag on your face!" It looks like she is suffocating him rather than providing any kind of care.

With a great heave, Sam pushes her off the bed, and Bertha lands on her rear. I walk through the open door, take the ice, and hand it back to Sam, who indeed covers his face and groans. I offer my hand to Bertha, who refuses my help but manages to get herself upright and then sits down again, primly this time, at the foot of the bed. She stares at me, daring me to say something deprecating. I am too worried about Millie to engage. All I can see is the swollen body of George being lifted on a gurney, and I can't stop the images of Millie lying still like that, underneath a sheet. I sit in the awful chair and rub my temples.

Sam speaks first. "Did he know where Millie was?"

"He says he doesn't. I don't necessarily have reason to doubt him outside of my intuition, but my intuition has been working overtime on this trip. Bertha did you see when Francis got back to the church?" Begrudgingly, I add, "You are pretty observant."

"The pastor? Never noticed. Only cars and one motor home, but the ones I paid attention to was Pete's and Sam's here. It's a pretty busy street between me and the church, lots of cars going by. You think I got them all memorized?" She says it with anger, but I see by her expression that she is giving the question more consideration.

"I drove up and down these streets," Sam says. "What kind of car does he drive?"

"I don't know," I say honestly. "I've only been in Pete's old, smelly car."

"He drives one of the four-wheel drive things. A silver pickup truck. It's not new either, but it's shiny. Bunch of junk in the bed to make bedrooms for those invalids." Bertha still looks lost in thought.

"Old people are not all invalids." This does not resonate with Bertha. "Pete is looking pretty guilty," I say without total conviction. "He is lying about something."

"He's been lyin' about everything," Bertha quips. "But he was pretty upset about that George fellow. Pete probably didn't do that."

"Probably is *not* an assurance." Sam gets up from the bed and checks his nose in the brass mirror hanging over the scarred desk. "I feel a little dizzy."

"Your nose stopped bleeding. That's a good sign. Maybe just sit a little while longer." I need Sam's help to find Millie, but I don't need a person fainting on me for real. "Pete must have packed a punch."

"Heh, heh," Bertha chortles. "He might still have it." Then she gets quiet again.

I've had enough time for contemplation. "Bertha, do you have a flashlight? And Sam, I don't have keys to my car. May I use yours?"

"Alva, it is almost midnight. You can't go out now." Sam stands again, a bit straighter this time because he is the man in charge.

"Sam," I say with equal command and stand myself, "it is eight-thirty."

He is momentarily shocked but looks at his watch and concurs. "Still late. I'm worried too, but I don't know what we can do until the morning."

"There is a time for sleep and a time for action. I need to find my sister, exhaust all leads, and then look for some more. There is no way I will rest tonight."

"*What the fuck,*" Bertha says, and my hackles rise. "I'll go with you. Gonna grab my flashlight. It has saved me more than once, maybe it'll save your sister." She hops up and heads for the office, giving me a little push out of the way.

"I don't like her. She's no lady." Sam has mentioned it before, and I would agree, except I am rethinking that "lady" title.

"She uses improper language, but she is a lady of *action*." And I have to say that Bertha is growing on me.

Alva

There is a short debate on who is going to be the driver, but ultimately Bertha wins out because she knows the streets better. Her aptitude for driving appears to be her long suit. She even signals, and there is no other car in view. Sam's car is older, too, but it is a deep blue Cadillac, and maybe Bertha is being careful because she really likes driving it.

We circle the church parking lot, but only the silver pickup truck remains. Where are the other mourners? I wonder if Francis has contacted poor George's family. I fight back tears because everyone should be missed, their life remembered. We know we haven't seen Millie walking on Main, and Sam said he circled around mostly between the motel, the church, and Mercy's Milestone (he talked to someone at the Dollar General who told him most old people go there), so I instruct Bertha to drive up and down the shadowy residential streets, slowing for every bench or picnic table in case she got turned around and couldn't find her way back. I try her phone again. It goes straight to automatic voicemail. She doesn't always remember to charge it. I call Mercy's Milestone and leave a message for Vivian Reynolds.

"What's next, Boss?" Bertha jibes, but she is listening to me, following my directions. *It's about time someone does.*

"Okay," I say, "that was the first step. Bertha, is that Texaco still open?"

She snaps her fingers. "That's probably it! You told me you were gamblers—"

"I didn't say anything like that—"

"She's probably in the back room playing those machines! People lose all track of time. Pete did." Bertha sighs despite herself.

"First, we aren't gamblers. Millie played cards for the first time at that casino. And that is what got us into this quandary. Second, I think you still love Pete, and you are overly cranky because your marriage didn't work."

"Well, aren't you the frickin' know-it-all," Bertha continues in a singsong voice. "*First,* I do love Pete, but I had to do something. 'Eat your betting money but don't bet your eating money.' That's what I said because I like to eat, and we couldn't afford groceries. And he wouldn't stop. *Second,* what is a quandary, and why do you keep using stupid words?"

"Ladies, ladies," Sam patronizes from the back seat.

Bertha slams on the brakes so that Sam's head lands on her shoulder. "Don't call me lady."

There are no cars at the pumps and only one parked out front, but the OPEN light still flashes over the station door. My knees creak as I get out, and I remember for a brief minute how old I am. Sam takes my arm as we head inside, and I shake him off.

"I don't get it." He is truly distraught. "I am just trying to be a good guy."

"Sam" I relent, "I know you are a good guy. Just right now, we need some focus on the mission at hand. Think of me as a partner, like we are working for the FBI. And think of Bertha as a junkyard dog."

"Got it." He growls at Bertha, and she growls back.

The convenience store attached to the pumps is fighting a losing battle against time and neglect. The linoleum floors are cracked and grimy. A tired fifty-ish man is sitting on a stool behind the sticky counter, smoking a cigarette. On top of that bad habit, he is wearing a cap indoors. *No manners.* There are shelves behind him with cigarettes, chewing tobacco, stale snacks, and a plethora of personal hygiene products: nail clippers, breath fresheners, toothpaste. *I doubt the clerk has used any of them recently.* He slouches in our direction and points his Marlboro at us, candy wrappers at his elbow next to the ashtray. He's going to start a fire.

Focusing, he says, "Hey, Bertha."

"Hey, Burt. Listen, we are looking for someone—"

"Who you lookin' for? Heard ol' George is dead. You lookin' for whoever killed him?" Burt's shoulders shake, and I think he's laughing. It's not funny.

"Who said there was a killer?" I say, suspicious of someone horning in my investigation, then realize it's a good thing that other people think a crime has been committed.

"Aw, I was just making that up. So boring around here, thought I'd start a rumor. But no one would kill sweet George." He yawns. "I think I need a vacation."

I think that this is a good job for him. No future in law enforcement.

"Is anybody in back?" Bertha understands our charge. Without waiting for an answer, she walks to the back of the store and pushes open the swinging doors. More smoke comes billowing out, turning the small space a hazy gray, and I can't even make out the Twinkies and Doritos anymore. I catch a glimpse of worn slot machines and more stools with vinyl flaking off the tops. "Anybody in here?" she yells.

"I could have just told you no one was," said Burt.

"Why didn't you?" says Bertha.

"Never mind." Burt seems a little afraid of her. Then he figures a way to taunt her.

"Pete was in here for a bit, though. This afternoon."

"God damn it," she mutters, and heads outside.

I see her grab a bag of Lays on her way out. So does Sam. He shrugs his shoulders, hands the guy a one-dollar bill, and follows her out.

"Thanks, man," Burt calls to the closing door.

I stand there for a minute, considering the possibility of Millie ever spending time in such a place. She wouldn't. "Let's go back over to the pawnshop," I say, but Bertha and Sam are already in the car.

Millie

"Am I dead?"

"No, but the future doesn't look rosy." Bonnie is in the room.

I sit up and try to swing my legs to the ground, but they are tied with twine to the undercarriage of the wire cot. I am in a tiny rectangular room, with just the folding bed, one straight-backed chair, and a hamper in the corner. There is a picture hanging precariously from the wall to my left of those dogs playing poker. *They did not spend any time or effort on interior design.* Bonnie is pacing, back and forth, on her phone.

"Daddy, please pick up the phone. I don't think George is going to be able to deliver these folks. Daddy? Damn."

Her deep voice seems incongruent to her childish pleas. My head is spinning, not because of any kind of blow, but the drugs. *The drugs!* I look down at my forearm, where my blouse sleeve has been unceremoniously pushed up, and see bruising surrounding needle sticks. *She could have given me a band aid. Now I have blood on my left sleeve as well as my right. The mosquito only got me once though, and it looks like she got me twice.*

"I have to go to the bathroom." I slur.

Bonnie wrestles a bedpan underneath me. I'm covered with a graying blanket, and I am not wearing pants. *Why am I not wearing pants?!* "There you go. Now keep quiet unless you want me to give you more of this," she says, reaching into her pockets and waving a syringe. "I just gave you a little. Old people don't really need that much. You already sleep a lot. Another symptom is that it may cause some dementia, but you probably already have that too."

I don't, but I might have to fake it in order to get out of here. "The needles cannot be sanitary if they've been in your pockets." But then I stop talking when she moves closer to me. I wonder how long I've been here. The smell of soil, a musky smell, assaults my nose, and I start to cough. I remember Alva telling me that coughing can propel germs at speeds close to fifty miles per hour. And I pray I am harboring a debilitating disease that will bring Bonnie to her knees. I hear cicadas buzzing outside, but I have no idea what time it is. I sense nightfall, but this room is windowless and airless. I feel my heart race, then my ears start to ring. A pulsating sensitivity. "Bzzz, goes a bug." Then the sense of cotton in my cochlea. Then the "Bzzz" again. I try to focus on the kitsch art on the wall, the dogs with cigars, cards on the table, the poker chips. It makes it all worse. Images return: the casino, the fur coat, Bertha, Chasten.

This is just not what I had in mind when I pondered the end of my days. I want to die at home, quietly, maybe knowing that my death is imminent and then purposely not pushing the panic button. Not here. I need just that, a necklace with a medical alert call button. I didn't think I was old enough to get one. But now, lying on this scratchy mattress with no pants, I am feeling beyond my years. I peek under the cover and see my once shapely legs, now covered with spidery veins and age spots, saggy knees stiff from not moving, and see the flesh-colored bedpan positioned under my hips. I yank it out from under me and drop it on the floor. Not much in there, but if it spills out it will be Bonnie's problem. She had turned her back on me to reach around the door and grab a tray from a cart stacked with a couple other trays. They must have stolen the cart from one of those motels with marginal room service.

"Breakfast for dinner." She mutters and drops breakfast at my feet, narrowly avoiding stepping into the modern chamber pot.

"Shit," she says, seething. "I hate this job."

I blink at her, expecting a reprimand of epic proportions. But she already is heading out the door. I see burned toast and an orange juice box at the foot of my bed.

"You can reach that when you are ready to eat something. Your arms are free and long enough. I'll come back for the bedpan. Bring ya' some diapers. Disgusting work." Bonnie mutters the last part on her way out the door.

I do reach for it because I haven't had anything to eat since the unappetizing lunch at Mercy's Milestone. I have to do some shimmying to grab the corner of the metal baking tray, not because I have stunted arms, but because, at eighty, I am not as limber as I use to be. Pulling it toward me, I notice that she has forgotten to bring me the little straw that goes into the box. *Dammit.* I struggle to unglue the cardboard and bite off the corner. Pouring it down my throat, I dribble orange on my blouse. *It's going to look tied dyed by the time I change clothes.* The toast has a little butter on it, and I press my finger in and lick it. I feel like I'm being treated like a child, and I comply. I am going to have a legitimate temper tantrum as soon as I can muster the energy.

Breakfast or dinner over, I revisit the pickle I am in. Bending my knees and leaning over the cot, I see where the ropes are knotted. I just can't reach them. Besides, each time I strain to grasp my tether, the ropes burn into the thin flesh of my ankles. And what? If I really could get a grip good enough to work the knots, this camp bed would fold up with me in it. How embarrassing to be so incompetent. Victims of crime novels are never lucky enough to have their hands free, yet here I am, and I still can't figure out how to escape.

Poor me. Poor Alva. She must be sick to death about my whereabouts. I'm very alone and very helpless. *Will anyone listen to her?* Will she know to look at Eden? There is no doubt that's where I am, but I am still flabbergasted by the contradiction. Laying back on the stiff pillow, I start to cry a little.

Alva

The pawnshop sits directly across the street from the Texaco. Frustrated with my coconspirators, now quiet in the car, I slide back in the passenger seat. "We could have walked, Bertha, it is just right. . . okay, well, pull over there." I gesture to the left. "The street parking in the front."

"No light on, no other cars," says Sam, pointing out the obvious.

"I've got a flashlight, you numbskull." Bertha lifts it up from the seat and turns it on, but it is not very bright. Sam leans over the front seat, so she pops him in the head with it. I'm not sure it was on purpose. The beam falters for a moment. Bertha shakes it a few times, and it brightens. "Sorry about that, but I think your hard head got it working. No harm, no foul."

"I'm the one that is supposed to say that to ease your conscience, but I won't since I have a bump on my head to go with my black eye," Sam pouts.

"Jesus, you're a baby."

"Shut up. Seriously," I say. I don't think I've ever said that to another adult before. I am definitely changing. For a second, I was rooted to the ground. Now I'm back feeling flushed with worry and anticipation. I open the door of the car before Bertha brakes and shoves it into park. A light drizzle begins to fall, and it cools my cheeks. "Get out and shine that flashlight into the windows." I think we are getting closer. "Maybe Millie is stuck in there!"

The lot is paved with faded asphalt, cracked, and weathered from neglect. A roll of barbed wire hangs from the back fence. Grass stabs through the surface. "Let's try the front door first, maybe we can see in the windows." The panes, like we saw earlier, are clouded with dirt and age, but I notice right away that the fur coat is not where it was hanging this afternoon. "Someone has been here."

"Of course someone's been here. Those brothers that own the place are always around," piped Bertha. She focuses the beam of light into the shop. Mostly empty jewelry cases box, a cash register in the center. A few fur stoles (probably fake fur) hang from old metal rolling garment racks. A mannequin is naked in the corner, wearing a hat with feathers. Nothing is moving.

"What do you see, Alva?" Sam is moving hesitantly to the storefront like a bogeyman is going to jump out of the bushes.

"Our coat is gone," I say simply, while circling around to the back.

"This the mink Millie lost?" Sam asks probingly and follows me at a distance.

I imagine that my sister spilled most of the beans to Sam. She probably told him about the casino robbery and everything. I have no idea why he is playing coy with me now.

"She didn't lose it." I have no patience for long stories. My mind is trying to work through different scenarios. *Millie could have bought the coat back and then got lost returning to the motel. She might have had a bout of heatstroke, carrying the thing around, and asked for help from someone living in the area. What if she didn't even go off in this direction? Or, most likely, considering the day we've had, Millie has been abducted.* I keep coming back to that.

I turn around and head to the parking lot. Bertha is behind me, jerking the flashlight from right to left, then up and down; shadows encroach on our progress, and I can't really see where I'm walking. We move in a single-file line toward the rear of the building. A solitary lamppost stands at the corner of the lot, but its dull light doesn't do much better than the bobbing beam to illuminate the area. I climb the two steps and stretch my neck to peer in the tiny window in the back door. I can't see anything.

"Let me see," Bertha bullies me out of the way, and I lose my footing, barely catching myself before I wind up on the pavement. I grab her arm to steady myself, and she pushes me away. Amidst our scuffle, my eyeglasses and the flashlight end up bouncing on the cement step and landing on the little patch of grass to the right of us. "Oh, fuck a duck," cries Bertha. "It better not be broken."

This time I appreciate Sam's arm at my elbow. I'm about blind without my glasses. I'm so used to them being on my face that I am momentarily frozen, afraid to move my head and see more darkness. Sam walks me down one more step, finds my glasses, and secures them on my nose. Bertha is lunging for the flashlight, now dimmer in the wet grass. *I don't know what she's thinking. Does she assume I'll fight her for it?* I take a step toward her, try to calm her down, but she is waving the thing around like a weapon. *What an odd woman.*

"It's the only flashlight I have," she bemoans.

"I'll buy you a new one when we find Millie," I say pragmatically. Because goodness knows, someone needs to be the voice of reason. She is humming "This Little Light of Mine." Perhaps a long time ago Bertha was a churchgoer.

"This thing here"—Bertha raises the flashlight toward the sky— "is what saves me during a storm."

"So, all this is because you—" Sam begins.

"I'm afraid of the dark, you asshole." Bertha is frank about it. No psychotherapy needed. She points it like a sword, then swings it around like one of those Jedis my grandson is always talking about. I gave him a lightsaber for Christmas.

"I'll chip in for a nightlight," says Sam earnestly, even though I know he's not earnest at all. "You probably sleep with a gun under your pillow, and I don't want you jumpy while I'm staying at the motel."

I turn my back on their banter and scan the area for any sign of Millie. And then I see something in the long grass at the edge of the asphalt. *Not trash.* "Wait!" I scream. "Wait, shine it back over there!"

Damp from the mist, I see Millie's hanky, the little square of faded floral fabric. "It's hers," I take deep breaths. Holding it gently in my shaking hands, I motion for Bertha to point her flashlight at it. "It's got blood on it." I say it to myself, but they see it too.

Alva

Leaving the scene and stumbling toward the car, I make a mental list.

1. *(According to Pete) Pete dropped George off at the church.*
2. *(According to Pete) Pete dropped Francis at Eden.*
3. *(According to Pete) He went to help George at the church and then went on errands?*
4. *Someone took our coat from the pawnshop.*
5. *The only people who knew about the coat were Pete and his accomplice.*
6. *They might have told Pastor Francis.*
7. *Someone took Millie from the pawnshop.*
8. *Millie is being held against her will.*
9. *There is not enough blood here to assume Millie is dead.*
10. *Finding George in the river is related. Blood or not, George is dead.*

There are a lot of holes. Back in the car, I turn on the overhead light, reach for my journal stuffed deep in my purse, and start scribbling. I need to put things in order, make a plan to find Millie. And the garden and thorn thing continues to haunt me like a recurring melody.

Flash! *It was some kind of accident. The seatbelt is holding me upside down, but I am alive. The belt protects me more than any knight's armor. I hang like a bat using my echolocation in the darkness. I listen to the whispering wind, hear the bumps in the night. Sometimes not knowing what's out there is better.*

Bertha's face comes into focus. She stares into the car window. I stare back. I realize I am not, in fact, upside down and that the pen is in my hand. The other still holds the hanky. I do not have time to write this one down. I've been wasting time. We've been here too long.

"What's wrong with you? Are we still looking for someone or what?" She shines her flashlight in my nose before moving back toward the shop.

Thoughtfully, I think, you know how people say, "Oh, I knew something happened to so-and-so, I felt empty right away." Or "I knew they were dead before anyone told me." Well, that is probably a bunch of malarkey, but I have to say that when my Irwin and my siblings passed, I did experience a sense of loss. Felt it in my stomach before I knew they were gone. At least that's how I remember it. I don't feel that now. Millie is waiting for me to rescue her.

Sam opens the car door and kneels. "Don't jump to wild conclusions Alva," Sam stills my hand that is stroking the cloth. "Do you know for sure if this is Millie's?"

"Of course I recognize the hanky. She has had this thing tucked into her sleeve for about seven years now. I'm not even sure she washes it." I turn it over and over. "There really isn't a lot of blood, not like she broke her nose, or not like she was . . . stabbed." I start to shiver. Sam puts his coat around my shoulders and tucks it around me.

I let him scoot me over and put a hip on the front seat next to me. *But I just need to get my ideas together. I'm not a shrinking violet,* I remind myself. I absently rub my face with Millie's hanky. I can smell her. Her blood and sweat, a little, but also her White Diamonds cologne by Elizabeth Taylor. It is a scent for the ages as familiar to me as my own Avon Timeless. Smells are stimulating. They bring back memories, sure, but they are also what leads the hunt. Sam is hovering at the car door, watching me intently for any signs of duress. My resolve only intensifies.

"Get all the way in the car—the back seat!" I bark at him. "Where is my junkyard dog?"

Bertha is sitting on the cracked cement steps, leaning against the back door of the pawnshop. She is holding the flashlight against her breast, the light flickering upwards toward the sky. The threat of rain fades away. A few stars wink back between the dark clouds like they are interpreting each other's Morse code. I remember learning about the timing of Morse's dits and dahs and that the spaces between them are called "a period of signal absence." I love thinking about that, a quiet moment that brings meaning to the onslaught of words. I needed just such a quiet moment. And now it's over.

"Bertha, you're still the driver, so let's get moving."

"Oh, sure thing, Miss Daisy," Bertha snarls but shines a path back to the Cadillac, flicking on the headlights and shedding light on our situation. "Where to?"

"To the motel." Sam is sure that is what I mean.

"To Eden."

"Oh yeah." Bertha smiles and shows her teeth. "Let's go get the Mi . . .uh mi . . .."

"The miscreants?" I offer.

"No, um, Millie. I forgot her name."

Bertha is getting on my last nerve. "Buckle up," is all I say.

Alva

"I know where it is," Bertha is leading us down more dark roads and then more dirt roads. Every couple of seconds, the windshield wipers scrape across the glass, smearing the dead bugs. The rain has stopped but the automatic blades insist on intermittent squeaking. Bertha turns on the radio, but we mostly hear static. The cacophony of unnecessary noise would make a fine soundtrack for a horror movie.

Millie. I only can think of Millie.

The Cadillac bumps along, and Sam makes his case for turning back. The rocks are ruining his undercarriage. *(He is fixated on his undercarriage.)* The branches are leaving scratch marks on his chassis. It is too dark to be breaking and entering.

Bertha rolls her eyes at every complaint, and I fear she cannot possibly be watching the road when the whites of her eyes are the only parts visible.

"Stop with all the sex talk," she says. "I can't concentrate."

Must be that I am oblivious to any innuendoes.

"Huh?" asks Sam.

"There's the sign," Bertha points to a vinyl banner attached with zip ties through the grommets and wrapped around two plywood posts. The posts aren't the same size, and the sign droops from the left to the right. "WELCOME TO EDEN." Another few feet and we are at the entrance. A chain crisscrosses a rusty gate, and barbed wire extends around the property as far as we can see. It is pitch black out here, so as far as I can see is not very far. I touch one of the barbs by accident, and pricks of blood dot my fingers. Scrub and bush hide the bottom of the barbed fence, making it too treacherous for us to veer from the driveway.

There are surely some nasty creatures out here: snakes and mosquitos. Maybe a few bears. Bertha shines our light between the rails in the gate. They are too close together for any of us to squeeze through. Partial frames of incomplete structures loom like forgotten skeletons, pieces strewn willy-nilly. The drive on the other side of the gate is deeply rutted, muddy from the rain. Discarded tools, saws, and shovels stick out of overgrown grass and scattered debris. We only see one trailer intact. It has a small porch and not-so-white exterior siding. One window is boarded up, and the roof is sloping. There are no lights on.

"*That* is the pastor's house," says Bertha, wiggling her fingers through the slats and pointing out the old mobile home. "There's some more buildings behind it, but I can't really see them from here. Not enough light left. You need to buy me some more batteries."

She is kneeling in the reddish, silt clay. Sam stands above her, staring at Eden. "I don't get it. This is where you think Millie is? Doesn't look like anybody is in there."

"That's what they want you to think," says Bertha in a weird whisper, and then just sits in the dirt.

"It's hard to tell," I say. "They would be sleeping now, right? I don't see Francis's truck."

"He's probably sleeping at the church. He does that sometimes." Bertha pushes Sam aside again. "I think I see an RV parked over there. One with wheels. And are those gravestones?"

"Where?" I say. But the flashlight dies. "Will you repark the car so that the headlights can illuminate the field?"

Bertha is already moving toward the safety of the car.

"I don't see any men wearing masks and wielding knives." Sam chuckles after her.

"Well, you can stay out there then; maybe I'll get lucky, and one will show up." Bertha hops behind the wheel, slams the door, and locks it.

"Dammit. Open it up right now." Sam starts pounding on the window.

Bertha turns on the inside lights and sticks out her tongue. She does not turn the car around. For a full ten minutes, we are at an impasse. Sam continues to bang his fist so hard that I think he may shatter the glass. Finally, I yell, "Bertha, if you keep running the motor and the lights, it will run out of gas and or battery power. And then we will be in *complete* darkness!" She glances down at the gauges and decides to take me seriously. The doors unlatch, and Sam yanks the driver's door open. He tries unsuccessfully to pull Bertha out.

"You are way too old for me, Mister," she says while brushing his hands away. "I'll call the cop."

"Are you kidding me? The cop?" I'm at my wit's end. My yell has turned into kind of a shriek with a tremor. "St-to-op i-t!" It zaps my energy, and I fall from my anxiety high into a deep pool of depression. I'm furious and frustrated and so exhausted. It's clear that I need to do this alone or find better accomplices. "Bertha, can you drive us back to the motel? It's too late for any rescue tonight."

"If Millie is in there, we will get her out. In the morning. Up and at 'em first thing. I was a Marine." Sam touches my shoulder, empathizing. *But he only has known Millie for a minute. He can't understand.* Since I do not respond, he straightens and salutes me.

"Nobody cares." Bertha puts the car in drive. "Both of you get in so I can get my beauty sleep."

"Beauty my ass," Sam mutters. "Did you bring all that dirt in the car!?"

Bertha moves her ass—dear me, I mean "rear"—wiping the remains of the reddish soil on his leather seat.

Alva

By the time Sam helps me out of the car, it is after midnight. All of Chasten's streetlights must be on timers; not one of them is working. The stars are back after the short rain, but they look farther away now. The Happy Family and the Texaco are the sole beacons of the town, and neither of them is welcoming. The Texaco isn't even open, and before we left, Bertha switched on the no-vacancy sign. I glance toward the church, and sure enough, I can just make out Francis's silver pickup truck parked close to the back entrance.

Without preamble, Bertha heads towards the office and, I assume, the little bedroom she has in back. She must have hit a switch because the neon motel sign fizzles. Sam takes both of my hands. "We will find her," he says. There is honest worry in his eyes, and I think I know then that his quibbling with Bertha is his way of coping with fear. "In the morning we will make the pastor take us out there himself."

I nod because we are both old and even in high-stakes situations, we know our bodies and brains need downtime. *A well-rested mind and all of that.* "I must try to sleep so that I can be strong for Millie. I'm going to talk to Francis first thing in the morning before he leaves the church. He won't be able to shirk me off this time."

I watch as Sam goes into his room, then unlock mine. Part of me believes that when I open it, Millie will be fast asleep in her bed. I'm terrified all over again when she's not there. Despite my fear and the urgency of the situation, my body is craving rest. I fumble with the alarm clock; thank God it is an old one with hands and big numbers. I'm no good at the digital ones. I think about changing into my nightgown, but I'm not ready for a bedtime routine, not without Millie here. Turning off all but the light next to my bed, I pull the top cover around me and reach for my journal. It is in my purse, but I don't have the energy to dig out the pen. *What would I write anyway? Millie's gone, and I am as empty as those new pages.* Instead, I read my last entries, looking for a clue to Millie's disappearance. There is something there in the words, but the darkness behind my eyelids grows and the soft ticking of the clock taps out the rhythm of a lullaby.

I wait for sleep to come. It doesn't.

Flash! *I'm on a farm. The sun sets with such a splash of red that I, too, am awash in color. It feels like the world is on fire. The animals sense it, too. They run in all directions trying to escape the imaginary flames. I will have to gather them back.*

Enough already! Mulling it over, I try to make sense of things. It feels like I'm sitting down for an exam without reading the textbook. The visions are important plot points, I think. I try to connect them. It's my story after all. I snuggle even deeper and hope that whatever comes my way, I'll be able to write about it later.

Almost asleep again.

Oh! And then these lids of mine snap up like someone throwing back the drapes. I got it! Just dreamed up a plan! I need to get into Eden, and my brain came up with a way to do that and get some real shut-eye. It's a win-win. Reaching into my purse, I find the mosquito repellant and dowse myself from head to toe. Then, adjusting the straps of my purse over my shoulder and clutching the bedcover, I peek out of the motel door. It is dead out now even the Texaco sign is turned off, leaving nothing but darkness in its wake. I walk as quickly as I can across the parking lot, sidestepping the sidewalk and staying close to trees and bushes. The church is right there, no lights on either. My adrenaline is working overtime, and I have to stop once to catch my breath and reposition the bedspread. I try to roll it up but it's ungainly, and I know that I've been dragging it through the dirt. But it's the least of my worries.

Oh, my heart is pounding! Undeterred, I approach Francis's truck and sidle up between it and the side of the church, quiet as a mouse. I have to thank God again that it isn't one of those with the oversized wheels, and it has a running board. I can do this. Bertha was right. There is a hodgepodge of junk in the back: some lumber, a couple of bags of cement, wire, old clothes, and stinky work boots. The comforter is cumbersome but with some effort I slide it in, then toss my purse in too. Standing on the sidebar, I grasp the edge of the truck's bed and hoist myself up. I may be almost 80, but I am strong when I am determined. And voila! I'm in. Well, I almost fall on my head, but voila anyway. Careful not to upturn anything that will make noise and alert the man in the church, I press myself into the corner of the truck bed, close to the tailgate, in case I need an emergency exit. I dig out a little space for me. I rearrange some of the old clothes, and chicken wire, and create a makeshift nest under the lumber that juts out. *Just like a bird,* I think, and plop down, wrapping the hotel bedding almost completely over my head. I remember Pudge, smile, and close my eyes.

Millie

She left me here for hours. Try as I might, I couldn't get out of the bed. *I should have signed up for yoga down at the senior center.* Maybe it's the drugs, or maybe it's the circumstance, but I am exhausted trying to loosen the ties, and I have to use the bathroom again, but the bedpan is on the floor, and I can't reach it either. I bend my knees and scoot my behind toward the foot of the bed for one last attempt when Bonnie or whatever she calls herself comes barreling through the door with a wheelchair in tow.

"Now what?" I say angrily.

"You behave like a good old lady," Bonnie says, and pushes me back flat. "It's almost dawn. Time to move you to a better place. You'd like that, right? A better place?" Her movements are hasty, but her tone is oddly humane. She goes to work undoing the ties that pin my feet to the frame, then lifts me up like a baby and sets me in the wheelchair. The idea that she could do that without laboring somehow starts me giggling. I *know* it's the drugs. Low one minute, and now I'm high.

"Uh oh," I hoot. "Have to use the facilities again." And saying "facilities" just like Alva did, makes me roar with laughter, and a little pee comes out. "Did you put something in that juice box?" I splutter.

Bonnie realizes that I still am not wearing any pants, and nothing under where my pants should be either. She allows me to use the bedpan, and then rummages through the hamper and finds an old hospital gown and throws it over me. "Residual effects. Mood swings." She stares down at me and then tucks the gown around my bottom.

"Isn't it dirty? It was in the *hamper!*" I am disgusted, but I am also not naked.

"The thing is," she continues, "I am not a bad person."

"Who are you talking to?" *Maybe Bonnie has been dipping into some of her own stuff.*

"I just wanted to be in charge for once. I'm good at things. Used to be a nurse once. I was just trying to get Daddy to notice me with all that circus stuff. Figured he was always telling me I was a clown, so I decided to enlist. But with all of this"—she waves her big arm in a circle— "I thought I could prove to him once and for all that I was a good daughter."

"So, is it working? Because he may think you're a good daughter, but I think you are being a bad person."

She shrugs her very expansive shoulders and starts pushing me down the hall to a back exit. She has to turn me backwards to roll it over the doorjamb and onto the threshold ramp. Once we are on the muddy path, I hear her gasping. It's hard going, even for sturdy Bonnie. We stop for a breather, her turned away from me, and I notice her shoulders are still heaving. Is it the effort, or is she crying?

"I am in love with George. And now he's gone," Bonnie murmurs.

"What? What? You are in love with George? He is so kind!" This is shocking news. Even being held as a prisoner, I have to feel sorry for her. Because I am sure that it is unrequited passion. I just can't see them together. "Where did he go?"

"Down the river." She whispers it so quietly that I strain to hear.

"Well, why don't you just take me back to the motel to Alva and go follow George? You never know. He might learn to love you back. He's not very smart." I don't feel that magnanimous.

"He didn't want me to take the money."

"You lost me."

"Never mind." Bonnie shakes her big head and continues to push me down the path towards the woods.

"Where are we going?" Because heading towards the woods does not seem like the most advantageous route to anywhere.

With a great big sigh Bonnie takes a scarf out of her enormous pocket—she could store a hell of a lot of doilies in there, and wraps it around my mouth. Ties it tight. Then she says, "To join the others."

Alva

It's barely dawn, and I guess I'd dozed off when I hear someone pounding and pounding. I dare to peek out from under my quilt and see Pete coming around the side of the church. I duck back down like a groundhog.

"Francis! Hey Pastor!" Pete shouts until Francis finally opens the door a sliver.

"Stop the hammering, Pete. I'm coming out." Still under my blanket, I spot a small gap—a narrow slit in the corner where the panels didn't quite meet. In this morning light, I can see Francis poke his head just out of the door, his eyes scanning the premises. He's nervous.

"You hiding from somebody?" Pete asks.

"There's this Cadillac," he starts, then stops. He slithers through the opening because the truck is parked so tight to the door, and he bumps the truck, and all the things back there rattle around, including me.

"What's your problem?" Francis asks Pete with disdain. He seems flustered. I wonder if Sam roaming around in his Cadillac is what is making him nervous. I can't imagine why.

Pete answers, "Why are you sleeping at the church? And my problem is that I don't know what you did with Millie or if you know anything about George."

Pete! I could almost look kindly on him if he leads me to Millie.

"Don't get your panties in a wad," says the phony pastor. His words are clipped. The air around him crackles with intensity. "Heading back to Eden now. Need to look for something. Millie is under Bonnie's care, meaning she's probably still sleeping."

"Yeah, but what are you going to do with her? You can't keep her sleeping forever."

"Of course I can." Francis sneers. "But another couple of doses of the sedative will muddle her mind enough—you can bring her back to her sister this morning. Say you found her wandering on the road. If she starts voicing any gibberish about our operation, just say she is imagining things. Now get out of my way. I've got something to take care of—"

"Alva won't buy it."

"Well, Pete, you'd better hope you can convince her. Otherwise, both are too risky to keep around." His voice is rising. "Right? *Then,* you will have to stage an accident. Hmm, maybe their car can run off the road, maybe into the river."

"Did you kill George?" Pete is livid.

I can't believe Pete is plucky enough to ask—straight out like that, too—and I almost gasp out loud. Then I think about it and figure, if he's asking, he can't have done it himself. *Hmmmm...*

Francis shoves Pete out of the way. "I didn't get back to the church until five or so. And I never go traipsing around the riverbank. Now move!"

"You need to take this more seriously. Alva is right. I think somebody did kill George. If the police come asking, I'm going to have to tell them about the money George found in your office. It was the kickback from the pharmaceutical company, right?"

I sneak a look and see Francis turning back to Pete. He grabs Pete by his shirt, shaking him. Pete might be in trouble, might be pushing Francis too far.

"Did you take the money, Pete? Where is that fucking money?" Red spots flare on his cheeks.

Pete holds his hands up in surrender. "Only reason I know you had cash in your office is because George showed it to me. You were damn careless leaving it out like that."

"It was in an envelope on my *desk*. No one should be rifling through things on my desk! What did you do with the money?!"

"I told George it was a donation to the cause, and I left it right there. And, I assume, George left it right there. He seemed uneasy though. What did *you* do? Lose it?"

"I don't have it. I think maybe Bonnie took it. She's been acting sneaky. I need to get to Eden and find the cow. Should've figured that one of you screw-ups would get greedy." Francis is flush with anger and his brows are knitted together.

"Bonnie is not going to go rogue. She's got the circus gig, and anyway, her father would kill her. And George is about the least greedy person in this town, and you know it."

"Then it was you!"

"Francis," Pete says in a mocking tone, "*you* are the greedy one. I just want out. I don't give a damn about the money anymore. I'm heading over to pick up Millie, my mom, and Harriet. I am going to ask them for forgiveness. You know, that thing pastors are supposed to teach."

"The fuck you are." Francis grabs a two-by-four from the back of the truck and swings it hard at Pete. It misses, but I flinch, and part of my cover slides off my head. I duck. I am terrified I am going to be seen back here.

"You did! You killed George!" Pete is yelling for all he is worth.

"You moron," Francis says, and I hear the board whip through the air again like a baseball bat, "George was going to be our driver. Free you and I up to do the construction and promotion. But now maybe it's you that's gotta go. I don't take kindly to threats." He growls it out and then takes another swing and connects. I can tell because I hear Pete hit the ground.

Francis runs around to the driver's side of the truck. He puts it in reverse, and I think he plans to run Pete over. Good thing he parked so close to the church. There is no room to maneuver; the truck brushes the siding, but the wheels don't reach Pete. I make a decision. I come to kneeling and remove my makeshift camouflage. Pete is on the ground. He looks up and sees me.

The engine roars, but I see Pete's shock and then hear him gasp. "What the hell?" Pete hollers. "Do I have a concussion?"

"Go get Bertha and Sam! I'll take care of Millie!" I shout back. "And your mom!" I wink at him.

Francis kicks the truck into drive, oblivious to our hasty conversation. We speed away, and I hope I am right to trust Pete.

Alva

I snuggle back into my blanket.

Off we go. It is a smooth ride at first, but when we turn toward Eden the truck jostles me back and forth. The stacks of material in the back topple. The gravel road is full of potholes and debris. It was a lot more comfortable riding in Sam's Cadillac. Then we swerve so violently to the right I almost fly out of the nest, and without wings I doubt I will live to see another day. Thank goodness the paraphernalia all around me rattles raucously, or I'm certain he would hear my yelps. I'll be of no help if Francis discovers me.

Bump. Bump. Bump. I am uncomfortable, but adrenaline is surging through my veins. *I'm coming Millie! Hold on sister!* The morning sun is hovering at the horizon, and those early rays are slipping through the trees. I sit up a little taller feeling the wind in my hair, and it braces me for the job ahead. Francis slows. I'm facing backwards so it takes me by surprise when the truck stops abruptly at what I assume to be the not-so-pearly gate of Eden. I hear Francis jerk the door open, work with the lock on the gate, and push it aside. He gets back in and drives through, and to my relief, he does not re-padlock that gate. I have an escape route, and if Pete does what I said, they will be able to enter to find us.

Francis seems frantic as he hits the gas again and races up to the complex. Before the brakes even grab, he is running into a trailer, screaming for Bonnie.

Time to get out and find Millie. It's a little harder to disentangle myself from the truck's mess. Things have settled in different positions, and I have to squeeze around a dislodged cement bag and lift a rake that is balancing right overhead. I pull the comforter along with me and drop it to the ground in case I land funny. Maybe not a good idea, but hopefully by the time Francis sees it, I'll have found Millie and backup will have arrived. Looking for better footing, I kick aside an old coat, revealing that pair of boots lodged underneath. They really do smell funny, and as I step on one, it squishes beneath my shoe. Why does Francis have a wet boot back here? I search for the other. Sure enough, I pull a soggy lace from under a toolbox and out comes its match. I pour the contents out on the coat. Brackish water stains the flannel. I hug those boots to my chest and suck in air. *Oh.*

Putting my purse back over my shoulder and standing on a paint bucket, I extend my right leg over and straddle the sidewall, then grip it hard to swing the other leg over. *I do so wish I had put on my trousers, but no one is looking.* Lacking any grace, I hang for a minute, toes missing the running board, and drop down. I take a minute to praise my foresight— taking that bedspread was a vision on its own. Getting off my rump, I straighten and survey my surroundings.

I hear Francis in the trailer, bellowing for Bonnie and tossing things around. I hadn't put it together that Pete's casino sidekick was Bonnie or that Bonnie was synonymous with the circus fat lady. If Pete hadn't come over to berate the pastor, I would have never had a chance to eavesdrop. Bertha had mentioned a big woman who was hanging around Francis and Pete at Eden. Now things are falling into place.

But my sister! They are drugging her? What was all that about a pharmaceutical company? At least I know that Millie is still alive, but I have to get her out of here before those drugs muddle her noggin and before Francis comes back out of the trailer. It doesn't sound like he's having any luck in there.

The sheds behind the trailer look promising. I doubt that he'd house the elderly in his own home. I sneak stealthily around back and push open the door to one of the structures on my right. Besides Francis's curse-filled rant, the whole property is remarkably quiet. Inside here, too, not a peep to be heard. I remember the clamor in Mercy's Milestone: wheelchairs colliding, women cackling, the click-clack of canes, the camaraderie, but there is none of that here. Stepping inside, there is a distinct lack of air-conditioning. I see an idle fan in the corner by a desk piled high with entertainment tabloids. I would have expected some kind of intake area with a computer and maybe some calendars for scheduling. Instead, there are fast food containers littering a table in the center, one wooden chair, and a large recliner that looks plenty used, damp with sweat. Passing through that room there is a narrow hallway with about four doors on each side. Only one is open, so I peer inside and whisper, "Millie?"

I get no answer but go inside anyway and look around. This looks more like a lab room at a defunct doctor's office. To the left is one of those prefab cabinets with a sink like the ones at Home Depot down the "for sale" aisle. Poorly laid vinyl squares cover the floor; there is something unidentifiable spilled. My shoes stick. One of the cabinet doors is ajar, and I can see an array of syringes, sponges, and two vials of clear liquid. First things first, I open the vials and pour the stuff down the sink. *There will be no more sedation on my watch.* There is one syringe sitting on the grimy counter near the faucet; the crystal-clear liquid doesn't have any bubbles in it, and there is a cap on the needle. Instead of taking the cap off, pushing the plunger, and emptying it, I shove it in my skirt pocket.

Next, I sidle down the hall, planning on opening the doors one by one. There are trays of uneaten food on room service trolleys in my way, and a few stained mattresses are propped against the walls. Maneuvering through the nightmare, I take stock. It is so odd, each room looks like there had recently been an occupant, but the beds are empty now. They are all pretty much the same, a nightstand, a wire cot pulled up close to the wall. A few of the rooms have two beds with barely any walking room in between, dim overhead lights, and flickering black and white televisions. The TVs are on with the sound turned off. The beds are rumpled, covered with sheets in childish prints, scratchy blankets, and worn pillows, some with restraints hanging from the metal frame. A few rooms have threadbare rugs and knockoff artwork. I hate that one with the dogs playing poker.

The "ward" is smelly and claustrophobic. I have yet to find a bathroom, but I see bedpans scattering the floors. I start to gag and head back the way I came. I want to shout for Millie, but I don't dare give away my position. Francis is still yelling; his preacher voice, not his indoor voice, echoes throughout Eden.

The next building is smaller than the first, but it's nothing more than a tool shed. Construction supplies like the articles in the back of Francis's truck are haphazardly stacked. There is a box of Bibles in there too. *My Lord, Millie isn't anywhere. I was sure this was where they took her.* I still don't know who the kidnapper was, if it was Pete, or Bonnie, or Francis himself, and I'm running out of ideas where to look. I head to the only building left on the property. It is some kind of chapel made from stone, or partly made of stone from ages ago, and now is supplemented with corrugated metal. It looks like there used to be a steeple, too. But now it looks more like one of those brick chimneys you come across in rural areas: the ones that were likely attached to a house, but the house has all but been reclaimed by the earth around it.

I tiptoe into the old sacred place, but it has gone to hell like the rest of Eden. Nature has been working overtime. There are weeds sprouting through cracks, mold growing on the two pews left in the place. There isn't even an altar, and I think that parts of this chapel must have been repurposed to fit the church of Chastain. An empty bird's nest rests in a rafter. Even the wrens see the writing on the wall.

Sitting on a pew and praying it holds my weight, I believe I hear a woman's voice. Not Millie's. Most likely Bonnie. Getting up, I take a looksie out the chapel door. Sure enough, I am right. She is talking to herself, or God, and waving those great big arms in exaggerated circles. No, I'm wrong. I didn't see the phone tucked under her double chin. I hear the one-sided conversation.

"Daddy, please pick up. Okay, well just listen. I found out a few things and you are going to see how I saved everything. I know you sent Francis the money from Phitec, but I really think that I can handle the finances better. Screw Pastor Francis, he's a nut job. And Pete is worthless, always worrying about his mama. And I didn't tell you I loved George. But—well call me back. I've got this."

I think I hear her choking back tears, but she could just be choking on her words. That middle-aged woman is too old to be calling her father "Daddy." I haven't seen her since the Ho-Chunk, but she seems more sorrowful and sweatier. She heads back to the building with the beds. I haven't figured out where to search next, so I watch her. She comes out immediately with an armful of blankets, yelling, "Who took my stash?!!!" Her eyes dart all around, settling her gaze on Francis's trailer. You can see her uncertainty. She hears him in there, but it is obvious she doesn't want to confront him. She wants to rescue her drugs, but she is ready to flee. She decides to run, heading into the woods. Her steps are ungainly. Where is she headed? I bet she knows where Millie is.

Alva

Then all hell breaks loose (excuse the language). While I am tracking Bonnie towards the woods, I hear Francis coming out of his trailer. I don't need him to find me on his property until I have a handle on Millie's whereabouts. Looking for a place to hide, I start moving helter-skelter. I'm halfway between the chapel and the woods when I step on loose soil and tumble into a shallow grave. Maybe not a grave, but certainly a hole with high hopes of entertaining a dead person. I lie perfectly still.

Flash! *The weight of the world is on my shoulders. I am in the newsroom when the anchor starts to cough. It begins as a tickle, then a bout so serious she can't catch her breath. Suddenly I am pulled from behind the camera and sat behind the big teak desk. "Just read it!" The producer points to the prompter. The enormity of the news staggers me. How ignorant I've been! Then, the anchor returns. "Take back the world," I say. But I shove kernels of truth in my pockets before I leave.*

My clothes are getting muddy. My mind is getting muddier by the moment. I don't know anything about the world. I am only starting to figure out the scope of the mess we are in. But, to be honest, I would be fine to turn back the clock and forget about this adventure. I'm face first in the soil, a lone old lady. My adventure with Millie was not meant to be the death of me. Or her. I turn over to lay flat on my back and do a quick assessment of my body parts. Everything seems to be working. Francis is coming nearer, but he doesn't seem to be looking for me. The fear of discovery keeps me quiet, even though I want to spit some dirt out of my mouth.

Francis is shouting for Bonnie, but he doesn't see her scurrying away, and he now heads into the main shed with the rooms, not the woods. As he goes in, I spy a dark green sedan speeding up the drive. The cavalry. (Guess Sam decided to leave the Caddy in the parking lot.) I stand up and wave my hands at Sam, Pete, and Bertha. The hole is only a foot deep, but when Bertha spies me, she stares like I'm some gnarled monster rising from a crypt. I am dirty, and a few twigs and weeds are intertwined in my hair, but I'm no creature from the Black Lagoon, or whatever that movie was.

I wave my arms more vehemently and motion for her to get over here, holding a finger over my mouth in the universal sign of *Be Quiet*. Pete is already running for the trailer with Sam hot on his heels. Bertha approaches slowly, her eyes scanning the tiny cemetery, of which I am now a reluctant guest.

"So, no one killed you then," Bertha says.

"You are quite the observer," I reply.

She reaches for my hands and hauls me topside like a sack of russets, turns her head, and takes in her surroundings. Then Bertha shrieks and points. "Are those *bones*?"

I turn slowly to see another shallow grave nearby, its soil disturbed. This one is inhabited by skeletal remains. I peer down.

Bertha stammers, "D-D-Don't touch it."

But I do. I touch an arm with the toe of my orthopedic sneaker. Finger bones protrude from the sleeve of a larvae-chewed wool sweater.

"I used to have a sweater like that," I say. "I bought it at JCPenney during that cold snap we had right before Irvin died."

"Is that all you have to say right now?" Bertha stares down into one of the eye sockets. The other eyehole is filled with dirt. There are little lines on the skull like a spider's web.

"Mine had a blue stripe, but this one's more of a coral color."

"*Alva, Holy shit!* I don't like to be out here." She jerks around, looking for ghosts or maybe her ex-mother-in-law.

"I've seen my share of dead people," I say, nonplussed. "You get to where most of your friends and family are dead. You know what I'm talking about."

"I don't know."

I sigh, "Dead is dead. Those morticians have some talent putting eye caps on eyeballs and the makeup, of course, but we all know it's just dress-up, and the bones are waiting underneath." I tap my toe. "Look, her little arm is reaching out for something. I hope when they bury me next to Irvin, I'll reach out and try to hold his hand, maybe do a little dance in the dirt. I've thought about it a lot."

"What are you talking about? Who is she? Who put her here?"

"I don't know," I say. "But I know who she's not."

It's not Millie, I think. *It's not my sister.*

Alva

We hear a shot and Bertha screams. Already terrified of bones and graves (and the dark, even though it doesn't apply here), Bertha isn't as tough as she pretends. She leaves me and heads for the chapel, crying Pete's name once or twice as she runs. The shot came from the 'ward', but she does not go in that direction. Prayer will probably do her good.

I'm praying too, that Sam is okay and that Francis has been neutralized. Don't really know what that looks like and don't care because no matter what is happening over there, I have a sister to save. It's all clear. Francis is a crook who got into the business of eldercare to shake a little of that big pharma money his way. According to the conversations I've overheard recently, he was taking advantage of Mercy's Milestone's predicament and providing temporary lodging for the old folks. Keeping them just long enough to transport them like produce. George was a sad, gullible figure; Francis hadn't had too much trouble pulling him into the fold. Bonnie is a sad case too, beaten down by a controlling father, trying to prove her worth. Pete, I don't know. Pretty sure he is the saddest of all—what else can you call a man smitten with Bertha?

As for the bones, they belong to Francis's mother. They've been there longer than Eden's recruiting, but it would take the wool fiber in the sweater at least six to twelve months to totally biodegrade. George said she lived out here, but he hadn't seen her for a while. Now we know why. As I've mentioned, I know my crime shows. Decomposition happens quickly when you are buried without a coffin. The maggots have long moved away from this one, but the sweater is hanging on by a thread. I stare into the shallow graves.

Flash! *The woods take on a sinister appearance, the wind kicks up, and branches snake out and coil around my arms. "I am Hercules!" I cry, even though I'm just Alva. There are women needing saving, drugged women, and I need to bring them up out of their hellish slumber.*

I stare for a long time. It means something. They all mean something.

The vision transforms into the here and now. Another gunshot. Moving toward the tree line behind the encampment, I see the Winnebago. There is a canopy of green hiding the fiberglass top and ripped awning, but the engine is rumbling, and there is a thin wisp of smoke sneaking around the foliage. As I get closer there are other noises, grunts, and groans. I watch Bonnie as she kicks the tires, then she circles around to pull the steps out from underneath the camouflaged portal to hell and drag them in front of the lifted door, obviously a makeshift replacement for the RV steps no longer attached. She stops abruptly, lifting her nose like she can smell me. I step on a brittle stick, and she faces me, crossing her arms over her abundant chest.

Clues click into place. My mirages are all part of my epic journey! Not in a real mythological sense, mind you, but in their own little way, figurative tasks in my quest for 'more'. *All that reading of Poirot—I should have recognized. Bonnie is my last labor.* She, with the (at least three) chins, stands guarding the trailer door with all the savagery of a rabid dog. She was discovered, after all, trying to sell souls out from under Francis. Desperate to please her father, who treated her more like a disappointing pet than a daughter, cunning enough to pull off a casino heist, nurturing just enough to sedate without killing, even wretched enough to mourn an unrequited love. She's a one-woman circus.

I have to smile. It is clever.

"Get away little old lady," Bonnie pants, and then quickly reconsiders. "Oh wait! Come on in! You are the one that matches Millie. I think there's more money for me if you are related."

"You have Millie in there?" I know the answer because it's the only thing that makes sense. Bonnie is attempting to kidnap at least three, if not a few more, of Mercy's Milestone ex-residents, and somehow Millie has gotten herself involved. There are many crisscrossing wheelchair tracks in the soft terrain, some deeper than others. *And does that mumbling coming from inside belong to my sister?*

Bonnie moves from the doorway and clomps toward me. She doesn't have a weapon, but she will definitely overpower me. I don't have heroic strength, so no way I can wrestle her with my bare hands.

"Listen, what's your name?" I try to establish a rapport.

"You know who I am. You were at the Ho-Chunk and at the circus the day before that. I saw you."

"But we weren't formally introduced," I say with my hand extended. If she takes it, I might not get it back. "I'm Alva. And you have Millie, my sister, in there. Do you have a sister?"

Bonnie shakes her head and stops her forward progress. "Never had no sister. My daddy always said there was enough of me to make a couple sisters, though."

What am I to say to that?

"Not in a mean way," she added.

"Well, if you had a sister, I am sure you would do whatever you could to protect her, right? Women are like that." She stares at me blankly.

"But I don't have my own sister. I have your sister. And she is doing me a favor by accompanying me to Ohio." She says it frankly, with no shame.

"Why Ohio?"

"Company wants to test a new drug, and they need some old people." She takes a big step toward me but doesn't reach for my outstretched hand.

"So," I say, making sure I have the pieces put together. "Francis lures residents from Mercy's Milestone to this ungodly place, then you transport them to a pharmaceutical company in Ohio. They use them as guinea pigs to test their drugs." He really is an evil entrepreneur. People don't miss the elderly, once they are out of sight. "They pay you?"

"Yep. A lot. And I'm going to need the money. Got a little legal trouble, I think." And then she sighs so sorrowfully I almost forget what we are talking about.

"Well, I heard you back there." I nod in the direction of the cemetery. "You were talking on your phone about George?"

"The thing is . . ." she whispers, "he saw me take the money, and he said he was disappointed with me. And then he walked away. I followed him down to the river and said I just wanted to explain. He was willing to talk, so we got in that little rowboat, the one tied down by the church, and he told me that we shouldn't be taking money from God. I said we were taking money from Francis, who wasn't a nice person, and from a big drug company, who wasn't a person at all. He kept shaking his head, and then I stood up, and the boat started to shake too, and then George fell out, and I saw his body float away."

Anguish is written all over her face.

"I think he's dead!" She weeps.

"He is dead," I confirm. "Do you still have the money?"

"I reached for George"—it comes out in a gasp— "and the money fell in the water."

Weeping harder, Bonnie grabs my hand tightly and pulls me into her bosom. I think that she needs a hug, but as I try to hug her, she lifts me up in the air and toward the open door of the camper. My feet swing and kick, and I feel hopeful that a few boots land with purpose into that jelly belly. But then Bonnie bends over, and my shoe gets tangled up in one of those big pockets. She has to drop me at the top step: I can't get off her, and she can't get me out of her petunia pouch. There is a lot of huffing and puffing and a flurry of karate chops that I learned from watching that Kung Fu show in the seventies. With my small bare hands, I try to wrestle with the giant, get a grip around her neck. Finally, she yanks my shoe off my foot and is about to lift me by my shoulders when I remember what I have in *my* pocket. Luckily her next bear hug pins me to her chest, which allows my right hand to search for the syringe. *Ah.* Flicking off the cap, I jam the needle into her backside.

Alva

Bonnie sits heavily on the ground and looks up at me. "Was that a whole syringe?"

"Yes, I think so," I say. "I pushed it all the way down."

"You would've killed me if I weren't so fat." Bonnie closes her eyes, and her head drops gently, into a pretty heap of leaves tinged with the upcoming colors of fall.

The news that I quite possibly could have been a murderer jars me. *Me. Alva. A little bit heroic but equally criminal? I don't like the ending to that story.* I guess when you choose a new path, there are always new perils. I'll have to write it all down.

Meanwhile, Bonnie's snores are interrupted by muffled shouts. *"It'ssssss meeeeeee Milllleeeee."*

Shakily, I get to my feet, one without a shoe, and reposition the steps. "I'm coming Millie. It's Alva, and I'm coming." I enter the dark trailer. There is a small kitchenette to the right, and just past that, a door revealing the cab, a well-worn driver's seat, and several half-drunk Big Gulps from 7-Eleven. To the left is a tiny living area with a table converted into a bed and a small, scarcely stuffed chair. Two figures lay motionless on the bed. Millie is strapped in the chair with a belt the size of Canada wrapped around her middle. She has a scarf tied around her mouth, and her eyes are red and angry. I put my arms around her neck and start kissing the hair on her head. I can't stop, the smell of her. *My sister.* I breathe in, and my fingers work on the knot until she finally breathes me in, too. "Oh Millie!"

Relief washes through us both. I never understood that phrase before, not like this. It is such an enormous feeling. We are soaked by it. Millie's voice is raspy, and it takes her a few minutes before she begins her story. I already know it, but I let her tell. Patty and Harriet don't open their eyes yet, but their bodies turn toward each other, and they hold hands. They sense their safety, even though they are huddled in a dinette booth converted into a vinyl cot that looks harder than a cracked riverbed. A curtain divides the camper, and we push through. Two more women who I do not recognize are in the back sleeping quarters. We stand over them, assessing. The room is dank, and an overhead bulb flickers. They are alive, but I'm not sure they are in anything but a dream fugue. I think of those drug trials and offer up a silent prayer that someone somewhere is doing some honest research. We work a tired bedspread into a pillow and prop them up against it. Eyes flicker without recognition.

Millie sits down next to them, gently rubbing their legs and offering little shhs of comfort, then looks up. "Pete kidnapped me," Millie says.

"Yes," I answer.

"But I don't think he meant to," she adds.

"I guess we will have to sort all that out. Francis is the one that is reprehensible. He killed George," I reveal. "Did you know George was murdered?"

"I thought he fell out of a boat and probably drowned. That's what she thinks." Millie draws up the shade and peers out at Bonnie, now on all fours but drooling over an ant bed. She lays back down, her cheek squishing the tiny pests.

"No," I say firmly. Pete found George behind the church in the reeds. If George fell out of the rowboat, he would've floated down the other way with the current. I think he must have gotten his footing and came back toward the church. Francis was waiting for him, looking for his money. It was Francis who hit him with the rock and tangled his body in the reeds. Francis's boots are in his truck, filled with earth and algae."

"You were always good at puzzles." Millie grins.

I pull out my phone and search for Director Vivian Reynolds's phone number. When she answers, I sit down next to Millie and the other two tiny figures, who have closed their eyes again, and start to relate the morning's events. I tell her, in no uncertain terms, that this entire operation is a matter for the FBI. Vivian is no-nonsense and says to stay put. She is already on her way. Bertha had called her with our location. *Will wonders never cease!*

"There was blood on your hankie, Millie, but I didn't think you were dead or anything. I would have known, you know?"

"I do know," Millie whispers. "And I didn't think you'd stop looking for me. I was going to just go down to that pawnshop and get our coat and convince you to get the hell out of Dodge."

"Right." My arm snakes around her shoulders, and we sit unmoving. "But we are stronger together. You should have waited for me to get my second wind."

Millie sighs. "You are the strong one Alva." And then, as an afterthought, she says, "I hate that stupid fur coat."

Alva

Francis said he had been administering his own brand of spiritual comfort to those at Mercy's Milestone yesterday afternoon. But it was his truck I saw in my mirage. The river water baptized the trunk bed, and his boots were the clincher. Vivian confirmed that he had not been back to the property that day. No twist ending. Sometimes, what you see is what you get. *Bad is bad.* Millie and I continue to share our stories, working out the lengths of Francis's subterfuge, Pete's part in the hostage plot, and George's demise.

A gunshot rings out, and we both jump. "Oh, my lord, Millie," I totally forgot that there was another drama unfolding outside. "Sam and Pete are out there, Bertha too. Francis may still be on the loose!" I stand up. We need to get back to Francis's trailer. I hear a scurrying up toward the front seats.

"What the hell?" Millie stands too, eyes me with real concern. "Why is Sam here?"

Millie looks paralyzed with fear. Or hope. Then we are both almost knocked off our feet. The floorboards rumble underneath us. I grab the curtain and try to steady myself. My eyes dart wildly to the front of the RV. Bonnie has managed to drag herself into the driver's seat. Almost. Her buttocks are squeezed somewhere between the swivel chair and the front console cup holders, a Big Gulp dripping down her pant leg. She has a maniacal look as she reaches up and maneuvers the gear shift into drive.

"Millie!" I scream over the roar of the engine. "You've got to hold those ladies in place. It's going to be bumpy. If they fall out, they'll break in a million pieces." I am not so worried about Pat and Harriet.

They are cocooned in the drop-down bed thingamajig. Words escape me. I look all the way back to see Millie wrapping her arms around the unaware duet, crooning her shhhhs much louder than before. We begin to move quickly, barreling through brush and tiny trees at the edges. The narrow dirt road isn't equipped to handle the breadth of this beast. Bonnie's upper left arm is the only appendage steering, and when I say steering, I mean, it's just sort of positioned over the wheel, the rolls of fat rippling, inching us to the left and then the right. We are going to die. All of us old people, old women (of course it is the women) all at once.

Luckily, the road to the back entrance of Eden is more or less straight. We careen for about a half a mile, branches slapping at the windows and scraping the fiberglass exterior. I can't keep my balance, so I am baby-stepping like I am on a balance beam. Never had been a gymnast, so it isn't anything near to graceful. There is loud rattling coming from every cabinet, the doors open, and a melee of pots and Tupperware come tumbling out, knocking against my shins. I manage to grab a frying pan as it flies toward me. *That's just what would happen in the movies,* I think, barely registering that I wasn't in one.

Wielding it over my head, I yell to Bonnie, "Stop this thing! Stop it right now, please!" How banal. The inappropriate politeness is glaring. "Bonnie, get the you-know-what out of my way!"

She tries to glower at me over her shoulder, but her eyes are unfocused, so she never sees the frying pan. I clobber her over the head, and she falls backward, wedging now on the floor between the driver and passenger seats, her arm slipping off the wheel, pulling us toward the right. I feel more than see that her thick arm has now landed on the gas pedal. The engine revs. We lurch forward again, and a big bump throws me on top of Bonnie, but then the road starts a gradual incline. We are still moving faster than I want to be, but thankfully, the vehicle slows just a bit. There is pastureland at the end of the access road, and I see a cow standing squarely in our path, big cow eyes watching our approach. I draw a line at killing a cow.

A siren wails in the distance. I shimmy up Bonnie. She's out cold, but probably from a combination of the drugs and the pan. I didn't hit her that hard. No blood. But to the problem at hand, I can't pull her arm off the gas pedal from this position. And her big paw has dipped under the brake pedal, so can't push the brake without crushing her hand. *A conundrum.* Crawling into the driver's seat, I frantically search for an emergency brake. *Is she sitting on the lever? For Pete's sake. Honestly, for Pete's sake!* I manage to position myself in the driver's seat and take stock. The camper jumps the shoulder and heads into the pasture. Cow dung flies. There is a yellow triangular knob on the dash. I'm so relieved.

"Bonnie! I see it!" She, of course, doesn't hear me and certainly wouldn't be elated, but I feel like I need a witness to my discovery. I push it over and over until I realize it's something you have to pull. There is a burst of air pressure from the bowels of the 'Bago. We slow more but do not stop. I have no choice but to take the wheel and steer, maneuvering around that first cow and then around in a big wide circle, like a cowboy rounding the other cows into the middle of the field. I carve a nice path, so the RV settles into the ruts and quits spitting rocks into the frightened herd. Millie bobs into the cab, her footing still not grounded.

"Alva? I'm getting a little dizzy."

"Well, I'm thinking about what to do about that." I am getting a little dizzy myself. The cow bodies are blurring, except I still see their haunted eyes following me as we go around and around.

"Alva, can't we just stop?" Millie hasn't taken in the entirety of the scene. Or not notice Bonnie's hand underneath the brake. I point out the obvious.

"Millie, maybe you can crawl down there and pull her arm out? There wasn't time for me to do it, or else I'd have murdered one of these mooers."

"Gotcha," says my sister without questioning the predicament. She kneels down, but we both notice the camper is losing momentum with each circle. Reluctant wheels creak, then hesitate. And then it shudders to a stop.

"Yeehaw!" Millie cries.

"Indeed!" I agree, breathing in deeply the dung-filled air. The siren I heard earlier is now quite close, and I hear familiar voices from behind. "Millie, if those gunshots we heard earlier actually killed someone, or if they even maimed someone, or if that gun is used against us, I would like it known or written on my headstone that today, I did not kill any cows. People need to know that I tried to do the right thing, didn't even hit Bonnie that hard. It's important to me."

"You'll be engraving my headstone before I'll be dealing with yours. Stop talking about things like that." Millie waves her arm toward the back. "All these ladies are going to live because of you, Alva. By focusing on farm animals, you are underestimating yourself. I thought that this trip was about self-worth?"

"Oh, Millie! Well said! Yes, self-worth." She's no wordsmith, but Millie nailed my emotional journey. "That is exactly what this is all about!"

Alva

"Code three. Shots fired; shots fired!" A two-way radio in the police car squawks the repetitive chant. Vivian Reynolds jumps out of the blue and white, which has arrived before the ambulance, and cautiously approaches the mobile home. Millie and I watch her progress out the front window, Bonnie still out cold and sardined between the seats. We hear another siren, indicating that some other officer must be dealing with the shootout in the trailer. *Wow, how'd they get more than that one officer from Steven's Point to show up? Impressive.* Then, another click of the radio, "Suspect down. All clear." Is Francis dead?

"Alva? Are you hurt? Is anyone hurt?" Vivian speaks loudly, in that beautiful, deep timbre. Her shawl flows from her shoulders in the wind. *A caped crusader,* I think, *has never looked so beautiful.* Her crusade, quieter than most, is evident as she swings open the door, glances around for just a moment, and then embraces tiny Ms. Werner and Harriet, tears flowing all around. Harriet's head rolls to the side and her eyes smile when she sees Vivian.

"You are a hero too," Millie whispers in my ear, as if she reads my mind. Again. We clasp hands and help one another from our perches, taking care not to kick Bonnie when she is already down. A paramedic joins Vivian to check on the two ladies, and we remind them that there are an additional two in the bedroom in back. The lone police officer, T. Johanson, a short young man with red curls and a scruffy beard, checks on Bonnie, and looks as though he's calculating whether or not the handcuffs will fit around her wrists. He struggles with the first one and then just cuffs the other around the steering wheel. It's easier. Then he calls for another ambulance to transport all our passengers to the local hospital in Norway. Hopefully, they haven't sustained any lasting injuries from the drugs or our bumpy tour of the pasture. Millie refuses to go, and I have to promise that we will get her checked out later once all this mess gets sorted out. I fully intended to, regardless of their recommendation. She has been through a lot. But now, we are both anxious to find Sam and, surprisingly, Bertha and Pete, too.

"Bertha kind of grew on me, Millie," I say as we step down from the trailer and try to shake off some of the Big Gulp drops from our clothes. "Hope to God that nothing has happened to her, but I think she was channeling a higher power when I last saw her."

Millie looks at me sideways, "I'm not sure she'll have any luck with that. A forgiving God is one thing, but she seems insincere about almost everything."

"You'd be surprised to know she helped find you, and Vivian said that it was Bertha who called her first. You know I gave Bertha Vivian's number, but I really didn't think she'd have the wherewithal to use it. I'm a little bit proud of her."

"To be fair," Vivian strides towards us, "she called to say Pete was coming up here and just might kill Pastor Francis. I don't think she wanted him to face jail time. Didn't mention you two at all."

"See Alva," Millie is righteous, "Bertha doesn't do anything good just for the heck of it. But if she brought Sam along, I'll be grateful. Unless, of course, he was on the wrong side of a gun." At that thought, Millie goes pale and leans heavily into my shoulder. She is weaker than I thought and is tripping over the hem of a stained hospital gown, trying to keep some decorum by pulling it tight around her hips. There are little ties down the front, obviously meant to be in the back.

"Millie, what are you wearing?"

"Well, Alva, you can see what I am wearing. And take a guess what I am not wearing." Millie stares at me hard, willing me to open my mouth. I don't.

"Here" says Vivian. Stopping to take off her shawl, she wraps it around Millie's waist.

"Oh no, I can't!" Millie struggles against her. "It is too beautiful, and I am very dirty."

"You are beautiful," Vivian says quietly, but firmly, and cinches the fabric tight.

With that, we leave the paramedics to deal with the senior survivors. Vivian ushers us into the cruiser with new urgency. "Tom!" she calls to the red-haired cop; "Can you bring us back to the compound?" Officer Tom glances again at the snoring Bonnie and nods.

"Let's see how the others are faring," she says with authority.

Alva

It takes another two hours or so for the whole story to be told.

First things first, Sam has shot Francis. In the foot, mind you, but still, he shot him. Seems he knew Francis from before. It turns out that Francis is Fred, the scoundrel ne'er-do-well his daughter Laura had married, and why she got saddled with the motel. Pete gave me the rundown on how Sam went into the trailer shouting "Clear. Clear," like he was in the FBI or something; how they surprised Francis, who took one look at Sam, his very angry ex-father-in-law, and dropped the gun. It went off, a bullet just missing Pete. Sam picked it up and gave a warning shot. But, after realizing who his enemy really was, and listening to Francis make excuses, just went ahead and shot him. It moves Sam up quite a bit in my estimation because I think my Irvin would have done the same. I am a little disappointed it's just the foot, but, being in my eighties, I also know comfortable feet are important, and Francis will find that out later.

Pete says that when the cops came in, Francis was crying about his toe, and I find myself smiling inside, and maybe a little outside, at the thought.

During the explanation the officers take turns checking on Bonnie, making sure she's transported to the county jail, and radioing in pertinent details to headquarters in Steven's Point, which, in turn, reports on to Madison. One of the locals from Norway works as an EMT, and they call him and Dr. Ames to the scene to check out Francis. The consensus is that Francis's toe is too shredded to reattach, so they clean it up well, elevate it for a while, and give him some stitches. The preacher has finally stopped wailing about his foot and wisely decided not to speak. Officer Wilson takes him over to the hospital in cuffs. *It's more than he deserves,* I think.

Real FBI agents are going to meet with Director Reynolds as soon as Francis, Bonnie, and Pete are transported to the city. I am going to make a statement attesting to the remorse Pete felt about his conspiratorial relationship with Francis and how he helped to bring the whole operation to light. Really, had Pete not changed sides and brought Sam and Bertha to the compound, I'm not sure how it would have all ended. Not well, most likely. I explained how I came to find Francis's wet boots in the truck and my supposition of his guilt in George's murder. I said "supposition," but I know darn well he did it. When the police go over the timeline, it's the only thing that makes sense. Francis will be put away for a long time. I think of the tiny fractures radiating in a circle on the skull in the shallow grave. I think of the other graves and even of the poor woman who fell out of a bed a long time ago. I think of George. Francis' modus operandi seems to be blunt force trauma. Maybe the shovel.

Millie will file her insights as well. She has the skinny on the money that Bonnie dropped in the water. Bonnie confessed that she had been to the church that day, and when George stepped out of Francis's office, she stepped in and grabbed the money. He caught her in the act, though. What a sad end. I really do think Bonnie loved that sweet man.

Bonnie will go to jail or a halfway house. Stealing drugs from the circus and injecting unsuspecting elders carries a sentence, to be sure. Maybe she can turn the State's evidence against her father. He just might be the worst human being. The feds were already following Mr. Berg's finances, questioning his social conscience. He was the original owner of the nursing home Francis, previously known as Fred, worked for in Eau Claire. Sam helped them make that connection. *Was it a coincidence that we met Sam first?* People always say they don't believe in coincidences, but in this case, maybe. *Or was it part of a master plan?* I don't believe that either. *Sometimes you discover a direction that's all your own.*

The sun is high in the sky as we walk out of the complex and to the cars. The remaining officer doesn't feel compelled to shackle Pete.

He is shuffling behind us, a few tears remaining on his cheeks. I told him about his mom and that she is safe and is being taken to the hospital for observation. His shame is palatable. We are all surprised when he takes off, racing toward his green jalopy. Officer Tom starts to pull a weapon but thinks differently when we all recognize Bertha stepping out of the car, yawning.

"Bertha! Bertha bear! Honey!!!" Pete is crying with relief. I hadn't been that worried about her, but I guess Pete had been. I thought she was probably still hiding out at the church. She didn't care for the police much; I figured she was probably going to redeem those lottery tickets I promised her once we all got back to the motel.

"Bertha Bear," I hear Millie snicker. "Look, oh my!" Millie is bent over at the waist, laughing uncontrollably. I stare at her, wondering if, in fact, she is really psychologically damaged.

"Look!" She points and guffaws.

Bertha steps away from the open door wearing the fur coat.

"Bertha the Hamster!" Millie is beside herself.

"It only looks like a mink on you," I join in.

Pete has the decency to stop and stare. He looks helplessly at Millie and then at me.

Bertha yells from her spot twenty-five yards from us, "Pete, where'd this coat come from?"

Millie looks at me. I look at her. We say together, "The casino!"

"That's why he was there," I add with a wink. "They had a special prize that day."

We are laughing so hard; we both look around for a bathroom.

"I hate that coat," Millie can't stop giggling.

"It's got bad juju," I say.

Alva

They said it was a small stroke. A month or so went by, and after that I was pretty much back to normal on the outside. But inside my head there were swirling pictures of possibilities. Perhaps "Peduncular hallucinosis" said the physician. *No,* I think now. *Better than that.* After Millie and I returned from our road trip, I called him back and asked, 'If I were younger and said I envisioned myself the protagonist in my fantasies, wouldn't I just be imaginative?'

My sister witnessed my budding. She ultimately believed in me, nurtured my growing confidence. We went on an adventure, got into some hot water, brought attention to some reprehensible characters, saved ourselves. She calls me a hero. I am uncomfortable with the title, but wryly, I think, *When is there a better time to become a hero? When does life throw you the most challenges? At the end, surely, when you are the closest to losing everything—your family and friends, your physicality, your control.*

Millie and Sam are spending more time together. I think I found him for her, but I can't explain it. She needs to be happy in case the "not dying out of order" prognostication is unfounded. For now, I will be their third wheel, spend time in my vegetable garden, pore over travel guides and maps. *I've never been to South Dakota.*

Acknowledgments

I owe a debt to my editor and publisher, Dianne Pearce, who helped me focus; who said things like "Really, finish the damn book," and "Why do stories about old people have to be sad?" I need to thank David Yurkovich, for being the design force behind Current Words Publishing—and especially for his kick-ass book cover.

Many thanks, to my book club, The Eclectic Eleven, even though we are down to eight, for always being supportive. Thank you too, to all my dear friends who listened to me patiently as I droned on and on. Too many to list here, but I couldn't ask for a better tribe.

Finally to my husband Sham, and our sons, Sam and Andy, I am thankful for your constant encouragement. I treasure every moment of our lives together. I love you to the moon and back.

About the Author

Emilie Khair is the author of the biographies *Passion's Piano: The Eddie Heywood Story* and *A Beautiful Puzzle: Nadia's Journey from East to West* as well as the children's book, *Kudzu for Christmas*. She holds undergraduate degrees in theatre arts and English education from the University of Minnesota, a master's degree in special education from the University of West Georgia, and a doctorate in sociology from Georgia State University. She has two sons and resides in McDonough, Georgia, with her husband of thirty-five years. While Emilie's roots are in Minnesota, her southern experiences are an inspiration to her writing.